The Flight of

The Flight of
Sarah Battle

Alix Nathan

PARTHIAN

Parthian, Cardigan SA43 1ED
www.parthianbooks.com
First published in 2015
© Alix Nathan 2015
ISBN 978-1-910409-60-2
Editor: Claire Houguez
Cover image: *Mrs Anne Hart*, Henry Raeburn, 1810, oil on canvas,
135 x 109 cm © Bildagentur für Kunst, Kultur und Geschichte, Berlin
Cover design by Mark Jennings
Typeset by Elaine Sharples
Printed and bound by Gomer Press, Llandysul, Wales
Published with the financial support of the Welsh Books Council
British Library Cataloguing in Publication Data
A cataloguing record for this book is available from the British Library.

To the memory of my parents

Prologue

She's sick as soon as the *Fair American* leaves the mouth of the Delaware and is out at sea. Recalls how they were both sea-sick when they left England three years before. There was ship fever on board then. Somehow they escaped it, the flushed and swollen faces, raging headaches, rows of prone bodies. They huddled under tarpaulin by day, driven below deck at nightfall by ice and wind to a hole of a cabin with nothing but an ill-fitting door between them and the shouts of seamen, the sounds of distant delirium.

In their cupboard cabin, as nausea finally left them, they celebrated escape. Sailing to the new land, they left lies and oppression behind, tasted freedom and joy.

Now, when the vein of Pennsylvania coast has thinned to nothing, there's only sea and the ship: neither America nor England. For the first time in her life she's alone. Sarah Battle. Wretched, desolate. And sick like a girl. Soda water helps calm her heaving gut. She refuses Peruvian Bark, distrusts it; can't bear the thought of the other remedy, chicken broth.

She leans on the rail. Lets the wind beat her face, strike her in welcome punishment.

Thinks to stand at the rail for the whole two-month journey. She's spent much of her life standing. Aloof, detached, even

1

when surrounded by men demanding drinks and attention. But two days of soda water alone cause her to crumple on deck, be carried below, lain in her trough bunk, a coffin without a lid. Where time is obliterated by sound: boom, roar, sough.

Seven weeks later, at the cry of 'England!', she has recovered her health. The journey from Philadelphia has been shorter than sailing to it, what with the following sea and a broad reach. She's exchanged the strangely intimate pleasantries of those thrown together by potential peril with a few others who, like her, are strong enough to resist the typhus. The passengers will never see each other again, can risk a little revelation. They'll remember her for a while, her youth, her sadness, then forget her.

At first she doesn't recognise the banks of the Thames. On the way out she observed nothing. It was winter then and the ship had crept through drifts of mist, its pilot cautious, dour. Propelled by their own urgency, by a longing to abandon, they had no time for apprehension, for anything outside themselves. Had willed the ship to hasten to the sea.

Now, at the mouth of the river a huge black-winged bird, immobile on a post, suddenly dives into the water, disappears. Distance no longer shimmers. The river edges curdle, clot with mud, marshland. No houses, no trees, only ships at anchor or passing the other way, sailing into their future, her past.

Fields at last; the banks nearing, a hovel here and there, shacks for cattle. Small houses support each other in tipsy groups; inns, waterside yards sprout up, their inflorescence timber piles, rope coils, nets, inverted hulls. Fishing boats pitch in the ship's wake.

Warehouses, mill-chimneys, stench of soap and tannery. The river fills with craft, rocking heavily at moorings or skimming across it. She feels a gladness that doesn't suit her sorrow; a homing pigeon's relief at the familiar window-ledge.

They approach the city and she begins to search for known buildings, steeples, waterworks, though it's not her part of London. Her fellow passengers crane and quip to each other with anticipation. They see new warehouses, bricks unblackened; rows of ships lining docks of gleaming stone. The new century shows its face.

In the upper pool at Wapping the *Fair American*'s anchor drops and watermen swarm off in wherries towards it. She steps up onto the quayside among justling, cursing sailors, lightermen, warehousemen. As she stands with her box, her feet unused to stability, she notices a pale girl holding a bag, waiting against a wall. Sees the girl's eyes frantically pin each passing traveller, how her whole body strains to find. She stares at her, wonders, pities.

But here's a porter who'll shoulder her box to a hackney. She must make her way back to Battle's.

PART I

PART I

1

In Change Alley lecherous sparrows nested in roofs, hopped on and off each other in constant copulation. Cheeping incessantly, they fought in the gutters at Battle's, her father's coffee house. Sarah Battle watched life outside her window high in the building every day of her childhood; on dark mornings she listened for the scratch of pecking, pelt of rain. After the Cornhill fire in 1748, begun at the peruke-maker's, Battle's had been rebuilt. There, twenty years later, Sarah was born.

Downstairs, light fed through large windows, but the Alley's other buildings, peering in, crowded out the sun. There was space in the big room to drink and eat at open tables, to mingle, move from group to group, even address the company, but also to huddle in private behind thin walls of high-backed settles. Where deals took place, stock was shifted by jobbers and brokers from the nearby Exchange, vital figures passed on or withheld.

To a little child the place was enormous, full of the noise and smell of men. One woman officiated at the curved bar in the centre, Anne, her mother, and a cook worked in the kitchen, but all the rest were men, loud, looming. They patted her head, laughed at her, asked her impossible questions, fed her morsels of bread like a caged goldfinch, though she didn't have to sing for them. Made her sip chocolate, teaspoons of punch when her father wasn't looking. She played with the puppy among their legs and feet, learned that they would be charmed by her presence through a rack of steam and smoke. Wondered why some kinds of rowdiness caused her to be removed to the kitchen or up to her little room where she knelt on her bed and gazed across roofs. Heard the shouting and thumping continue floors below.

Often if the puppy was asleep she watched unobserved. How men picked their noses and teeth, rubbed their thighs, scratched their groins, clapped the backs of their friends, causing showers of white dust. She saw wigs slip, staring to see if fuzz, matted strands or naked skin lurked beneath. Saw eyeballs roll, lips purse at the man who read aloud the morning news each day, watched earnest talk, handshakes, secret signs, money pass and fingers touch their lips when they saw her see.

Her childish view fixed on the peculiar, absurd, self-important. She smiled to herself at singular expressions, habits, movements supposed unseen, food and drink slopping and dripping, fish bones flying, chops dropped, crusts lodged in odd places, men no better than babies. Hid under tables when overcome by giggles.

She might have continued to decorate Battle's with her innocence. Sam Battle, brought up to the business by his own father, knew her value, but her mother had modest ambitions for her daughter and, egged on by educated customers, put Sarah to school. Where she learned the necessary elements and failed to enjoy the companionship of girls unlike herself.

The best thing about Sarah's early life in the coffee house was Benjamin Newton, who made her sit beside him while he drew pictures which to her were real. Through him she'd learned her letters, whole words: *bottle, pie, goose, wig* and graduated to sentences: *the goose wears a wig, swigs the bottle and gobbles the pie.* She began to read from books plucked out of his apparently infinite pockets. Through him she heard about existence outside her smoke-thick, closed-in world: sea, ships, animals strange beyond belief, other lands, snow-deep, heat-dry, Turks, Lapps, Scots. Before long, recognising a shared attitude with his child companion, Newton sketched regular customers in familiar poses, their characters or weaknesses exposed: greasy tricorns, fantastic shoe-buckles, popping eyes; men who fiddled with their ears, gawped at scandals in the *Morning Post*, snored then gasped themselves awake. Among his sketches, the formidable Sam Battle occasionally appeared, armed cap-à-pe, as did Miss Sarah Battle laughing behind her hands with a scrawny, bird-like friend labelled B—n N——n.

Newton was young, unknown, sold his drawings to print shops when he could. He rarely paid his tab but Sam didn't press too hard, seeing that men enjoyed his satires, lingered, ordered more coffee, more punch. Her mother, Anne, was glad to have the child off her hands. For Sarah, Newton was a private magician, drawing for *her*, casting his delicate smile at her alone. He wore no wig, his hair was wayward, his clothes unkempt, and he hummed sweet tunes. While he sketched or read a book of verse, she pulled off thrums from his ragged cuff; held a hoard of short green threads in her pocket to keep him always present.

'Look, Newton,' she'd say, poking him in the side, annoyed by his absorption. 'Over there.'

'Where? What?'

'*Look*; where I'm pointing.'

'If you point they'll see and stop doing whatever they're doing that's funny.'

'*Oh*! The man behind the man warming his arse at the fire.'

'You ought not to say 'arse' if you're going to grow up into a lady,' he'd say, mumming disapproval.

'The man at the table behind the man at the fire. Look at him, he's sliding off his chair.'

'Well observed, Sarah! And if someone moves the table even slightly down he'll go.'

'Quick, draw! Draw him! Quick!'

She rushed back from school, imagining that he'd spent the day waiting only for her return. And he did, indeed, always have some newly-drawn absurdity with which to make her laugh. In turn she would mock her teacher voraciously for him, tell half-invented tales about the other pupils, watch them appear in wonderful exaggeration on the paper before her. It was like conspiracy with an angel: Newton was her authority, Newton, his books and his drawings.

They were always side by side.

'Man behind you. Don't look *yet*.'

'Is it seriously funny? I thought you were reading that poem.'

'He cut up his meat into pieces. Sucked the gravy off each one in turn, then he put them to dry round the edge of his plate. Now he's slipping them into his pocket. Look, *look*!'

She prodded him. He'd stopped humming. In repose Newton's face looked sad. It felt like a threat.

As she grew older and it was seen how well she could read, others made her stumble over the *Morning Chronicle* and *Gentleman's Magazine*, birthday odes for the King, even significant bits of Blackstone's legal *Commentaries*. She obliged, though their amusement was greater than hers.

*

In June 1780 thunderous heat kept casements wide open all night. Mephitis of cesspools replaced the pungent pipe-smoke and boiling coffee steam which hung in clouds in Change Alley. Returning early from the school she hoped soon to leave, Sarah found herself suddenly pressed up against buildings, pushed aside by crowds surging past from St George's Fields, across London Bridge and down Cornhill. The banners they held up said *Protestant Association*, they waved flags, sang hymns and wore blue cockades in their hats.

'Is you a papist?' a woman glared into her face. 'Git you indoors if you is.'

Sarah was familiar with her father's view of papists (Irish weren't they?), though he'd not ask questions if Irish customers paid well and caused no trouble. The woman fluttered a pennant on a stick at her. *No Popery*, it read.

The mood was sprightly in Battle's.

'North's a dismal fool. We've enough Irish; we don't need more. Every other house a mass-house.'

'You *would* say that, Bullock.'

'Want us overrun, do you, Thynne? You'll be bringing in the French next.'

'And what *I* say is Lord George Gordon's mad. A third son. A lunatic.'

'That's calumny, Thynne! Gordon's a leader. Looks every bit the part – you've not heard him speak, have you? The man's a great Protestant.'

'And that's *all* we need. A precise puritan begot between two stock-fishes.'

'*There's* toleration for you! I thought you drank toleration with your mother's milk.'

11

They ignored Sarah whose dreams splintered at sounds of disturbance all through the night.

She and her mother went to church as usual on Sunday where for once the sermon held the attention of the congregation, supporting the Protestant Association while not actually mentioning the word 'papist'.

On her way back from school on Monday she walked rapidly past bands of men with rolled-up sleeves and bludgeons. And a cutlass, she thought, but kept her eyes on the ground, the stones of the street quite black where huge fires had burned out, leaving singed hinges and locks, handles and doorknobs on beds of ash.

She ran straight to Newton. A reserve had grown in her; she was no longer young enough to speak to adults with impunity. With Newton there was more: a smear of jealousy when, for a time, he came less often and was said to spend his time with 'Maria'. She'd challenged him then and felt sudden regret as his face seemed to tumble downwards and he didn't reply.

Now she could offer him something; needn't wheedle.

'There are men in the street with sticks.'

'Thank whoever's in heaven you're safe, then!' He put his arm round her shoulder and hugged her to his side, which smelled deeply of tobacco and dust, and she lapsed into a hopeless fug of love for him.

'Tell me what else you saw.'

'Draw it while I tell you.'

'I shall.'

'They were fierce. There were lots of them, shouting at each other. They wanted to punch somebody I think. Not me: they didn't notice me. One had a cutlass. Give it to *that* one. And the others all have sticks. Big ones. That's right.'

'Any women?'

'There were the other day when they marched. Do them marching. I can tell you what was on their banners.'

'Later. What else did you see today?'

'They've had fires. Some were still burning. The street was black. Oh, and they were getting up the stones with picks and putting them in sacks. Horses will fall into the holes, won't they?'

'Break their legs, poor beasts. Carts will topple over.' He was already drawing tilting carriages, passengers tipping like barrels down a chute. 'What else, Sarah?'

'One of them suddenly called out "Mansfield!" Then they *all* called out "Mansfield, Bloomsbury Square!" and ran off.'

Newton sketched everything, somehow just as she'd seen it. He included her, a diminutive figure, half hidden, watching behind a lamppost. She spread the sheets out on the table and called to the waiter, Bob, to bring Mr Newton a dish of coffee. She pored over the drawings and others came to look, as they often did, anxious to see which of them he'd skewered today. They saw legs, arms, staves, distorted faces, fires, smoke, picks, sacks of cobbles. Just as she'd told him. But no one laughed.

On Tuesday they kept her at home and bolted the coffee house shutters despite the heat. Sam Battle's mood was grim. Of course trade increased with new customers in flight from the mob, which was good, though someone had to risk their lives for more meat and fish from Leadenhall market (he sent the fifty-three-year-old boy, Dick). More to the point was the danger to Battle's itself. For the mood of the riot had shifted. Chapels were attacked, Catholic houses stoned, but people wanted more: MPs, ministers, justices too soft on papists, in favour of Catholic Relief. Libraries of burning books and papers lit the streets, the distorted faces of the crowd; grand homes were sacked, furniture and wainscoting sought for a particularly fine blaze. Destruction became delight, looting the lust of the moment. Sam knew it would only take one known papist sympathiser to duck into Battle's for the building to be attacked by the mob: its windows gouged like eyes, doors wrenched out like teeth, tables, settles, barrels heaped in a crackling pyre.

News flew in. The crowds were on their way to Newgate, armed with the very labourers' tools so recently used to build the huge new prison. You could hear bellowing as the keeper's house was stormed and fired, for Newgate was not far.

'They're freeing the prisoners!' someone pushed through the drinkers, shouting and waving his arms. A cheer broke out at one end of the coffee house.

'Liberty! Freedom!'

Yelling and cursing greeted this; fists shook.

'They'll go for the other gaols. King's Bench, Fleet, Clerkenwell. The soldiers do nothing.'

'Magistrates won't give the order.'

'We want no massacres.'

At which point a fight broke out. Sam Battle, purple with fury, hauled man off man and her mother hastened Sarah upstairs to bed. There, in fear and fascination, she saw the flames of Newgate lick the glowing clouds, smoke out-blacken the night. And back and forth, between the fires, figures of men dancing triumphantly on the roof.

*

Nothing was normal in London on Black Wednesday. In the coffee house men woke from under their coats on benches, raised their heads from tables: so many hadn't dared go home the night before. Fire was re-lit under the coffee cauldron, water pumped, grounds measured and soon the smell disguised the night stink of bodies in unchanged clothes. Fortified, they crept away to worried wives, or joined spectators viewing the ruins of Newgate, watched Protestants plunder the Old Bailey Sessions-house.

'They've done it,' Bullock said, returning in a sweat at midday. 'King, Privy Council. Orders to shoot – without the Riot Act.'

'There's gangs with iron bars,' someone said.

'Going from house to house demanding money for the poor mob or the true religion.'

Thynne glared at Bullock.

For a while there was a lull. Waiters skimmed back and forth, silent water beetles. Sarah sat beside Newton, but he was pale and wouldn't smile. Wouldn't draw a thing.

She pulled at his sleeve. He was missing an excellent scene between the emaciated, sharp-chinned Thynne and Bullock whose lumpy nose looked as if it awaited slicing in the kitchen with the rest of the vegetables. She plaited and unplaited the longest thrums from his pale green cuff. Could see that the coat had once been fine.

Later there came a noise greater than any they'd heard yet. Not quite the same as Newgate though the engine wheels and yells were there; but ten times as loud.

'They've fired Langdale's, Langdale's distillery,' shouted the latest messenger, his face sooted over. 'The vats are going up, and most of the street with them.'

'They'd be better off drinking the stuff than igniting it. Lunatics.'

'You can be sure they'll have drunk as much as they could first.'

'There's pools burning in the street, they say.'

Roaring, blazing alcohol, a lurid light flashing in, even to the dark end of Change Alley. Silenced them all. A roomful of hares, quivering, poised to run. In Sarah's mind black shapes continuously jumped among flames.

Her mother rushed in from the kitchen.

'Sam, I must go to Charlotte. See she's safe.'

'Damn, no! You shan't, Anne, it's all afire out there.'

'I must. My own sister. She's only in Poultry; it's further on is the fire. I'll bring her back with the baby.'

Sam scowled, would have locked her in his office, but he wanted no scandal. And that damned sister. Good for nothing.

'I'll go with her, Sam. I'll see she's unharmed,' Newton offered and hurried her out before Sam could stop them.

The day palled. With Newton gone there was no diversion from the strangely silent room where everyone listened. They drank of course, smoked, chewed, spat; but sat, clamped, askew.

Surges of violence, like days of battering gales, became a background. On the whole they seemed distant, sometimes moving nearer, but not too close. The massive boom of the burning distillery ceased. Then came a new noise to Sarah's ears: Smack! Snap! Mid-chew, mid-puff, diners and smokers stopped at the crack of muskets, a different kind of shout, of orders issued.

Eyes widened in alarm, messages flashed from face to face. Shoulders hunched as if ashamed. Without Newton there to explain, to draw what he heard, she guessed. The men with the rolled-up sleeves and bludgeons, the ones who'd set the gaol alight, who'd capered on the roof, who'd stolen things from shops and houses, attacked fire engines, were being shot by soldiers. Shot and killed. She'd never seen anyone killed.

Not seen anyone dead, though once a chair-mender was stabbed with his own knife by a rival and when she walked past later, there was blood on the street.

She looked towards the door each time it opened.

'Shot some on Blackfriar's Bridge,' somebody reported. 'They were setting the toll houses on fire. Militia are drawing chains across the streets now.'

Sam sent Sarah to bed. There was no refusing her father; it was already late. She took Newton's sketchbook to give him tomorrow. She'd have to wait till the morning to see Charlotte and the baby safe. Through her half-open window countless fires glowed and flickered, doubled in the panes. Musket shots and screams sank into the distance. The smell of summer burning was different from winter fires. She shut the casement. There were no figures jerking and hallooing on rooftops.

*

The sound of violence moved out of hearing of Change Alley. For two days shopkeepers wouldn't open and people lurked indoors, the streets given over to soldiers and armed volunteers. Looters and thieves hauled away more spoils, shots were exchanged south of the river but destruction was done.

London was ravaged. Buildings blinded, smashed and blackened, hundreds killed by musket balls, bayonets, not a few from falling masonry, burning spirits, glass-severed arteries, too many gulps of neat gin. Among those shot were Anne Battle and Benjamin Newton, mistaken for rioters as they rushed across Poultry to rescue Charlotte and the baby, their bodies hauled into St Mildred's Church before the second round.

When they told him, Sam Battle scowled, snarled, just as he'd done before she left.

'*Told* her not to go,' became his refrain for months after.

Sarah cried aloud and was taken into the kitchen where Mrs Trunkett, the cook, near smothered her in apron and panic. They sent her off to school once it was clear the riots were over and there the lessons continued as though nothing had happened.

In the coffee house the customers treated her with caution as if she might bite, with embarrassment as though it were their fault her mother was dead. She rejected their pity. At night she mourned into her pillow, realising before long that her greater loss was Newton. For most of Sarah's twelve years Anne had been too busy to do more than occasionally cast an eye on her daughter from the other side of the room. Ben Newton had drawn for her, laughed with her. They'd conspired. She had no other friend.

She tried to imagine him dead and couldn't. She turned the pages of his sketchbook, to find that what made her smile made her cry at the same time. Would she never laugh again? She told herself it was her duty to laugh at Newton's witty drawings, he'd be cross if she didn't, but it was a long time before she obeyed herself. All the while, gusts of sparrows fought and swifts screamed in the dusk.

Sam Battle's relief that his premises had survived, fought with his fury that his wife had got herself killed and could no longer run the coffee house with him. But then he thought of a simple solution, obvious *and* money-saving.

2

Sarah learned quickly and grew into the part. She must make up the daily orders for meat and fish for cook to poach, roast, bake, fry; supervise the grinding of coffee beans, measuring of pumped Thames water; the mixing of sugar and milk with ground cacao in readiness for the sweet-toothed; the boiling of sassafras for saloop. Who else but she must tick the inventory of flasks, glasses, pewter pots, cloths, coffee dishes, cutlery, aprons, debt-books, pencils? Ensure that orange peel not used for punch was collected, dried and stored for lighting the fires. Chase the dog, now elderly, out of the kitchen.

After two years, when she was almost fifteen, Sam saw that Sarah's maturing female charms would draw the men, cause them to linger, chalk up another. He sacked the woman who'd served for years. From mid-morning Sarah must stand behind the curved bar, the comely girl pouring port, claret and porter, whisking egg into cups of chocolate.

She was a reluctant beacon. Heat and steam drove her naturally high colour to a perpetual blush. Her strong bare arms prickled. Men strode or sidled up; barked their orders from heights or leaning, lisped; intimidating or intimate, she struggled to keep them all at bay. Her emerging womanhood drew most of them, but there was more to Sarah for those few who troubled to look: hearty peasant origins precluding neither intelligence nor strong feeling. She longed to shake her hair out of its mob cap. Learn more of the distant world described by Newton.

Instead, she must rehearse names of customers and drinks, quantities, proportions, when to order more loaf sugar, nets of lemons, when to call the boy, Dick, when to hail a waiter. She disliked her prominent position but worked hard, in part from an urge to defy. For, though unspoken, there was a belief no girl could do it all. Sam never praised nor encouraged, only criticised as his father had done before him.

For a while her nightly ritual of grief gave way to recitation of lists: port, sherry, claret, cherry wine, arrack, rum, usquebaugh, gin, Brunswick mum, aqua vitae, metheglin, cider, perry, scurvy-grass ale, Welsh ale, Dorchester beer. Prices for a glass, a bottle. How much ale to put in flip, the exact amount of brandy, Madeira and green tea for Battle's famous punch.

In the day inner dialogues with Newton held her. *'Draw this face, that scene!'*

'Which scene? What face?'

'The man with all the chins.'

'He's leering at you now.'

'Yes, yes, pin him down in your sketchbook. Get all those chins and whiskers!'

'And the scene?'

'Table in the corner. Man trying to sell watches. Pulling one after another out of his coat. How many has he got? They must be stolen: the Runners'll be in and Father'll be furious.'

How they'd have laughed. No one guessed why she would suddenly smile. Some wondered it her wits had turned from grief. Most, seeing her ride a crisis unperturbed, remembered that Anne had been tough, as you had to be to put up with Sam Battle. Thought it was that.

'You're so like your dear mother,' they told her when they judged enough time had passed since Anne's death.

She knew better. It was as though she dedicated the life of her mind to Ben Newton: cried for him at night (once the lists were memorised), mentally conversed with him during the day, helped by the feel of the knot of green threads lodged deep in her pocket. She grew a skin of detachment that some disliked, others found provocatively attractive. She soon hated compliments.

She longed to stir up the dense stodginess of the place, to shake the ruck of customers who sat behind papers for hours at a time. There were eight morning papers and one evening newspaper at Battle's; Sam bought in several copies of each. Sarah pictured a Newton sketch where each man was nothing but a newspaper with a pair of legs and fingers gripping itself. As a child she'd sat among legs, looking up at men, some of whom were still there, appearing much the same, perhaps more lined, shabbier, more fixed in their ways. Now, from behind the bar she glanced down upon them, recognised their peculiarities from a distance.

'They say Percy's has lectures every Friday, Father. Let us have lectures *here*, too. Or concerts.' She had only a vague notion of either of these, though surely Newton would have wanted concerts. He often hummed to himself.

'Many people would come, not just these stock-jobbers making their deals.'

'Whatever's got into your head?'

'I want to raise Battle's up a bit. Everyone is dull here.'

'*Dull*? *Lectures*?'

'Well, *I* should like to hear some music.' Twice on her way

21

from school she'd passed musicians in the street. Had wanted to whirl and fling herself about.

'I'll not have it. We've the auction room upstairs for a sale once in a while. That's enough. Think of the sandwiches. I'd have to pay another hand in the kitchen to cut all morning.'

'More sandwiches but fewer chops, less venison. Let us do it, Father.'

'No! Damn, no! There were *consultations* here when I was a boy. Corn-cutter did all the coffee houses one after the other. He died and Sally Mapp did bone-setting. Place was full of hobbling and coughing. I did away with it. I'd rather have an East India giantess on show than *instruments*.'

'Let us at least have books here.'

'I don't mind a learned pig that knows its letters like the one in Pall Mall. *That'd* bring 'em in! No! Newspapers is enough.'

She didn't try again, worried away at her knot of thrums, abandoned dreams.

*

Having lost her youth with her mother and Newton, Sarah became humourless, existing on a pulse of memory. She carried out her tasks with efficiency acknowledged by Mrs Trunkett, Dick and the waiters, if not by her father. Efficiency had a satisfaction in itself. Severity towards easy leers also became habit. A sense of apartness had begun with Newton, watching others, not joining them. She was contained, fortified, even against the physical turmoil of becoming a woman: accepted change, confusion, the onset of blood, thought little of it.

She'd had two models of womanhood: the woman who used

to serve at the bar and her mother, Anne. Charlotte, well, that was the woman she was supposed *not* to emulate; with a dear little boy, no husband, poverty. Mrs Trunkett was more like a grandmother. What had they done, those two overburdened women, her mother and the barmaid but work hard at the beck and call of men? She knew of no alternative.

At first she was unaware of offers made to Sam Battle for her hand in marriage or simply for her person. He dismissed each without hesitation. When she did hear, she was glad he turned them down, for no one resembled Newton.

Eventually she was left dispirited. Too many years passed. Cauterized years. She remembered the warmth of Newton's body next to hers, the joy of pressing up close to his fusty jacket. Knew the memory would thin.

At twenty-two, welling desperation compelled her to notice some of the customers not as caricatures but as men.

One man, a head above the others when he joined the crowd at the bar to order port, sometimes scribbled at a table or read a book. And watched her. She turned away, then couldn't help but notice how often he was there. He was different from the rest. His thin face, shadowed eyes, his concentration began to fascinate her, so when one day he introduced himself she was not displeased.

'James Wintrige, Madam.'

'Oh?'

'Clerk in the Customs Office.'

'Ah.'

'Custom House, near the Tower.'

She asked him what he wrote so vigorously. Newton would have drawn him drowning under an enormous wave of paper inked over with tiny words.

'A play. I hope they'll take it at Drury Lane.'

'Oh!' Playwrights rarely came to Battle's.

They spoke a little more each day. Or, rather, he spoke and she listened. It was not the first play he'd written; he had great hopes of performance this time because he knew a famous actor. He mentioned a name and over the weeks more names speckled his conversation, currants in a new-baked bun: writers and thinkers he knew, authors of books he'd read. She'd heard of none of them but swiftly understood that here was someone whose life was of the mind, just the kind of person she'd once envisaged attending lectures, even *giving* them, in a superior Battle's coffee house.

Of course plays didn't make money, he said. His post in the Customs Office paid him to live. And it wasn't only plays that he wrote at his table, sipping coffee from the dish, sometimes smoking a pipe, eating rarely. He penned letters, the minutes of meetings.

She experienced the thrill of the illicit. Not that the new Corresponding Society was illegal, not *yet*. Battle's customers were split politically; it was not a coffee house like some, allied to one party or faction. Many regulars came straight from the Royal Exchange where views depended on financial success and financial success depended on the protection of markets and stopping incompetent wars. On the whole they supported the government, but not always and there were plenty of gradations of whiggery and radicalism among those who drank and ate and smoked and joked, did business and argued. But anything that smacked of Jacobins, as he insisted on calling them, was anathema to Sam Battle. And of *that* Sarah was well aware.

James Wintrige was a secretary in the Corresponding Society which, he explained to her in low tones, wanted reform of parliament and votes for all adults.

24

'Are they *Jacobins*?' she dared to whisper.

'Certainly not. Reform, not violence.'

'Ah.'

He spoke of the ideas debated each week by members of the society.

'This is the great Age of Reason,' he informed her, staring at her nose, her mouth all the while with half-closed eyes. 'Why do we have Reason if not to use it? And with it we see that too many suffer at the hands of a few. The few have wealth and power because they obtained it from their fathers or friends or they bought it or stole it.'

His voice mesmerised her. Words slipped through lips that barely moved and these, when he stopped, he patted with long fingers, as if to check they were still there. Such thin lips, wide beneath a long philtrum. For a moment Newton intervened: '*His mouth is like a frog's.*'

'*Surely frogs don't have lips?*'

'*This one does.*'

'All men want liberty,' Wintrige intoned.

'*Do frogs want liberty?*'

'And women?' asked Sarah.

'Of course! Women want liberty too. By 'men' I mean women. That is, women, too. The tree of liberty has begun to grow. In Paris for instance.'

'Oh.' It was 1792. 'I thought that in France…'

'Beware to whom you listen. Here it will grow peacefully because all men want it, even if they don't yet realise that they do. We must enlighten the nation.'

The burr of Wintrige's voice intoxicated her as alcohol had never done. His was not great speaking; his rhetoric was borrowed, which she didn't know, but its stuff was strong, rolled out relentlessly.

She had never thought about power, wealth, the many, the few. The world outside Battle's came in daily to drink, eat and smoke. That was enough. It was not Newton's world of sea, ships and exotic lands. Outside were violent, inexplicable lives glimpsed through her window, seen hurriedly in passing on a few streets, heard about:

'Sarah, your mother is dead.'

'Dead?'

'Shot by soldiers. An accident. They took her for part of the mob.' (She had wanted to laugh at the absurdity of her mother with rolled-up sleeves and a bludgeon, while yet she cried.)

'And Newton? Ben Newton?'

No longer a child, she must face this outside world. If James Wintrige told the truth, it was not a violent place but a rational one. There was hope of change for the better, he said, if only men employed Reason.

He wooed her with his luminous phrases. *Enlighten the Nation*. *Tree of Liberty*. Here in cobbled, brick-brazen Change Alley, where the sun found it hard to break in, people knew little of trees. Sarah, deprived, watched sparrows on slates. And 'en*light*en'! Did Wintrige realise how the word shone in Sarah's imagination?

He wooed her with names, knowledge, superiority. How could she resist?

He would be her revolution. Through him she would have the courage to encounter life outside Battle's. Through him she would touch a world of intellect, ideas. Her mother might have wanted that, she thought, gradually understanding that there was more to her mother than she'd perceived. She could release herself from her father's blinkered views, his crudity. Five years after the Gordon riots he'd bought a print of Rowlandson's *Wonderful Pig* picking out letters to a tittering, fashionable assembly and hung it in a prominent place. He hoped that new customers would think the wonderful animal had displayed its literacy in Battle's.

Yes, through James Wintrige she could enter a higher sphere. Moreover, she could surely abandon the tedium of flattery; the stink of tobacco and charred meat that hung about her like a garment. The misery of swollen feet.

This curious courting took place in moments of lull in trade, for Sarah hardly ever left Battle's. She couldn't. Too much depended on her.

Of course there was Sunday, when Battle's was shut. Her mother Anne had been evangelical. As a girl she'd heard Wesley preach, stood in a thronged field, watched men and women collapse on the stubble, groaning as if in death. Sam would have none of that, arguing that trade would suffer if she was known to attend meetings where people behaved like madmen. So Anne had taken Sarah to St Mary-le-Bow instead, with the injunction to listen to the preacher. Each Sabbath they'd come away, Anne complaining of the miserable divines, the shocking behaviour of the congregation, talking and laughing throughout. Sarah's sense of compulsion was mixed with the unpleasantness of her mother's mood and her own boredom. After her mother's death she continued to go each week through a sense of obedience to the dead woman, though more to get away from her father for a few hours.

Sunday afternoon, then, was the one time she might meet James, though only after she'd lied to Sam, telling him she was visiting Charlotte and her little boy, which was bad enough. She could certainly not go to a play with him in the evening, nor did she think they could risk being seen walking in Goodman's Fields. On two occasions they took a stroll to Ludgate, looking in shop windows, hoping not to be noticed by coffee-drinkers who might tell. They were never completely alone. Yet somehow his proposal was uttered, murmured out of the side of his mouth and received as he pressed his lips nervously with his fingertips.

'You must ask my father,' she said, guessing the outcome.

He spoke to Sam Battle in a private room, emerging after less than five minutes, his eyes sunk in their shadows and left the coffee house.

'I'll not have it,' Sam told his daughter.

'He has a good post. He's a gentleman.'

'Pfooh!'

'He's well schooled. He writes plays!'

'*Pfooh*! They tell me he's a damned *Jacobin*.'

'That's not true. And father, I am turned twenty-two. I am a woman. I can decide.'

'And me? *Me*? What of me? Running Battle's all on my own?'

'I...' Her father pushed her out of the room.

'*Another sketch, Sarah!*'

'*I know. A variation of your previous one of father.*'

'*Yes: Sam in full armour, two hands grasping a massive sword with ME! ME! written on it. And you in mob cap and apron thrusting a tiny knife and fork. The title? Battle of Battle's!*'

With admirable speed Wintrige suggested an arrangement. While they would live elsewhere as a married couple (he was already searching for rooms), Sarah could continue to work at Battle's and return home each evening.

'We'll employ a housemaid to keep our place in order,' he promised when Sarah's face fell.

They married in St Michael's, the vicar a customer at Battle's who took pity on Sarah. Sam refused to attend despite

28

being not displeased at James's 'arrangement' and after the ceremony they walked all the way to their rented rooms in Winkworth Buildings at the Moorgate end of City Road.

Mr and Mrs James Wintrige. Sarah went straight to the window. No sparrows, no view over the city's dense forest of chimneys and steeples. The glass was darkened by the proximity of the house opposite. She watched a cat creep across the roof towards an open window, saw the reflection of James as he came up behind her.

*

Their lodgings were a brisk walk from Battle's. Neither convenient for Sarah, nor for James, though he liked to lope along on his thin, stockinged pins. The maid lit a fire and heated water early, for Sarah must be at Battle's by six in the morning. Betsy washed sheets, removed cobwebs, spread a cover for the evening meal. She had no need to cook, for Sarah carried back their supper each night wrapped in several cloths to keep it hot. Bottles of wine clinked in the basket.

James set out his books, his writing table, told her not to call him Jem. Gave Sarah pamphlets to read while he wrote. She asked about his meetings, what the men in his division discussed, what they resolved by democratic vote. He told her little. Had to be cautious even with his own wife, he said. She was startled at his severity; stopped asking. Opened the bedroom window to catch the early robin song in February, trilled from the top of a bush in the yard.

With food from Battle's kitchen, they ate well. James was often preoccupied, would rise in the middle of supper to write something down that he'd just remembered.

'Ah,' he'd say, leaving the table, sometimes mid-mouthful.

'Yes!' He never explained, looked always as though he were reading something inside his head.

'*His eyes are not frog-like*,' she said in her imagined dialogue with Newton, which marriage had failed to diminish. '*They live in slits under his eyebrows*.'

She tried asking him about the stage, his plays, the actors with whose names he'd enchanted her when they first met. She sought detail of people and places about which she knew nothing, but his replies were vague or else dismissive as though her questions were ridiculous.

It was only late at night that he paid her close attention, pouncing as she began to unpin her hair, nibbling, pecking at her, his thumbs sinking into the flesh of her upper arms. Once he'd secured her in bed, he'd strew his clothes in heaps round the room, pull on a nightshirt and leap onto her as if to prevent her escape.

Sometimes, as they ate, he said she reminded him of his mother and grandmother who'd brought him up. The same rosy colouring. Forgiving nature. She wondered what he meant.

The world of intellect remained elusive. She struggled with the pamphlets, James too busy to help her understand, longed to hear more of the ideas he'd uttered during their courtship. Her life seemed barely changed. Each day she supervised, checked, ordered, mixed, stood for hours behind the bar, not smiling, ever redder, an accidental siren. Each night she walked home through the streets in a private fume of broiled steak and tobacco. Dick, the ageing, arthritic boy from Battle's, who was also first grinder and shoe cleaner, escorted her to protect her from footpads.

Her father treated her as he'd always done, ignoring her unless she made a mistake. He never asked about her other life, never mentioned James's name. Working in the coffee house with an unseen, unmentioned marriage was like when she went to school after her mother and Newton were killed and no one said a word. Had it happened at all, she'd wondered then? Was she married at all, she wondered now, or had she imagined it? James, chill, preoccupied, painful, was he a phantom? Perhaps she should take the stairs to her childhood room at the end of the day, climb into the high, narrow bed of her girlhood, listen to sparrows under the eaves, cheeping in the dark.

Exhausted at night, she returned to find James writing rapidly or, more often, out at a meeting. As she must arise before five she sometimes ate alone, one of James's books propped up before her. She gradually made her way through *Macbeth*. Went to bed and fell asleep before he returned. He jerked back the covers after two a.m. smelling of wine, shreds of meat in his teeth and crushed her dreams with his heavy bones and long, cold, ink-stained fingers.

And his income was erratic. Once, he gave up the Customs Office to pursue the performance of a play he'd written. Went to Margate. A satire on gaming, it closed after one act to howls of derision, he said. His coat was spattered with egg.

'Oh,' she said, disappointed for him and for herself.

'I should have acted in it myself. It would have been a success if I had,' he said.

'Might someone else put it on, here in the city? I thought you knew actors.'

'No hope of that.' How can he grin, she thought, while uttering such words? 'No. No hope. But how often do great writers go unrecognised?'

She had no reply to give but in any case he suddenly laughed aloud and asked her what she'd brought to eat.

Somehow he retrieved his position at the Customs Office, but apparently there was little left over after the landlord and Betsy had been paid. It was out of the question for Sarah to leave the coffee house, he said. They couldn't live without Battle food and wine, Battle money.

3

For two years the city is feverish with war. When the French execute their king and declare war on Britain and Holland, volunteers pull on uniforms and march about; mercenaries from Hesse and Hanover reinforce the King's Men against expected invasion.

Opinion is divided in Battle's. There are those who pledge competitive sums to defend the realm; those who complain with disgust at the draining of the Exchequer.

'We know quite well who will don the uniform of these new militia,' snarls Bullock. 'It's what all those Irish traitors have been waiting for. Free weaponry!'

'You smell traitors round every corner, Bullock, hopping out of every cesspool you peer into along your way,' says Thynne, his chin jutting ever more sharply at his opponent.

'Pah!'

The military diversions are good for those who employ quick wit in crime, like William Leopard, a lawyer with a fine living from excise fraud. But then people become disgruntled with war, its colossal expense when harvests are poor. Riots break out like the pox. There are too many Runners about the place, too many Extra-Constables, and now they're onto him.

A warning to Leopard from a 'friend' comes wrapped in a

parcel of sprats. He has no time to destroy evidence, gather cash, a clean shirt and stockings, escapes across the yard at the back of the house, flees over the bridge, darts along Tower Street, down Beer Lane to the quays. Porters' Quay seems deserted until he sees someone chucking stones at gulls.

It's a boy with an accurate throw. The birds are quicker of course; like crows they sense hostility before it strikes. If he sits next to him nobody'll look twice, will they, seeing two anonymous backs along the quay? They'll think they're fishing.

The constables will start with Hardman, obviously, his partner in law. He didn't have time to send on the sprat parcel. But if they're busy with Hardman, it'll give *him* more time. Eventually Hardman will squeal, of course. His name's a nonsense! Then they'll pick up on the copemen in Tooley Street and the light-horsemen, but they're *far* too canny to be caught out.

The bills of lading game is shot. He'll have to mizzle quick, get right away. Soon.

He's fat, out of breath, needs to sit down. The boy's legs hang over the slimy stone, a pile of chippings on the ground next to him.

'You're good,' he says. 'Ever tried a pistol?'

The boy looks up, startled. Leopard notes: clean, well fed, not living on the streets. Sensitive, self-absorbed. About fifteen. Blue and yellow bundle nearby, his discarded uniform.

'Shouldn't you be at school?' Still no reply. The whole quay is oddly deserted. That's good. He'll easily hear if steps approach.

'William Leopard,' he extends his hand though it isn't taken. 'May I sit here with you?'

'As you wish,' the boy growls, voice new-broken. 'Shouldn't *you* be at work?'

'A nice point!' Leopard laughs. 'Give me one of your stones, will you?'

Before them are barges lashed together three deep, stretched six along. Wooden chests marked B E N G A L. So easy for scuffle-hunters! Perhaps straight theft is better than false papers. Damned bad luck. But he'll not stoop to jemmies and night work. Too much effort, no sleep.

Gulls stand in a row on the outer edge of the barges, fly up, screaming, dive and fight for booty, return to the row again. Leopard aims, misses. As he expects, the boy picks a missile, lines up and drives a bird, screeching, into the air.

'Bulls-eye!' What did you say your name was?'

'I didn't.'

'No, you didn't.'

'Matthew Dale.'

'Matt?'

'Matthew.'

'Wouldn't it be better further up, Matthew, fishing from Dice Quay?'

'I'm not fishing.'

'No, but if you went further up you could.'

'Can't take fish home.'

'Ah.'

'As you said, I'm supposed to be at school.'

'And which school is that?'

But the boy isn't going to say, just as he, too, will keep certain facts to himself.

'What is *your* work?' the boy asks Leopard suddenly, plucking at erratic courage.

He looks at the man and finds him extraordinary. His clothes are grimy, tight-fitting, stained yet made from good cloth. He's educated too, as well as prying. Must be cautious, can't have the man report him. Yet he doesn't look the reporting type. Too unshaven and amused.

'The law,' says Leopard. 'I'm a lawyer. Doing a little business.'

'*Here*?'

'A somewhat difficult transaction. Merchants have need of lawyers, you know.' He waves his hand vaguely.

'Oh.'

'Sugar, brandy, wheat. There's seventy-seven thousand tons of iron due from Petersburg,' he sighs.

Matthew yawns.

'I see you have no interest in trade, young man.'

'No.'

'I'll wager you're a revolutionary. A Jacobin – I bet *that's* what you are.'

The boy blushes. His features are small, unfinished; bear the burden of transition, of daring in conflict with caution.

'You hate this corrupt world, don't you, this vicious self-seeking government. I'm *sure* you do.'

Matthew hunches himself. The man is laughing at him. Any minute now he'll reveal himself as an unusual friend of his father's and trudge him back home.

'I'm serious, young man. *I* hate this corrupt world, this vicious self-seeking government.'

'Then why do you work in it?'

'How precise you are! Have you read Tom Paine?'

Matthew wishes the man would go. He knows they'll find out and beat him sooner or later, but later is what he hopes for. He's here because he hates his *life*, not because he hates the government. *Wishes* the man would go.

'Look!' Leopard rummages in his stuffed pockets and pulls out a book. Thumbed, greasy. *Rights of Man,* Part I. 'Have you read it?'

'It's banned,' Matthew says. Embarrassed at the folly of this remark he stutters: '*And* I've read Part II.'

'I knew it! A man after my own heart. Shake hands, citizen!'

The gulls fly up at this burst of activity and noise from the quay.

'What a book it is! Who has done more for the world than he? But here, you won't have seen this.' He thrusts a creased pamphlet at the boy. *King Killing*, it's called, published at the British Tree of Liberty, Berwick Street.

'Take it! Still, it's no good reading banned books behind closed shutters, is it? You're too young for action, I suppose. But sitting on the quayside's not going to help the world.'

'*You're* sitting on the quayside, too.'

'Yes, yes, *now* I am. But not for long. Well, no doubt dodging school is a start. What is your father?'

Matthew mumbles.

'A *chaplain*! A man of the cloth! Oh Lord! Then I admire you, Matthew. You defy your school, you defy your father. You've started on the right road.'

'Are *you* on the right road?' The boy's voice squeaks infuriatingly. He's unused to praise; isn't sure that's what this is.

'I myself shall go to America.'

'Ah!' Matthew sits back and stares at this surprising companion with the blackguardly face. Pocked skin, lank hair, all-seeing eyes.

'France *was* the place, as you know. Once. But the French have defiled themselves, betrayed their principles. They have not drowned corruption in all the blood they've spilled; it has surged up again. America is the only place to be. Paine knows that himself, of course.

'But you have made a beginning, young Matthew. The right road, as I said. Already you are countering authority. Is there not something even bolder you could do?'

'Perhaps.' As he hesitates an idea forms. Of striking simplicity. 'Tomorrow. I think I can do something revolutionary by then. Will you come again tomorrow?'

'Well, young man. I *could*. Yes, I could do that. I need some time to make arrangements, in fact. But maybe we should meet somewhere else. Mustn't arouse suspicion. These new river police are on the prowl looking for men with hogsheads stuffed down their trousers.' He laughs immoderately. 'How about the beach below the Tower? At low tide.'

'*No*! Here's better. There's nobody about, is there?'

'True. Tomorrow might be different, though. Well, all right, here then. But look. Should anyone ask for me, you haven't seen me. Have no notion who they're talking about. Nobody of my description. *Could* you describe me?'

'Easily.'

'Well *don't*. And *I* haven't see *you*. Truant? Never met one! Agreed?'

They shake hands. 'Porters' Quay, eight o'clock!'

Matthew watches the insolent set of Leopard's shoulders as he walks briskly up the street. He turns back to the river. He can't go home for hours yet.

*

It's clear and hot soon after daybreak. The river teems with boats. Barges form an inner margin below quays and wharves, dredgers, lighters, floating fire engines lie by. Mid-stream, masted ships rock, their sails half furled. They can go no further up-river for London Bridge stands in their way on all its legs. Brigs, cutters, West Indiamen, their cargoes unloaded into small boats by lightermen. Over the rest of the water dart skiffs and rowing boats, sculled, punted; fishing, scouting, ferrying.

At eight Matthew is pacing the quay. Smiles break on his taut face. Leopard is late and he can hardly bear the wait.

At last, some twenty minutes later, the man arrives, walking rapidly, panting slightly. They shake hands. Matthew notices that Leopard wears exactly the same clothes. A strong sourness suggests he slept in them.

'Citizen Dale! Did anyone ask for me? No sniffing quay guards?'

'No, Citizen Leopard. Not a soul.'

'That's a relief. But let me warn you, Matthew, I am a little jumpy today.'

'Oh?'

'My business has not gone well. I cannot stay long. But now, let me see. No one found *you* out either, then? Your parents do not suspect? The school?'

'So far not. But have you forgotten, Mr Leopard? Have you forgotten my revolutionary act?'

'Ah! No, by god, no! What have you done then, citizen?'

'I should like you to guess.'

'How can I do that? I hardly know you. It's impossible.' He looks around him and back at Matthew, taps his right foot impatiently.

'What I have done can be seen,' says Matthew proudly. 'It can be seen from *here*.'

'From *here*! Well! In that direction I see ships, more ships, London Bridge, waterworks, Hanks's timber, Fowler's, Clove's.' He tails off. Must he play *games* for this final 'transaction'?

'Wrong direction.'

'Oh. Behind me then?'

'No.'

'Then that leaves the river itself, barges, ships. Nothing revolutionary that I can see. All looks the same. Wharves, warehouses on the other side. Left is all that remains,' he swings round slowly, 'the walls of the Tower.'

'The Royal Arms are flying,' says Matthew, 'for it's the King's Birthday today. June 4th.'

They both look towards the White Tower.

'Good God! Do my eyes deceive me? Did *you* do that? *Did* you? Your revolutionary act. The work of a genius! Citizen Dale!'

From the ramparts of the White Tower a second flagpole protrudes and from that flagpole the French Tricolor flutters in the glory of the June morning.

'Did you do that?'

'Yes.'

'But how? How on earth?'

'My father is chaplain of the Tower,' says the boy, ashamed and proud.

'You *live* there then?'

'Yes.'

'Is it true there are apple trees in the grounds?'

'Yes. But what of that? I was up early. No one saw me – not even the lions in the menagerie. And *still* no one has noticed else it would have been struck by now.'

'Where did you *find* a Tricolor?'

'We made it. My sister and I. We sewed it last night from pieces of silk we found.'

'So, you're not in this alone. Did you tell her about me?'

'No. But in any case, Lucy will not tell. Nor shall I tell of *her* when I am found out.'

'Then surely you had better not return. And I...'

They are stopped by an immense booming.

'Don't worry. It's not the powder mills exploding!' shouts Matthew, for Leopard has nearly jumped out of his skin. Cannon are firing from St James's and suddenly, very close, they're answered by those at the Tower.

'It's for the King. Yet my flag still flies!' The boy laughs like a child.

'Matthew. Tomorrow I take a ship to America. To freedom. The only land in the world where liberty, equality and fraternity truly live – better by far than your France. No, don't be downcast. The flag's a grand gesture. You have proved yourself.'

Leopard paces around the boy with tense steps.

'Come to America with me! I shall escape my little trouble here and you will escape punishment. For what will they do when they find that it was you?'

The boy's delight has gone. He watches the sharp eyes darting like flies.

'Yes, come with me. We can meet here tomorrow before the sailing. It had better be nine o'clock; we can't board before the tide's in. Bring as many clothes as you can fit in a single bag. I believe the winters are cold there. And bring as much money as you can. For your passage.'

'I shall have to steal it.'

'Is stealing worse than hoisting the flag of the enemy on the King's Birthday? We are at war with France! That's *treason*! Punishable by death!

'Now Matthew, think only of America. Your future lies there not here. Here there's only repression and punishment. The ship sails to Philadelphia. I shall set up a law office and you, with your precision you could take up the law yourself! Oh, there'll be all manner of opportunities. And women, Matthew! There's women aplenty in the land of liberty!'

The boy looks down, oppressed by youth and desire. Leopard glances about him again. His ears prick up, cat-like.

'Come now, Matthew. Let us shake hands on it. If I'd a bottle we could toast ourselves. To America! Till tomorrow! Nine o'clock!'

And he's gone. Along stones still black from the stream of liquid fire when the sugar warehouse went up. Matthew feels utterly dejected and excited beyond anything he's ever known before.

America. Freedom.

He looks up. The tricolor is no longer there.

*

June 5th is hot again. A burning sky dries the sludge at low tide, magnifies the stink of fish and sewage. The upper air is clear, the lower clammy with steam and smoke, hops, malt, pitch. There's little activity on the river, the barges beached, boats bobbing only in mid-stream. The gulls at Porters' Quay have flown up-river to Fishmonger's Hall to await the flounders and smelt, shad, lampreys, jack, perch, chub.

The tide returns, boats breathe again, ships shift. The gulls, satiated, swoop back to their spattered row on the barges that knock against the stone. The boxes from B E N G A L have not been unloaded. Porters' Quay is deserted. No one comes all day.

4

What with the rioting and the burgeoning number of radicals, Government winds tight the wire. Even in Battle's someone's arrested for giving out handbills urging on the rioters. Sam is disgusted, as near as he can to being ashamed it's happened on his premises. Sarah looks away, knows she's like to be blamed.

Not that James is seen in Battle's: it's not known where he drinks. But Sam assumes that his daughter goes along with her husband's views as a woman should, even with *those* views. After all, his own wife curbed her Methodism at his command. And he's right for the wrong reason. Sarah's feelings diverge: she is drawn to the ideas, no longer to the purveyor of them. His attraction for her was an odd thing from the start.

She and James see each other rarely: she's up and out before six, he comes in late. She leaves supper for him; they write notes to each other.

James,
Betsy says the coal is low. Please call in at Seagur's.
Sarah

Sarah,
I have told Betsy to wrap the rolls each in two napkins so
they remain hot. I dislike a cold roll for breakfast.
Did you give her her money?
Jas.

Occasionally they walk out on a Sunday as Sarah no longer goes to church, and of course they've no need to fear recognition as they did during their stilted courtship.

'Now this will amuse you,' he says, knowing from somewhere before that she likes to be amused. When *was* that? Yes, when he first sat in Battle's and watched her, red in the heat, competent in all she did, not flirtatious. Saw her smile to herself momentarily.

After two years of marriage neither one knows the other. He sees no reason to change his pre-marriage calculations. Her visions from that time have vanished.

'A cricket match. Team of Greenwich pensioners with one leg against another with one arm. Tars against tars.' He gives his short shout of a laugh that's more shout than laugh. 'We must go south over the bridge to Walworth. Someone's put up a thousand guineas. Think of that! The one-armers will win, surely.'

'It will be painful to watch, not amusing.'

'Painful? To *them*, maybe. Haha!'

'No, James. I should find it a painful spectacle. You go. I'd rather see if the porpoises are still in the river. I heard they swam up yesterday.'

'I'll go to Walworth later. I've finished all my notes. The game will last the whole day and longer. Bound to be slow.'

They join the crowds along the banks at London Bridge. Gulls wheel; thousands of clacks and whistles issue from starlings on nearby buildings. Three porpoises leap and dive as if playing to the audience and when the rain comes on sport all the more. Sarah feels a childish joy at the sight; the ghost of a sensation in her elbow to jog Newton into sketching the scene.

'Look at that!' A cheer goes up at a spectacular double leap and turn.

'Swum away from the French, eh? Right up the river.'

'No, no! They've come to see the flag now the Tower's gone revolutionary!' A round of cackles at this.

'Ate up all the smelts, them poipoises!' a fisherman complains.

'It do indicate an 'ard winter, I've 'eard. Just you wait and see. Freeze over it will.'

James wonders if porpoises are good to eat.

The rain becomes heavy and people disperse.

Back in Cheapside they remove their drenched outer clothes to drape and steam before the fire. James creeps up behind Sarah and clamps his hands on her breasts. She jumps. Shrinks.

'Come now, Sarah.' He turns her to face him. 'We are *married*.' Out of their shadows his eyes fix on her mouth.

'I'm chilled from the rain.' It's the truth, but she won't tell him the rest. Cannot say that she married the *idea* of him, had never much cared for the body. And the idea turned out to be false. He was to have been her escape into a better life.

His stockings stink. His nibbling lips are thin, his fingers long and cold.

*

He mentions a huge gathering in St George's Fields at the end of the month. She thinks of the luminous phrases he discarded when he ceased his courtship.

'I shall go,' she tells him.

'I'll get a ticket for you. Did you know that people were killed in the Fields some years ago, shot by redcoats? St George's Massacre. 1768.'

'The year I was born,' she says.

But she must go. Hear, see for herself. She lies to her father, asks for a free afternoon. Draws his permission like a pulsing tooth.

The June day shines. Her walk is long: from Lombard Street into Gracechurch, Fish Street Hill, over London Bridge and along the Borough where soon she's moving in waves of women and children, families, even babies, towards the fields. She's not been near crowds of people since childhood. Remembering, she looks for bludgeons, cutlasses, sees none, though plenty of sleeves rolled up in the heat.

Acres of field, walled between the Obelisk and King's Bench prison, already surrounded by mounted troops, their horses snorting, pawing the ground impatiently; packs of nervous militia, for each man a musket. She won't look at them, sees, instead, sand martins swooping over dirty pools. Hundreds and hundreds of people, thousands, she can't guess how many. James is there somewhere, making notes with his pen and portable inkwell to transcribe later that night.

She shows her ticket, seeks out a group to join, for the space is so huge it terrifies her. Someone offers a corner of their blanket and she sits there among dock and burdock with wives and children of bakers, shoemakers, cordwainers, a watch-face painter. Men climb onto the wooden stage and silence drops on the thousands. The speaker begins – 'Citizens!' – and the people stir like one body to his words. They flinch, smile, tense with emotion, fill with glory, and in moments Sarah, too, is swept quite out of herself till she weeps and shouts with the rest.

'Are we *Britons* and is not *Liberty* a British RIGHT? There is no Power on Earth shall silence the Voice of an injured Nation!' Of course she cries for the injured nation. Cries for the injured, weeps for the dead. Her mother and Newton. Shot by soldiers. Lost to her. But her loss washes out into a sea of ideals that surges round her.

'The Voice of Reason, like the Roaring of the Nemean Lion, shall issue even from the Cavern's Mouth! Universal Suffrage! Annual Parliaments! Men may perish but Truth shall be Eternal!'

Elation pulls citizens to their feet. It's a huge gathering. Yet peaceable: no shapes caper among flames in Sarah's imagination, let alone on the field. There is no violence. Horse and foot guards slink away unused.

She is inspired. Carries the day home with her, compact in her mind, to be kept alive for ever in layers of memory. James is already writing up his notes when she arrives home; must have taken a ride in a cart. Puts a long finger to his lips pursed with determination.

I have faced the world, she tells herself, *I have sat on the ground with it, shouted with it, risen up with it*. It is not as she once envisaged. Now when she hears of bread riots, of anti-crimping riots against cruel press-gangs, she is moved. When she hears that someone has thrown a stone at the King's coach she closes her ears to the bursts of disapprobation led by her father. Habeas Corpus is suspended; new acts against seditious activities and treasonable practices are drawn up. Her negligible marriage has brought her something after all. A real cause.

5

Not present at St George's Field, his dues unpaid, his membership lapsed, is Joseph Young, an engraver, in his last apprentice year.

Now it's well past dawn. He's spent most of the night at Wood's, a cock and hen club he visits whenever his mood begins to plunge. He's still a couple of streets from his lodgings in Albion Place, the upper floor of an ill-patched house, three-quarters of a mile due west of Winkworth Buildings, City Road.

In a doorway he sees a girl. It's the bag that catches his attention first, then the clothes, she's no beggar, and pretty, though he can't be sure in half-light. He'd not have noticed her at all if it hadn't been this late. He'd cleared off early from Wood's when a raid threatened, dodging the Watch with his long stride.

'What are you doing here?'

She looks up at him, pale, opens her mouth but doesn't speak. Perhaps can't. Her position suggests she collapsed, unable to stand any longer.

'Let me help you.'

She closes her eyes.

'You must come indoors. I live nearby. You can shelter there for the rest of the night.'

She shrinks back against the wall, her eyes still shut, banishing him.

'If you don't come, one of the Runners will arrest you.' She looks at him then and he reaches down, lifts her, takes her bag, holds her upright with his other arm. They shuffle along, scuffing summer-baked mud.

He puts her in the one upholstered chair and takes the blanket off his bed. The room is chill: he'd dowsed the fire before leaving. There's nothing to eat but when she mouths 'thank you' as he tucks the blanket round her, he realises she's too dry to speak. He's out of water, will have to go down to the yard and pump some, but here's an almost empty jug of beer.

'I expect you won't like this but drink it, please.' She sips, grimaces, sips again.

'Sleep now. You're safe here. I'm an engraver; quite respectable.' Well, quite. 'In the morning I'll get you something to eat.'

But she's already asleep.

He removes her hat, wants to loosen her hair from its pressed hat shape to sketch her in her exhaustion, doesn't, stands looking at her hands clenched tightly beneath her chin and goes to bed in his coat.

*

Despite the hangover he wakes after three hours and lights a fire. When she opens her eyes he asks her to watch the kettle while he buys food.

Perhaps she's an orphan. He remembers when his mother died and his father went to pieces and apprenticed him to

49

Digham. He was fourteen, his life cut, deadened until he grew to love his master like a father. William Digham. On a surge of affection for the dear man he buys hot rolls from a street seller, cheese, butter, milk. Later he'll fetch a baked dish from the Eagle.

She's stoking the fire. Has warmed the teapot, replaced his blanket, folded neatly on his bed.

'Please tell me your name,' she says.

'Joseph Young. And yours?'

'Lucy Dale. I think you saved my life, Mr Young.'

'No, no. You were nowhere near dying.'

'I'm sure I was.' She pauses, then indicates the chaos of his room. 'I couldn't find any plates or cups, Mr Young.'

'Call me Joseph. I expect I'm not much older than you. All this? Well, I live and work here. Alone. People say I'm disorderly. I'm sorry.'

He finds a plate under a book, wipes it with his cuff, locates his own unwashed cup and an unused one hanging on a hook on the wall. They share the plate which he balances on a wooden chair.

'I'm terribly hungry.' He can see she is, beneath her polite gestures. He sits cross-legged at her feet, there being nowhere else to sit.

'When did you last eat, Lucy?'

'Breakfast two days ago.'

'Had you no money?'

'A little.'

'You could have bought a pie or a cheesecake.'

'I decided to speak to no one.'

'So you spent the first night in the streets?'

'Yes. I walked about. Sat on steps when I needed to rest. I didn't close my eyes once. I didn't dare to.'

'Where did you intend to go?'

'I don't know.'

She fascinates him. Pretty, yes, if quietly so. Resolute and helpless all at once.

'You can live here!' he says. 'That's it! There's plenty of room. I'll move a few things. I know it's a muddle but I could clean it up.' Not that he's ever cleaned anything in his life. She turns from his gaze. 'Oh, but perhaps you have a home to go to.'

'No. I shan't go home.'

'So you have a home.'

'It's not a home to me any more.'

'You've fled.'

She holds her cup in both hands; perhaps they're still cold. Yet her face is faintly flushed. He observes the shape of it, the set of her eyes, her small, determined mouth, her hair much fairer than his own. Her beauty is delicate, but certain: his fingers itch to sketch her.

'It's because of my brother. Matthew. Papa beat him. I could hear it a whole floor away. And Mama wouldn't stop him. Then they beat him at school, too! When he came home Papa said he must go back and live at school. He's arranged it with the headmaster. He must stay until he's eighteen. It's like sending him to prison.' She breaks into sobs.

He casts around for a handkerchief, sees only inky rags, the one in his coat pocket filthy, but she takes one from her travelling bag.

'What did they beat him for? How old is he? What in heaven's name did he do?'

'Oh, Matthew is fifteen, a year younger than me. But we're friends. We've always been friends. We never quarrel, unlike some brothers and sisters. I shall not live at home if Matthew is not there.'

'But what did he do that was so bad?'

'He hoisted a French flag on the White Tower on the King's Birthday. They said it was a crime.'

'Oh lord! What an extraordinary thing to do! And how on earth…? Was it his idea?'

'Yes, but I helped him sew the flag.'

'Oho!'

'We found pieces of silk in my mother's box of stuffs. A proper sized flag: three yards wide. Matthew attached it to rope.'

'You're revolutionaries! Wonderful! I've known several myself, but none like you, for they're all men. Lucy, you are the first revolutionary woman I've met.'

He begins to sweat. Holds his fists hard on his thighs. Forgets his lack of sleep.

'I cannot claim that title – I'm not sure I believe in revolution.'

'I was once in the Corresponding Society. Have you heard of it?'

'No, I haven't. All I know is that Matthew is angry the whole time. He hates where we live. Hates the school. Oh, poor Matthew! But it's no use my crying about him, is it? I shall make a plan to rescue him. Though I don't suppose … At least I can write letters to him. Do you think they'll let him receive letters?'

'I don't know. Perhaps not. I'll help you, Lucy.'

'Will you?'

'We'll secrete letters to him somehow. I have friends of all kinds. But where do you live that he hates so much?'

'The Tower. We live in the Tower. We already live in a prison, you see! The prison for traitors. My father is chaplain. The soldiers there must attend services; sometimes the King comes.'

'Heavens!' He scrambles up heavily from the floor. 'Then I salute Matthew. I salute you both. What a remarkable thing to do! What courage! And I have only ever posted bills and bored myself at interminable meetings! Oh, how feeble! Lucy, I am honoured to have found you!'

He takes both her hands, pulls her to her feet.

'I must sketch you. Stand there. Just there!'

He steps sideways, knocks her teacup and dabs violently at her clothes with the nearest rag.

'Oh! Have I ruined the gown? How careless of me. You shall have another.'

'Are you so rich, to buy food for two people and new gowns?'

'No, not rich. My father left a bit of money. I'm almost through it. I shall finish my apprenticeship next year. But I'm very good, you know. Digham says so and he's the best engraver in London. I'll draw you now!'

*

A while later, she watches him mix a ground of asphalt, resin, wax, spread it onto a plate of thin copper. The smell of resin speaks of unknown forests. He takes his etching needle, deftly reproduces his charcoal sketch in reverse, an image of herself cut into wax. With care she would not have thought possible from his previous clumsiness he dips the plate into a small bath, warns her not to touch the nitric acid, dilute though it is. Lifts it out, dabs varnish on the deepest grooves, dips again.

Rags, more rags, discarded clothes. Under a pile of them she finds some finewed bread, grey and hairy, another cup, a hard-boiled egg half eaten, but doesn't distract him with her finds.

He removes the ground from the copper plate.

'And now to Digham's', he says. 'Will you come? He has the press, you see. When I've earned enough I shall buy my own. Meanwhile I etch and engrave here and take my plates to him to be inked and printed. And sold if he likes them.'

'How far away is it? I don't want to be recognised.'

'Paternoster Row. Not far. Pull your kerchief over your face.'

She barely keeps up with him for he walks ahead as if forgetting she is there, the carefully wrapped plate under his arm.

'Lucy!' He turns, calls to her. Waits. She has kept her eyes on his head above the throng, the fair, tied-back hair bouncing on his coat, the pockets of which are bulging.

'What have you in your pockets?'

'Oh, I don't know. Books.'

They must pass through Smithfield. A comical pair, the tall young man striding with a parcel wrapped in old shirts, the girl, her face half hidden, running to keep up.

It's a great wide area, a field opening out from closed-in streets. Thousands of sheep shove each other in tight-packed pens. Lines of cattle and horses nudge and nose, rear suddenly, bellow, whinny; men whack them with switches. The air stinks of hot hide and the dung that will be carted to market gardens in Stepney and Chelsea at day's end. Shouts and cries of pudding-, sausage- and mutton dumpling-sellers punctuate the lowing, neighing, baaing, bawling, the rattle of auctioneers' patter. It's summer: young women, perspiring, sell strawberries, scarlet strawberries, round and sound five pence the pound Duke cherries.

He buys her a penny stick of cherries and bends to hear that she'll not eat them now for fear of revealing her face. He plunges on, she hastens to keep up, fearing to lose him in the press of men. For a while a dog runs with them. On towards Christ's Hospital, past new-built Newgate's enormous walls, down Warwick Lane to the narrow gloom of old buildings at the skirts of St Paul's.

At the top of a flight of stairs she waits in a dark doorway. Altar-like, a printing press stands in the middle of a room, in light pond-green from a tree's dense leaves outside the back window.

A short man in an embroidered felt hat looks at them through thick lenses.

'Joseph! And who have you brought with you? Come in, come in.'

'William, this is Lucy Dale. A heroine. I found her. Lucy, this is William Digham, my beloved master. The best engraver and etcher in town. I have learned everything from him.'

'Delighted, Miss Dale. A heroine you say, Joseph.'

'Yes.' Apparently he feels no need to explain. 'And, Lucy, this is Batley,' indicating a brawny man sweating and heaving with his arms and knee on the huge star-wheel of the press.

Batley nods mid-turn.

'Please sit here, Miss Dale.' Digham places her at a bench by the street window. A glass bowl of water on the sill magnifies light onto a small area of the bench. 'Can you draw?'

'Why yes. I've had a few lessons.'

'I thought so.'

She contemplates paper, pencils, charcoal, pens, while Digham questions Joseph under lines of prints pegged above their heads like washing on a still day.

'Now, young man Young, have you brought me a new apprentice?'

'No, William. I've a plate to print. I'll ink it, then you'll see.'

He unwraps his plate, rolls ink over it until the grooves are full, wipes it clean, lies a damp sheet of paper on it, places it in the press. Batley pulls with both arms, pushes with a podgy knee, the paper passes through and Joseph grabs it delicately.

'Ah!' he says and pegs it to dry. 'You'll see shortly.'

'I understand,' says Digham, gazing at the print moments later. 'He has a great talent, Miss Dale. Look. He has not flattered you, it's entirely true to life. Mirifical! Such touching symmetry of feature. Lovely!' While he shows her the print Joseph stands opposite scanning her face.

She reddens, pleased, embarrassed, unsure what to do or say.

'And shall I suggest how much you should charge, Joseph?' Digham asks.

'No, William. I'll not sell it.'

*

He constructs a bed for her of sorts for she won't hear of his giving up his; comes home with a mattress on his back that doesn't look too bad. She offers to cook for him so he picks up a frying pan and saucepan from a street-seller. She tidies and cleans one end of the large room, not daring to touch the other half where he works.

She gathers together the books she finds scattered on the floor, on the mantelpiece, under heaps of paper, and places them on shelves. Recites the titles to herself like a prayer of worship: *Paradise Lost*, *Paradise Regained*, Paine's *Rights of Man* Part I (Part II lives beside his bed), *Age of Reason*, Volney's *Ruins of Empires*, Martin's *Philosophical Grammar*, Shakespeare's plays, Cowper's poems, Defoe, Goldsmith, Voltaire, Homer. In between she wedges pamphlets: Priestley's

'The Importance and Extent of Free Enquiry', Thomas Day's 'The Dying Negro'.

'I don't suppose I'll read most of those books again,' he tells her. 'I have far too much to do. A paragraph of Paine is about all I can manage these days.' She takes a couple for herself: Bewick's *General History of Quadrupeds*, Johnson's *Lives of the Poets*.

They discuss Matthew's 'rescue' with scant hope and she begins a letter to her brother. He works at two plates for Digham, breaking off frequently to sketch her as she reads, as she writes. At other times she wonders if he remembers that she's there at all, so engrossed is he in drawing and etching at his bench. Then sees how he stares at the wall before him, not moving for minutes at a time, in a paralysis of concentration.

She gives him all the money she has, for her keep. It's not much and he accepts it.

'I shall take in fine sewing,' she tells him. 'In another week, when perhaps they have stopped looking for me. When that money runs out.'

Joseph grunts. He is busy: with his right hand he clasps the wooden mushroom handle of the burin, pushing its lozenge point into metal, forcing out curls of copper that cover the floor around his bench. With his left hand he holds the corner of the copper plate which rests on its leather pad, turning it to accommodate the burin's movements. The hands move in harmony with each other, creating harmony. To her he is a master.

A few days pass. Lucy's ways are quiet; she is the visitor, the intruder. Joseph is kindly, smiling; impatient, tetchy. Loud, boisterous; silent for hours.

One morning he doesn't rise.

'Are you ill?' she asks, but he waves her away. She tries to read.

'Go away! Leave me be!' he shouts at her later when she asks again.

She hears him groaning into his pillow. Dares approach.

'Worthless. My work is worthless. I shall abandon it.'

'Joseph, your work is wonderful! William Digham says so, not just me.'

He ignores her. 'Yes, I'll give it up. I'll buy a cart, a horse, collect night soil. What's the difference? It's muck. What's the point of these *drawings? Prints!* It's no good, any of it. To the dung heap with it! I might just as well set up as a goldfinder!' He moans, clutches his head with both hands.

She wants to cry, to laugh. He is ridiculous. Or is he? Eventually he gets up, counts out countless drops from a ribbed glass bottle. His head crashes onto his desk and he seems to sleep. Awake, he leafs through his sketches, flings them on the floor, stands before the fire staring at his feet. He has not spoken for more than a day.

'I'm going out tonight, Lucy. You will not mind?' He looks into her face so intently she turns away.

'How could I mind, Joseph? You rescued me. You let me live here. I am indebted to you.'

He growls, leaves and she feels entirely bereft. Lies down on his bed to retain the sense of him and wakes the following morning.

He returns after dark, dishevelled, his eyes faintly glittering.

She has tidied his bed, washed, drunk tea, eaten nothing. She is alarmed at the smell of him, too inexperienced to know its various origins.

'Don't stare at me! Miss Perfect. Miss Virginal Perfect.'

She can say nothing.

'Miss Perfect Welcomes Home the Evil Artist. Hah! There's a subject for a print. Now, you're turning away from me. Don't!'

'You told me not to stare at you.'

'Don't stare but don't turn away from me. Never turn away from me, Lucy! You are innocence itself. I need to see that innocence exists. Especially here.

'When I was your age I was innocent, too. You don't believe me, do you? It's true. Then one day I found myself in a house of ill-repute. By accident. It's true! And do you know, I heard someone sing a wondrous song in that place. It was the most beautiful thing I'd ever encountered.'

What can she say to this? She struggles to understand. Fails completely.

'We are all of us round-packed sinners. Perhaps even you are. It's just a veneer that perfection of yours. Think of your name. Lucy. It comes from lux, light. But so does Lucifer. Which are you, light or dark? Ha. Haha! Lucy Lux Lucifer!' He slaps his thighs in delight while she looks at him dumbfounded. 'There now. You're shocked!' He falls onto his bed and sleeps immediately.

She's utterly bewildered, stupefied with dread. His words are inexplicable, except she realises he has some other life. She hardly knows what a house of ill-repute is; has heard half-tales about soldiers, diseases. Was that where he was last night, all night?

Coldness shades, invades her. She is no help to him here, when she'd thought she was. She thought he liked her, was even charmed by her. Self-flattery! She understands nothing except that there can be no reason why he'd want her to stay. It was stupid to imagine he wanted her to. He hates her, despises her. He can live without her, work perfectly well without her. He must have held back for days from going to this other place, out of politeness to her. She is mortified.

Must leave. Where can she go? Not home. Not now. She envisages her parents' disgust, their execration. They would punish her. Matthew is shut away. Could she throw stones up at his window? Which window? She knows no one.

Then it comes to her that William Digham seems kind. And he understands Joseph. Perhaps he can explain him to her, and at least he might take her in or know of somewhere she could sleep. She imagines herself resting her head on the bench by the window in the pool of light, the sweaty green darkness of the room comforting, requiring nothing of her. She thinks she can remember how to find his house. St Paul's is unmissable: you can see the dome wherever you are.

She packs her bag quietly before realising that Joseph's sleep is deep, he'll hear nothing. The last of the coins she gave him lie on a table; she won't touch them. Pinning her hat she sets off, drawn and repulsed by the sounds and stench of Smithfield, her vision dulled by tears that have yet to run. She is jostled by herdsmen thwacking cattle, called after, shouted at. She seems to be in everyone's way. Stumbles against a legless beggar on a wheeled board who curses her bitterly.

Her bag begins to weigh heavily in her hand. She stops at a shop window, puts it down, pretends to stare in and cries properly. For herself. For Matthew. Leans her head against one of its panes. Sobs for the misery of the world.

He's grasping her shoulders, turning her to him.

'Where are you going?'

'To William Digham. I am a hindrance to you. Perhaps he can find me somewhere to live.'

'You mustn't leave like this. Come back. Please, Lucy. You

must live with me! I need you to live with me. I need your innocence, your perfection. You mustn't leave me.'

She looks at him amazed. Miss Perfect. Miss Virginal Perfect. Lucy Lucifer.

But she cannot argue or protest. Allows herself to return with him, following as he strides ahead with her bag, till back in his room he holds her to him for the first time, kisses each part of her tear-smeared face, gazes at her, promises, apologises, assures. She is confused, relieved, saddened. Joyous.

6

Toil in Battle's is alleviated for Sarah by her new cause. Where once she had escaped to her imagined dialogue with Newton, now she dwells in a remembered, passionate world, populated by crowds of people more like her than any of Battle's customers.

Not that she spoke to many on that day in St George's Fields. When they learned her father had a coffee house so near the Exchange their faces fell. She watched them furtively, especially the women her age with their children and babies, the families cheerful on their day out. But as the speeches began, they listened as one, the fervency felt by all, simultaneously. Then she was no longer different; a fellow-feeling moved in some new-found depth of her being.

Newton would have drawn them, of course, sprawling all over the field, their children running after each other, soon dirty, crying, laughing, babies at the breast, the women released, shouting and waving their arms, or listening, intent.

But Newton would have been *for* them. She's sure of that. Why else had he lost all his mirth when the soldiers began shooting? Why else had he rushed out so readily into the mobs on the streets? Of course he would have thought as she does! It's a small revelation that fortifies her.

The oddest thing is James, whom she can no longer connect to the cause to which he'd introduced her.

'I've never seen so many people,' she says the day after the great meeting. 'It was a wonder to me. May I read your report?'

'It cannot interest you.'

'It does! It will remind me of everything that took place, who it was who spoke and so forth.'

'No. It's not for you.' He covers it with his arms like a schoolboy.

'I can do no harm by reading it.'

'No! My, how red you are from sitting in the sun all afternoon, Sarah. What do we eat tonight?'

She longs to talk about who spoke, what they said. But not with him. Evidently it bores him. And yet he is secretary of his branch of the Corresponding Society, writes up notes assiduously. She knows that even if it didn't bore him, he'd kill the event with his lugubrious tones.

*

In Paternoster Row Digham advises Joseph.

'Lucy is a girl of some quality, not merely pretty.'

'I know. I love her.'

'Oh?'

'I do. I've told her.'

'She loves you, I dare say.'

Joseph doesn't answer.

'It's luctiferous, Joseph.'

'Luctiferous?'

'You'll only cause sorrow. You know how I love these old words on their death beds. It's like the old methods. Watch

63

out for the wooden press gasping its last breath, young man! Iron is coming. Even stone. They say stone won't wear away like copper does.

'You should return her to her parents. Perhaps they will give you a reward!'

Joseph snorts.

'Then you must marry her. And give up your Sal or Moll, your drinking and smoking club. Wood's is it? Where is that?'

'Wych Street.'

'Cock and hen is it, or a free-and-easy club? Don't think I haven't known since you began. I was glad for you then, knew you'd learn about the world that way. Make a better artist. As a boy you were so bookish, Joseph, dawdling at bookstalls whenever I sent you out. Of course, I swallowed a few books in my youth. But you! You needed to see life. And you have. By God, you etch like an angel even if your subjects are the devil! But you must not damage Lucy.'

Still no reply. Joseph tramps round the room bending his big head beneath the lines of pegged prints, a turkey in a coup.

'Not that I think much to marriage without love on both sides.' The old man sighs.

'I told you, I love her.'

Digham's turn to snort. 'You may today, but will you tomorrow?'

'Her parents will hardly approve of me.'

'Then let me intercede for you. You say her father's deputy chaplain at the Tower. I'll go, speak for you. I've always seen myself as a father to you, Joseph. I'll go first. Smooth the way. Burnish the copper.'

Joseph looks down and Digham clutches his upper arms, embraces his large ex-apprentice.

'You are a father to me, William,' the young man says, stooping to the old face. 'I promise I shall get all those tedious plates done that I owe you, the trade cards for Casaltine and Matthews, Scattergood, the lottery tickets and all the rest. I'll do them now in double quick time. And you can be a father to us both.'

'I'll certainly accept your promise of the plates which are well overdue, but this I shall do from love. And I've had another thought. Let me teach Lucy to hand-colour and earn a little money at home colouring prints. She can do mine, she can do yours. Even some for our rivals. I suspect she has the talent to limn accurately.

'So, young man Young, I shall look forward to my visit to the Tower. I've always wanted to see the lions in the menagerie there.'

*

The Rev. Mr Henry Dale and Mrs Dale agree to Digham's request that they meet Joseph Young. But the interview with Digham is awkward and they are disinclined to believe the whole of his story. An engraver, a printer of satires, why should they trust a man with such odd speech? Lucy ran away, bad enough, but this apprentice of his... The shame of it! And following so soon upon the disgrace of Matthew's incomprehensible crime! Mrs Dale had taken to her bed for a month but finds herself just well enough to join her husband after his preliminary discussion with the wretched apprentice.

The room is dark-panelled in the style of the previous century. There are brown portraits of earlier chaplains, a glass-doored bookcase, heavy chairs and tables. Mr Dale is a very small man made even smaller by his black clothes. His wife is helped into the room by a maidservant, tucked under a rug on the only comfortable piece of furniture. Joseph searches for Lucy beneath her mother's puffy, weary skin – finds the symmetry, a mouth that had once been firm. Fair hair aged to the colour of dust. Mr Dale shows tall Joseph to a low chair and remains standing.

'My dear, as we were informed he would, Mr Young has asked for Lucy's hand in marriage,' he says in a sharp rasp. 'I have explained to him that we shall not settle a penny upon her in view of the circumstances. And in any case my own fortune would not stand it, would it, my dear.' He looks at Mrs Dale with an old resentment.

'He has assured me that he can earn enough to keep them in modest comfort as a married couple and that Mr Digham is correct in assessing his prospects highly.'

Against her will Mrs Dale finds Joseph Young intriguing. He looks older than his twenty-one years – she was expecting a brutish boy – and has an attractive confidence which has yet to spill over into contempt. Before he left, Lucy washed and brushed him, advised him to wear his other coat, which she patched discreetly, a clean shirt, a striped waistcoat whose stains could not be seen. All of this, she told him, would help placate her respectable parents.

'My future is certain, Mrs Dale.' Joseph bows in her direction. 'I can engrave and etch perfectly and I use stipple and aquatint, both of which are desired by those who buy prints nowadays.' He looks up at the walls of the room with their archaic, carved panels and wainscoting, so valued by rioters seeking flammable material. There are no prints: they won't know what he's talking about. 'In five years I shall be the most well-known engraver in London.'

Mr Dale turns away from this distasteful boasting.

'And, for a while at least, Lucy will learn the art of hand-colouring so that together we can create finished prints.' Now it is Mrs Dale who turns away at the thought of this man and her daughter together.

'Of course, were I able to buy my own printing press then we should be dependent upon no one. We could be successful much sooner. At present I must use Mr Digham's press, you see. Even a small settlement could help me achieve the goal of purchasing my own.'

'Mr Dale?' says his wife, feeling a bubble of generosity begin to rise through habitual self-pity. Mr Dale ignores her query.

'Mrs Dale and I agree to your marrying our daughter Lucy as long as you do so as soon as possible. A pity Marylebone Old Church is no more. There you could have done it immediately. We shall not attend the ceremony of course.'

'Though I shouldn't presume to speak for Lucy, yet I am sure she, too, would prefer that you didn't attend,' Joseph says with disgust at parental heartlessness. It is a mistake.

'You will be good enough to inform us when it is done, Mr Young.' He pulls on a bell-cord. 'Bessy will show you out. Good day.'

*

St George's Court
Albion Place
Britton Street
14th November 1795

My dearest Matthew,

I wish I could know that you are well. I wish I could know that you will even receive this letter, but since I shall take it myself and try to persuade the porter to give it to you I am hopeful.

You will see from the address that I am no longer at home. I ran away when they took you back to the school and shall certainly never return so long as you are not there.

In any case I have found a friend who rescued me when I was fainting in the street – I had collapsed in a doorway. We are to be married! He has asked permission of Papa and Mama, which they have granted, though they want nothing to do with us. His name is Joseph Young and he is an engraver, so skilful and clever that I know he will become famous. And I have begun to learn how to be a limner, to colour his prints with watercolour paint so that we can sell them.

I know you will like him. He thinks you are terribly brave. He belongs to the Corresponding Society but is not such a revolutionary as you.

Oh Matthew, I hope and pray that they are not beating you any longer! Please write to me and tell me how you are.

Your ever loving,
Lucy

*

Joseph accompanies her to the school as she finds it hard to remember his directions, so anxious is she about her letter.

It takes an hour, avoiding the main roads blocked with carriages and carts, cutting through filthy, unpaved backstreets.

'Joe!' In Cross Street two men hail him through smog. ''Ow are you? Is it Joe, or is it a phantom?'

'Where you bin?' says the other. 'Wood's ain't the same wivout you. Not seen you in fourteen days.'

'Fourteen nights!' the first man says and punches him on the arm in mock fight. They look Lucy up and down. She's standing aside, shy, preoccupied, unused to working men on friendly terms. She feels their gaze all over her.

'Oo's the pretty wench, Joe? Friend o' yours? Sister, mebbe?'

'This is Lucy, Lucy Dale. Yes, she's a friend.'

He says nothing about marriage.

'Glad to meet you Miss Dale. 'Ow d'you like our clever friend Joseph Young? Good at drawin', ain't he?'

'Yes, he is.'

'Good at all sorts o' things is our Joseph,' they say and laugh raucously. 'Sandman Joe!' they shout and slap him on the back. One of them begins to sing:

He star'd a while then turned his quid,
Why blast you, Sall, I loves you!
And for to prove what I have said,
This night I'll soundly f...

'I've an urgent errand with Miss Dale,' interrupts Joseph. Miss Dale? 'We must hurry on.'

'Urgent.' They wink at each other. Oh well, off you goes. We'll give your greetins to ve lads and lasses, shall us, Joe?'

'Yes, of course.'

'Tell 'em you've urgent business vese days?'

'Tell them I'm busy, Jack. It's the truth.'

'Vey'll be sorry to 'ear it. George Quinton and Barnabas'll be sorry.'

'And Charlotte. You know, ve one always talks about her sister shot and killed in '80.'

'We miss you, don't we, Hugh? And Fanny, she'll be a lot sorry, eh?'

'We must hurry on now.' Joseph gives Lucy a small shove and walks her away. The men bawl out:

His brawny hands, her bubbies prest,
And roaring cried, white Sand O!

7

One evening in Battle's a man asks after James. Sarah knows spies sit in every coffee house and inn. James warns her to be careful what she says, though she's hardly garrulous.

'Mrs Wintrige?'

'Yes.'

'Do you know where your husband was this afternoon?'

'I have been here since six o'clock this morning.' She heard a thrush sing from a roof ridge on the way. 'He was surely at the Customs Office today as usual.'

'He was expected at a meeting this afternoon. He never came.'

She pays no attention. Nowadays they close before nine. Staying open late causes suspicion.

Two weeks later he comes again. She recognises his red neckerchief, his lively push through the press of men around the bar.

'Thomas Cranch, Mrs Wintrige. Enquiring about your husband again.' He catches her eye. 'I'm from the Society,' he says quietly.

'Yes?'

'He is ill, I hear. He sent us a letter today. He's too ill to attend the meeting. Coughing blood. Can we be of help?

71

Recommend a physician?'

Leaning towards him to hear, their foreheads touch. She draws back hastily, sees surprise, pleasure hop across his face. He drinks porter. He is short, thickset, his black hair cropped, his movements energetic. Printer and bookseller, he tells her.

'British Tree of Liberty. 98 Berwick Street, Soho.'

Or so he says. She warms to him despite herself.

James slips into bed about midnight, undershirt smelling of anxiety.

Half-asleep she asks: 'Are you unwell?'

'No. Been at a meeting.'

'Have you coughed up blood?'

No. Why do you ask?'

She turns over. Shifts away.

Stares into the dark with indignation: he has another woman.

She fails to sleep. He snores. Perhaps several women. Whores.

She's in Battle's at six, her father grumbling, a waiter late. She sets about seeing that fires are laid and lit under the coffee cauldron and in the fireplace where men toast their backsides, pat the dog, read aloud the latest news, hold forth. Checks that floors are swept, meat is prepared, onions sliced, clean glasses and coffee dishes lined in ranks.

Another woman. The words embed. She was told of a common law wife before their marriage whom he left. She finds relief in the pattern.

Later she remembers a conversation she once overheard. She knew the men. Knew they were radicals who drank at the Red Lion but dropped into Battle's occasionally to test the mood, check on the opposition. They were reluctantly tolerated by Sam because they came so rarely, always paid and were discreet. They'd not been seen for some time.

'Wintrige,' she'd heard.

'Our old friend Wintrige,' the man called Baldwyn said and laughed. They all laughed: Pyke, the oldest, Hadfield with the scars over his eye, down his cheek, Harley the young one. Slapped their thighs in merriment. Newton would have caught them all on a page, with their oddities, looking conspiratorial.

'Is he honest?' asked the one called Coke.

'Well, he's no Iago.'

'I should hope not. But can you *trust* him?'

'Can you trust a man that foolish, that silly? He's taken minutes enough times. He'd play the buffoon, only he hasn't the wit.' They laughed again. Left as soon as the government spy Nodder appeared with his threadbare moustache.

Foolish, silly? Buffoon? It isn't the Wintrige she knows. The man to whom she's married. But the day takes over; she can puzzle no more about it.

He's out when she returns. Dripping wax on his papers she rummages. What does she hope to find: a message in a woman's hand, a diary of assignations? There are books and books of minutes: once he'd actually been president of his division, now he's secretary. She reads the endless names, dates, subscriptions, sums of cash paid out to wives and children, which taverns for the next meeting; all in his tiny, neat, sloping letters. The life of the Corresponding Society about which he'd been so reticent is exposed: harassed by Blackheath Hundreds; justices terrified the landlord, moved to Angel, High Street; considered the best means of defending the several imprisoned Citizens; experienced a very narrow escape from the Bow Street Runners; adjourned at three o'clock in the morning; appointed as delegates Jas. Wintrige, Joseph Young.

There are those starry, overwrought phrases: *Infant Seed of Liberty; Hydra of Despotism; Strong Arm of Aristocracy; Yours with Civic Affection.*

And then a sealed letter addressed to R. Ford. Which goes the next day.

That night they coincide, unusually.

'Who is R. Ford?'

'Ho, ho! Been spying on me, have you?'

'I saw a letter, yes. Is it a man or a woman?'

'A *woman*? Why should you think that? You, with your apple cheeks!' He pinches them hard. 'It's for the Society. Our new strategy. We shall demand a meeting with the Duke of Portland. Don't trouble yourself with thinking. You couldn't understand.'

He shouts his loud laugh, mirthless, and his eyes slide away into their shadows.

She finds out nothing about the other woman. Yet their marriage is also nothing. Has almost always been nothing. Rare meetings. Pared-down questions; opaque answers from the edge of the mattress.

*

Winter sets hard. Yesterday's horse-dung is frosted. House martins, swifts have long flown the city. Carrion crows stalk the streets.

Tom Cranch comes often to Battle's. Stands at the bar, drinks, waits to hear treasonous tones, she assumes. Yet men are cautious now; he can't have much to report. His own speech is enthusiastic. She listens. He has a good disguise if he's a government spy. He tells her about America.

'There's wilderness with bears and wolves, eagles and

74

catamounts. But the wild men have made peace. Americans honour wise Indians, you know. They've even made a saint of one, St Tammany.

'Philadelphia is built to a rational scheme with straight roads and plenty of space to make the city healthy. In truth, it is a new-created world.'

'All built on the backs of slaves. Deny it if you can, whoever you are.' A bystander, listening in.

'Thomas Cranch, printer, bookseller, Berwick Street. In fact, sir, Pennsylvania abolished slavery in 1780.'

'Don't you believe it.' The man stomps off.

Tom Cranch is not fazed. He describes a future where property is unimportant, where *everyone* votes for members of parliament and no one starves. She has to remind herself that he's a spy and is trying to trap her.

She looks forward to his smile of pleasure, his latest tale of a reformed world. Knows what he says is true. Does he *really* not believe it himself? How can he speak like this yet actually think it's treason?

He charms her into talking to him, holding his head at an angle, bright-eyed, like a blackbird listening for a worm. Or, because of his red neckerchief, a robin. He brings her some verses by a poet he's just met called William Blake:

The Sun does arise
And make happy the skies...

'If you like it, I'll lend you the book. The illumination is wonderful, unlike anything you've seen.' She folds the paper, tucks it into the pocket of her dress.

She tells him she was in the great crowd at St George's Fields in June among the dandelions and flattened grass. That she'd never been to such a thing before; how she'll never forget it. He was there, too, of course, he says. In fact he printed the tickets for the meeting. Yes, wasn't it wonderful? There've been two huge gatherings of the Society since. He wrote and printed reports of those. Now there's to be a final one, near the Jew's Harp House, Marylebone, where city succumbs to open country. The great men will attend, the heroes, to speak against the Acts. Will she come?

A sudden surge of men from the street breaks her imagined flight.

'Three bottles of your best claret to begin!' they order, roaring.

'What a man you are, Byng! Bagged woodcock near St Martin's and snipe at Five Fields. Will you cook them, Miss Battle, when they've hung enough?'

'Yes,' she says to the men who've never noticed her marriage. 'I'll give them to Cook.'

'No,' she replies in a low voice to Cranch when they've moved away.

Her father won't give her the time off, she says. It was bad enough in June. He bawled red in the face about the mob when he'd heard where she'd been. Said they were sticking the French flag up all over the city. He'll guess she's doing the same again, for she no longer has the excuse of visiting Charlotte and her little boy since they moved away. And her father's gout is like the fiend. He says he'll kill it with a dose of colchicum.

Some nights James doesn't come home at all. Is this what he had in mind when he spoke of her forgiving nature? Should she write him a note? Should she leave him? No. Return to Battle's would be too great a humiliation. And of what can she accuse him?

'Come now, James. We are *married*.' She could throw his words back at him. But she needs evidence to avoid a sliding denial, cold shout of a laugh. His fathomless eyes.

She locks the door, rummages again, more extensively. This time there's something on the floor. She's under the table picking up torn foolscap when the door rattles.

He doesn't come in – the key's in the lock of course. It rattles more. There's furtive knocking. She gathers the shreds together and into a pocket, turns the key, opens a crack.

'Please let me in,' says Tom Cranch. 'I've escaped from the spunging house. Bailiffs won't think to come here.'

She draws the bolt behind him. Has he brought her the book of poems?

'Ran through my money.' He's breathing fast. 'Those reports of general meetings all printed by me – T. Cranch at the Tree of Liberty, 98 Berwick Street, Soho – and I've had *no payment*! No one from the Society has *paid* me! I've nothing. Can't pay my bills. Bailiffs broke in, took me up.

'I was lucky, though. The man was drunk. There was a window.'

His eyes are wild with urgency. She could stroke his dark, cropped head.

'I must leave the country. Besides, the Acts will be passed at the end of the month. There's nothing for it. Boat to America. Come with me.'

He needs her money, she thinks. It is always so.

But he embraces her. With undeniable energy. Delight.

She stuffs a bag with clothes, a loaf, her store of cash from the pearwood caddy. He watches as she casts the shreds of foolscap from her pocket all over Wintrige's papers, snatches up an undelivered letter.

*

Screeching terns are left behind. When sea-sickness has passed they huddle together, fend off icy blasts. Rip open the undelivered letter to R. Ford.

17 December 1795

During the whole of the last Five Years I am sure, sir, I was always regular in my Reports to you and anxious to do Everything in my Power for the service of Government. Never once have I stinted in relating Every Detail of information to you.

Not a Person on earth, not even my own Wife knew of my Connection to your Office. What Reward I have received has been concealed entirely. You know yourself that Discovery would have been attended with great personal Danger. My Part was ever to declaim the Beliefs of their Society, to be One of Them, and to allay Suspicion by playing the Fool in their meetings.

Spy. Spy to spymaster. No other woman.

En route to Philadelphia. They eat the bread, embrace again and again.

PART II

PART II

1

Rev. Mr Dale and Mrs Dale wait in vain in their dark, panelled Tower rooms to be informed of the marriage of their daughter. The subject becomes one they will not raise with each other. On the other hand according to the headmaster, Matthew is contrite. Obedient, concerned with his lessons, he has made no attempt to escape when, during several school vacations he's confined to a small room in the inner courtyard.

It will not be long before he leaves and goes up to Oxford to follow in his father's footsteps. Mr Dale quashes Mrs Dale's wish that he should spend the weeks before the university term at home.

Lucy hears nothing from Matthew. She writes letters that convey little except her love and longing. Sometimes they are taken by friends of Joseph. She believes, hopes they are delivered, not destroyed.

She earns her keep hand-colouring in Albion Place. Enjoys the easy attention it requires, keeping within the lines, the pleasant feel of the fine bristles smoothing paint onto paper, the patterning of repeated colours. She is part of Joseph's world: artists, engravers, printers and their train of nameless colourists in cold lodgings and backrooms, wives, sisters, kept women.

To those who pay her she is known as Lucy Young – even Digham calls her that, though he knows the truth. She is glad to have abandoned her previous name and her life with Joseph does resemble marriage to an extent. But Joseph is unpredictable. He ignores her for hours at a time, absorbed in his work or mysteriously contemplating some unseen thing before his eyes. Some vision playing on the wall. She keeps quiet, finds ways of doing her tasks with little noise.

'Lucy, why are you creeping about like a mouse?'

'I don't want to disturb you.'

'But you disturb me by creeping about! Sit still or go out!'

She comes to accept his outbursts, though she rarely guesses when they'll take place. She does not complain that he is often out at night, reluctantly accepts his explanation that visits to taverns and places of obscurity are necessary for his work. Some days he springs up, puts aside the burin and clasps her in his arms as if he's just discovered her.

'How beautiful you are, perfect, a flower. And to think I found you! I might have passed you by. Or I might have stayed at home that night and found your corpse in the morning.'

Must she be thankful to whomever he was with that night? For detaining him long enough that he might rescue her? But she's glad enough of his affection when it erupts.

'Let me draw you while you colour those prints.'

She sits at the table and dips her brushes. It's simple work, though the subjects are puzzling, unsettling. They're mostly satires, some etched by Digham, some merely printed by him. Some are Joseph's and some from other engravers.

She colours Bond Street fops and the latest female fashions parading in St James's Park, at theatres or seated round faro tables. Charles Fox, swarthy, unshaven in buff and blue, thin, spinous William Pitt, the Prince of Wales bursting with excesses edible, drinkable, female; the demi-monde at the Pantheon, masquerades at Vauxhall; cockneys, Irishmen, the Persian Ambassador's beautiful wife, quacks, Quakers and Methodists. When she gets known for her fine colouring, William tells her, she'll be given topography or sporting prints, but for now it's caricatures, humorous prints.

Joseph's own satires shift from overt attacks on the follies of the monarch and Prince of Wales to witty depictions of demotic foibles. That he should hang around the Bow Street lock-up or sundry round-houses and watch-houses is understandable when the results are hilarious prints of pugilistic or hopeless inmates, ludicrous or fearsome keepers and constables. Capering against gloomy backgrounds, each is as absurd as the other, the catchers and the caught. His constables spill into taverns, too, though here a partiality for one side over the other is apparent. His apprentices, labourers and servant girls heartily enjoy themselves in their cock and hen clubs: red-cheeked, amorous, tipsy, bare-breasted, their features hardly caricatured at all. In burst the Officers of the Watch and the Runners, brutal, distorted, their lips and chins extended, bent, eyes misplaced, bawling, beating, lusting in heavy, black lines.

These prints sell well. Satires they are, but for Lucy they display Joseph's other life: drunkenness, flesh, roister. She realises her wretchedness is to be placated by money, that her heart must harden. He always returns with folders of new sketches, so that much of his explanation is true. But his breath smells of beer and tobacco, his clothes of other bodies, strong, rank.

Nothing she colours is as disturbing as the drawings she finds one day when Joseph is at Digham's. Bleak with incomprehension at his insults that morning, she seeks for clues about this man to whom she clings, peering at the disorder of his work bench, lifting papers carefully. Opening drawers. To find sheets and sheets of half-dressed men and women on plump pillows, in carts, on sofas, tables, propped up on gates, unhidden behind walls, bodices gaping, skirts up, breeches rumpled round knees, hats askew; buttocks naked and immense, breasts, thighs, parts minutely drawn, exposed, enlarged, red-tipped. Expressions of ecstasy. Gorging.

She's aghast. They're his work. From his mind. When he's gentle, affectionate to her do these images lurk yet in his thoughts? She thinks of her own timidity, her fright even when he first encouraged her into his bed; how demure she is, how utterly unlike these great women with their hair and breasts, shameless in their desire. Has he drawn these for himself or are they to sell? And one woman, with black locks and big, seductive eyes appears again and again in the drawings, her body and limbs arranged in ways Lucy could not have imagined. Voracious.

She is crushed. Barely closes the drawer when he returns and finds her staring, pale and shocked.

'Lucy, what is it, my love? You're faint. Here! There now, that's better. How lovely you are, even when the colour's gone from your cheeks. Perhaps especially then.

'William has just paid me. Look! It's cockshut time. Twilight. Time to shut up the cock! Let's go to the Eagle and eat a broiled steak.'

In the warm, dark bonhomie of the Eagle her horror dims. She wonders vaguely if there's a room here, upstairs, where unspeakable things take place. Half listens for the sounds she supposes are made by those couplings. She dare not ask him about his drawings, is soon enveloped in alcohol and cheer.

Later, back home, he carries her over to their bed like a precious being that requires the utmost tenderness.

*

Now there's his latest project: a series of prints of Shakespeare's women. Not satires, these will express all the different sentiments of both the heroines and the wicked women, even the lesser roles of Shakespeare's best-known plays. He'll employ stipple engraving, the effects soft and subtle as brushwork.

'Collectors will want to buy each new one as it appears,' he says, bouncing with excitement, 'or perhaps I'll have subscriptions. A set for fifty guineas.'

'Will you give up the satires, Joseph?' Might she have him to herself at last?

'Good heavens, no!'

'How will you have time for both?'

'I'll stop working on trade cards and advertisements for a start. I'm sure William can find someone else to do those. Besides, Lucy, here's the main point. You will be my model!'

'Oh?'

'You will make a perfect Desdemona, a wonderful Ophelia, an upright Cordelia.'

'A Lady Macbeth?' She smiles faintly.

'Haha! I'll find someone else for that. But I'll begin with you – all we need is suitable clothing for each character.'

'Flowers for Ophelia.'

'Yes. Let's start now! Desdemona, I fancy. Come, sit here – you're listening to Othello's tales of his life.'

'But what about my clothing? And surely you need an Othello?'

'I have a friend who looks just the part. He goes to Wood's. Clothing's a minor matter and everyone knows the story. It's her face, listening enthralled, that will be wonderful to see. We don't need Othello, yet. It's Desdemona's face that people will buy.'

'What is Wood's, Joseph?'

'Oh, it's a club in a tavern in Wych Street. Come on!'

He pulls her up, sits her on a low chair, arranges her head, her hands, her hair. Steps back to look and look again. Smiles with pleasure at the prospect of his task. Looks at her as an artist, not a lover, not a husband.

*

The sketches of Desdemona are so good that Joseph decides to produce paintings first, and then make engravings of them. The original paintings may themselves sell well. Moreover, he thinks there should be several different poses for various dramatic moments in the play. In the first painting Lucy is shown seated neatly, hands clasped in her lap, her face upturned in rapt concentration to the telling of an unfathomable tale, her delicate beauty not much changed from when he found her, for all her unhappiness. The second painting will show Desdemona pressing Othello on Cassius's behalf, flirtatiously questioning, unintentionally irritating her husband, rubbing on the new sore of jealousy. Lucy thinks this difficult until she imagines how, if they really were married, she might try to persuade him to give up his other world. He begins the painting with her on half of the canvas, the other half left blank until his friend shall appear to pose as Othello.

Digham comes to see the work. He casts short-sighted glances round the room, taking in their life.

THE FLIGHT OF SARAH BATTLE

'You have made a teratical difference to these living quarters, Lucy.'

'He means big,' Joseph explains.

'I mean prodigious!'

'And you accused me of being bookish, William.'

'Not at all the same. I just like to hold on to the words that will shortly die. But what an excellent draughtsman you are, Joseph.'

'I've always drawn, ever since I was a boy and had a few lessons before I came to you. Everything else you taught me.'

'Yes, yes, but this is more than exercise. He has a great talent, Lucy, frappish though his mood may be at times. And you, Joseph, you have a perfect model.'

'Oh, she has learned her part well,' he agrees, offhand.

'No. There's more than that in her face. Lucy, you have felt for Desdemona, with her, that is obvious. And Joseph has understood it, my dear, else he could not have conveyed it.'

Here is a man who is kind!

*

Despite the frequency of Joseph's nocturnal absences, Lucy is not inured to them. After a night away he returns accompanied.

'Lucy, this is Fanny Lobb. Fan, Lucy Dale.'

She recognises the big, dark woman from his hidden drawings, if in reality less sumptuous than her portrayal.

Something prevents Lucy from running from the room or vomiting at their feet. Fanny has smiled at her without triumph. She cannot smile back, cannot speak, her body shudders inside her clothes, she longs to sleep.

'Fan will be Emilia to your Desdemona, Lucy. I'll need to make you somewhat thinner, eh, Fan? You're a servant, see, to Desdemona, Lucy that is. You must look subordinate. And you're married to the most evil man in all Shakespeare!'

'So you said, Joe. What's that make me then?'

'Oh, you're not evil, Fan. In fact you kill yourself out of love and loyalty to Desdemona.'

'I never!'

'You do. But I shan't paint you killing yourself, don't worry.'

Fanny fails to catch Lucy's eye. There's common cause here, Fan thinks, both of them attached to odd, intoxicating Joe; clever Joe, full of surprises. A looker he is, with his long fair hair, but moody. The girl loves him, he's told her that himself and she obeys him like a slave, no doubt of it. She can't delight him as she, Fan, has done all night, her body still thundering, her clothing sticky. However, this Lucy is perfect. With woman's eyes she sees how the girl's features are delicate and neat, small, exquisite as she could never be. Like, like a little cake she once saw in a pastry-cook's, all scalloped edges with tiny, shiny fruits. He wants her for how she looks, she supposes. Needs her, Fan, to fuck him good and proper when he's drunk, smoked his smoke and she's entertained the club with her singing, rotating her hips to 'Sandman Joe'; needs this other one to look pretty about the place. Patch his breeches.

'The willow song, you remember?' Lucy begins to cry.

'If it's a song as you want I'll sing it, eh, Joe? Ain't 'eard me, 'as she?'

'It's not like that, Fan. Different song altogether. A lament.'

'Oh lord, no. Let's 'ave us something to eat, I say. Got any bread and cheese, Miss Dale? Bit of bacon? Some of us ain't eaten since yesterday.'

Lucy gathers plates and knives, food from the press, warms the teapot. Joseph yawns. Passing Fan as she lays things on the table, Lucy identifies at last what she's smelled on Joseph so many times. A rankness from the woman's clothes, the body beneath.

There's knocking on the street door. Rapid. Repeated. Joseph goes to see and the women listen, try to consider how to act in his absence, but in no time two sets of feet leap up the stairs, burst into the room.

'Matthew!' Lucy runs to the slight young man standing, hesitant, next to Joseph. She sobs, can't stop.

'Lucy, Lucy. Now, now. It's not so bad.'

He cannot know how bad it is.

'Have you escaped? Thank God!' She drinks him in, clutches his hands as a thrown rope. 'Oh, but Matthew, this is Joseph.'

'Your husband. We introduced ourselves just now, and I'm very glad to meet you, Joseph.' Fanny, astonished at the news of Joseph's marriage, is ignored. 'Yes, I have escaped. Can you hide me for a day or so?'

'Of course,' Joseph says. 'I shall be proud to. But will they not think of coming here to look for you?'

'First they'll try the Tower. Do my parents know this address?'

'I don't think so. I was deliberately vague about where we live. You haven't written to them, have you, Lucy?'

'Certainly not.'

Matthew hastens on. 'I shan't stay for long. I have the name of someone. He'll tell me where it's safe to go.'

Fanny says: 'I'm going 'ome, Joe, then. Another day, eh?'

'I'll show you out, Fan. Don't worry, Matthew, you can trust Fan not to tell, eh Fan?''

'I ain't seen nobody. Swear to God. Au'voir, Miss Dale,' she says, nods at Matthew and is taken downstairs.

'Miss Dale?'

'We are not married, Matthew,' Lucy's lips tremble. 'But you are surely hungry. Eat something, as much as you want. Tell me how you escaped. Oh Matthew, I'm so happy to see you. I'm so happy.'

*

'You're quite certain about the lady?' Matthew asks Joseph when he returns.

'Yes. I know her well. Besides, I've given her a little something to make sure.'

'If the constables come is there somewhere I can hide myself quickly? Or a window I can climb out of?'

'There's a cupboard behind my bench, Matthew, with two sets of doors, upper and lower. See? I keep paints and tools and well, all manner of things in the top part. You'll have to go under the bench to get into the lower half. But there's room enough for a man. I'll make two small holes in the doors for air. I'll clear it out immediately.'

Barely able to squeeze himself into the space, Joseph crawls under his bench, bangs his head, curses, pulls out armfuls of papers, objects, clothing. Lucy and Matthew smile to each other at the sight of long legs protruding, at the shuffling, scuffling, papers, ever more papers.

'If I may say it, Joseph, you look like a huge terrier digging for a bone,' says Matthew.

'I am!' Joseph backs out, his patched breeches showing need of further mending. 'A terrier worrying at authority.'

'I want to do more than worry authority, damn them to hell.'

'Lucy has told me what you did.'

'Oh. Oh, that was nothing. A schoolboy's trick. To impress someone.'

They are silent. Lucy's pride shakes.

Of course he is no longer a boy. Two years have passed, in which she herself has changed greatly. Matthew's voice no longer squeaks, his limbs, even his features have hardened with a fierce assurance that hadn't fully formed before. He'd embraced her as a man, not a little brother.

'Joseph, I must get a message to someone. Could you deliver it for me? Better you than Lucy, who would be noticed. At the George in St John Street. Tonight.'

'Of course. It's near here. Whatever I can do.'

'That'll be a start. Are you willing to do more?'

'Joseph has so much work, dear Matthew, I doubt he has the time.' Lucy feels events swirl away from her. Imagines both of them in hiding, both in danger. Her life dissolving into terror. 'Many people buy his prints now. And there's the new project, isn't that so, Joseph?'

'Yes, yes. But I have always supported the cause.'

'What cause do you mean?' Matthew asks, sceptical.

'Why, liberty and equality of course. I am a friend of Democracy. I used to be a good member of the Corresponding Society. Did you ever attend the great meeting in St George's Fields? Not that I...'

'Oh the Corresponding Society. All talk. Debate.'

'Debate is good. Ideas are disseminated. Those get to hear who might not otherwise have done.' Joseph springs up. He is much bigger than Matthew, expects to dominate. 'We used to send letters and pamphlets all over the country, encouraged men north, south, east and west.'

'And what good has that done? You can no longer meet in big numbers, can you. No more than twelve! So many are in prison. Spies are everywhere.'

'Matthew.' Lucy has watched him without cease. 'How do

you know this if you have been confined to school all this time?'

He blushes. 'Oh. I can't tell you. I have been reading.' He dismisses her. 'But I must act. It is useless to read, to meet, to talk. Read, meet, talk. Nothing changes.'

Joseph has been searching through portfolios. 'This is how I used to act, Matthew.'

The boy glances at the sheets. Neither laughs nor smiles, replaces them.

'I admire your talent. But these are old things. Who doesn't laugh at the Prince of Wales? Or Farmer George or Pitt. Who ever heard of a king *laughed* off his throne? It's not enough. The monarchy must be overthrown. A republic established.'

'An impossible quest without bloodshed,' says Joseph crossly.

'Indeed! The Irish know what to do and how to do it. And French ships are waiting for the word.'

'The French, Matthew? The French are up to their necks in blood. They kill their own. Jacobins guillotine Jacobins. We had our civil war a hundred and fifty years ago; we don't want another. Look how people constantly cry out for peace!'

'Would you execute the King and Queen?' Lucy asks, barely audible.

Matthew turns to her, flat certainty on his face. 'What difference between the King's turds and mine?'

He pauses, waiting for her reaction. Hoots with boy's coarse laughter. She has lost him.

2

Shouts of 'land' echo from the crow's-nest to the lowest deck and all who can run up, pushing for a glimpse. At first there's nothing to see, except great numbers of porpoises leaping and blowing close to the bow of the ship, without ever touching it. Sarah and Tom watch the energy and apparent joy; dare to think it an emblem.

The banks of the Delaware appear, passengers jostle, straining for something familiar: trees, horses, a man with a cow. Two miles of broad river to Philadelphia, temporary capital of America, city of brotherly love. *Charming Molly* moves slowly, so slowly, as though allowing each passenger to absorb similarity, difference. Almost all are sailing to a new life. The voyage, a kind of purgatory, has tested, purged them; now they must ready themselves to step out into paradise.

Many are taken ill during the eight-week journey, numbers die. Somehow, Sarah and Tom avoid the worst disease, though they're sick for a while. At least their thinner, paler selves are safe from pursuit, they think, but their future is unknown. They have no home. No one awaits them. Yet better that than met by the master to whom one's youth, one's life is indentured.

The crowds lining the sides of the ship become silent in the search for familiarity, like myopic scholars constructing a language from fragments: black smoke buffeting up from boiling tar, barrels rolling, men with axes, a whole hedge of fishing nets. They near the main dock and river traffic thickens as it does on the Thames. Gulls circle. Now they understand the pilot's slow approach, for small skiffs and dinghies shoot here and there among the schooners and merchantmen, avoiding strings of barges, plunging carelessly into pathways and wakes, across fixed routes of solid scows.

Sparse houses, small white churches, snow-covered jetties, piles of lumber. Grey plates of ice. Wharves, stores, boat-builders, warehouses, houses crowding the river's edge, taverns: Ship-A-Ground, Boatswain and Call. Finally cranes, crates, shipyards, lines of docked vessels, tangles of masts and ladders, sailors everywhere, porters, lightermen, sacks round their shoulders for warmth. Faces through steam and smoke, black, white, brown, square-boned Indian. Recognisable and utterly strange.

They turn to each other at the same moment, feeling that strangeness. It's like waking from a long and troubled sleep, changed. They look at one another as if they're marvellous beings. Astonished at what they've done. What they will yet do. Laugh aloud. Hold each other close.

They have little to carry, wave away carters. Agree they should find the centre of the city, said to be the most beautiful in America. The air is cold; it's hard to ignore blasts of heat through tavern doors. Travellers and sailors fill the roads, ponies, traps, horses, carts churning up a sludge of snow.

They trudge on boards past river-licked wooden houses. Freezing mud becomes icy cobbles, roads widen, broad pavements appear, buildings grow in stature. Red-brick villas, rows of four-storey dwellings, steeples, municipally confident steps, tall windows, columns.

Sarah stumbles. Tom takes her bag.

'You're faint, Sarah. We must eat.' They smell coffee from a squat building on the corner of the street.

'Old London Coffee House! Would you believe it?'

'I didn't think they had coffee houses in America, Tom.'

'Everything will surprise us here.'

Sarah drinks coffee, Tom hot toddy, quite unlike the punch she prepared daily at Battle's, for its main ingredient is rum. They order two plates of stew. Men stare at them, assessing their provenance, their wealth, their relationship.

The stew is warming, the meat unidentifiable.

'Raccoon, sir,' the waiter tells them. 'Where're you from?'

'London.'

'No raccoons in London?'

The room, a simpler version of Battle's, tables, chairs, smoke and coffee fumes, handwritten advertisements on the wall, begins to fill with takers for a sale, jaws chawing, spitting on the black tobacco-juice floor.

'My wife and I have just arrived from London,' Tom tells the owner, a wary Irishman with long sideburns.

My wife.

'We need rooms for a few nights. Where do you recommend?'

'Your occupation?'

'Printer and bookseller. My wife's father owns a coffee house in London. We need good, clean rooms.'

Another man might have taken up the connection. 'No tippling houses for you, then. Keep clear of Helltown!' he laughs, unfriendly. 'The Bell, North of Arch Street. Eighth and Sansom. Tell Dobson I sent you.'

It's begun to snow. A group of some fifteen black youths and girls stand in the freezing slush.

'The sale!' says Tom.

'Are they slaves? Some of them are children, Tom.'

'Bonded labourers, Ma'am,' says a man. 'You British?' He spits.

Tom takes Sarah's hand, hastens her away.

Matthew Dobson, the Bell's keeper, is jovial, his tavern a small new building pressed between taller dwelling houses with a yard and stabling at the back. He checks their credentials, shows them a room under the roof, overlooking the street. Flakes shutter the panes.

Two candles illuminate them.

She removes her bonnet, shakes free her hair. 'I keep expecting to be knocked off my feet as the ship rolls.'

'We should rest. I'll seek out Robert Wilson soon and hope he'll have work for me. We'll need an income in a matter of days.'

'I too must find work.'

'Think what you could do with that coffee house, the Old London. Write to Sam and ask him to buy the man out. Don't look shocked! I'm not serious!'

'I think I'd rather forget the past.'

'In its entirety?'

'Of course not! But I want to remember only what was good. Working in Battle's was like living under water. Now I realise it. I couldn't breathe. I knew nothing about life on land.'

He takes her hands. 'My dearest,' he says, 'it's our honeymoon now, our honey-month. We've had our wedding night, have we not, squeezed into our corner of the ship?'

'It was like going to bed in a drawer!'

They laugh at the memory of the awkwardness, the promise that it drew from them nevertheless.

There isn't much in the room under the Bell's low roof: a chair, wash-stand, jug and basin, a small grate in which Dobson lights a fire. The mattress is lumpy with straw and corn husks: after the voyage it's luxury. They don't leave it till late the following day. A new world.

*

They find Robert Wilson's shop on Second and Chestnut, the street unpaved. In its double-fronted windows are books, bottles of ink, inkwells, pens and writing paper.

'Ink!' Tom says. 'Altogether a bigger place than Cranch's in Berwick Street. But no matter. I'm certain he won't be too grand for me; Baldwyn spoke well of him. I'm optimistic.'

He links his fingers in hers. Their reflections, side by side, smile back at them from the glass.

Robert Wilson's eyes are an extraordinary blue, unblinking. It's what you notice first about him and for a while notice nothing else. He reads Baldwyn's letter while they wait and glance round the shop, both sides of which are filled with books.

'Tom Cranch! Excellent!' They shake hands. 'And Mrs Cranch!'

They've decided to pass for man and wife until they make true friends who will understand. Many in Philadelphia are Presbyterians or Quakers who might be offended, they think.

Wilson is a Scot.

'How is my old friend Baldwyn? We grew up together, wee lads. I tried to persuade him to move here, but he went to London and stayed.'

'He is well but sore-pressed as all are in England and, of course, Scotland too.'

'Is it a social visit you're making, Tom? Or have you and Mrs Cranch chosen to live in this boom land in stead of the old country?'

'We hope to live here, Robert. But we made no arrangements except for Baldwyn's letter, for we left in a hurry. You may know how the government is closing in on those of radical mind. The Anti-Sedition laws were about to be enacted. We brought little with us, either belongings or money. I have abandoned my business, not doing well, it's true, though I'll surely sell it. Sarah was working in her father's coffee house, Battle's near the Exchange.'

'In other words you are in need, my friends.'

'Yes.'

'You bring nothing tangible with you, but you have talents, so that any man who helps you may anticipate a return, eh?'

'As Baldwyn says in his letter, my business was similar to yours. Printer at the British Tree of Liberty. 98, Berwick Street, Soho. Although,' looking about him, 'much less prosperous.'

'Ah prosperity! Philadelphia is certainly prospering; printing, publishing, bookselling are all doing mighty well. Everything else, too. Roads are being laid, canals cut. Masons and wrights won't take less than two dollars a day. This is as good a time to flee the old world as any. And,' he suddenly stares at them, 'I perceive you are newly married.'

They look at each other.

'Is it so obvious?' Tom asks.

'Och, yes! You even blush in harmony. Now let's talk business. I take it that's what you want. You have not come to beg for money, eh?'

'I hope you might have work for me. And Sarah does not want to be idle.'

'Come through into the back of the shop and we'll toast your arrival. You'll soon notice how we find any excuse for a toast in this city.'

Robert's office is dominated by a huge desk spread with papers. Cupboards round the walls, some with doors, some without are stacked with yet more paper in piles, rolls and boxes. On shelves to one side stand numerous earthenware bottles of ink with neat labels:

Robert Wilson's Patent Indian Ink
or
Robert Wilson's Patent Writing Ink
Sepia

Or blue, green, red.

Beyond the office they glimpse two printing presses. Robert pours out three glasses of Madeira.

'Here's a welcome to you, Mr and Mrs Cranch! You're supposed to drain your glass, Mrs Cranch.'

'I have lived with drinkers all my life,' she says. 'I have filled hundreds upon hundreds of glasses. I find I can only sip it.'

'Och well, all the more for Tom and me, eh?'

'Here's to you, Robert!' Tom proposes. Sarah raises her glass, the men drink another and Robert refills.

'Here's to the future!'

They drink, Sarah sips. The future has arrived.

'If you'd remained in London would you have continued with your business, Tom?'

'I was printing more and more of my own pamphlets. You shall see some shortly. I was hoping to shuffle off the printing, move to publishing purely.'

'The very thing! How remarkable! We are of one mind on that. Look now, sit down both of you and let me tell you about myself, so you know what you're in for, eh? I came here fifteen years ago, in '81. Began in quite a humble way.'

'Why '81?'

'Oh, did I see the writing on the wall, eh? Well, no. But too many printers were crowding the market in Edinburgh. As a Scot I preferred to keep out of England. A wholly new place pulled me to it.'

'I can understand that.' It's Tom's way: he can't resist a life story.

'I started in South Street making ink and printing; then I graduated to Front Street and finally to here. Perhaps it's the wrong end of Chestnut Street, too near the docks, but the books sell well. However, printing makes little money. There's always trouble with journeymen: they're unreliable and forever demanding more dollars.

'So I've begun to publish and put out the printing to others. Let them have the headache! The presses are up for sale. I shall keep the bookshop and publish. Much more lucrative!'

'And what do you publish, what do you sell?' Tom asks.

'Whatever makes money of course! But I favour a Democratic Republican view whenever I can. That's what we are here now: Democratic Republicans. I even sell Jacobin stuff, far too extreme, but there are folk who'll buy it. We publishers sell each other's work: I'll take something I wouldn't read myself if they take my new guide books.'

'What do you think of these?' Tom jumps up, produces the pamphlets he had on him when he was arrested, pamphlets for which the Corresponding Society had failed to pay him.

Robert reads rapidly, his eyes blue hoverflies darting, probing.

'We could put them out in a matter of days, Tom. We've an election this year: republican readers will be pleased to hear a radical London voice. They'll buy them in armfuls.'

'Then there are these.' He hands over *King Killing*, *The Reign of the English Robespierre*, *The Happy Reign of George the Last*.' Remains on his feet, too excited to sit again.

'By God, you're a Jacobin yourself!'

'I published them, I didn't write them, Robert. Bloodletting is not my line.'

'They're damned provocative, all the same. You put yourself in danger. Och, no wonder you fled!'

'The place was thick with spies! You couldn't mutter in an eating house without being reported. But, good Lord, there are plenty of Jacobins in Scotland, Robert.'

'Not me, man!'

'Well, I anticipate a purity and simplicity here I've never yet seen.'

'Don't count on either. But I'll take you to meet every Democratic Republican I know and that's a good many. Then you'll quickly learn how to identify the enemy, the Federalists. There's a lot going on. And now, Mrs Cranch, shall you be content to sit at home and sew and instruct the cook, eh?'

He turns his buzzing blue eyes on Sarah and suddenly she sees how huge his hands and feet are, long and broad. As if he should be wielding a mattock in a field, not a pen at a desk. When he speaks he's sometimes a Scot, sometimes an American. He disconcerts her.

'I have worked all my life: I cannot sit at home.'

'Robert, Sarah has great understanding. I know this perfectly, for once we were over our sea-sickness, we talked to each other every day for eight weeks.' He moves next to her, discreetly strokes the back of her neck.

'Och, and your marriage survived! I admire you.'

They look at each other as he speaks. Their 'marriage' will never be mere survival.

'She has great ability. Don't mind my saying this, my dearest! I've watched her in Battle's enough times, managing scores of customers, unfazed. But she was wasted there, I strongly believe. She will find a new way in this new world.'

'Can you teach?' Robert asks, overriding Sarah's embarrassment. 'There's a charity school, begun in '94, at the Second Presbyterian church where I worship.'

'I have some education but I've never taught. I'm not sure I'd be good at it. I'll try if need be.'

'Well then, here's another idea. See what you think. There's a great appetite for guides among book-buyers these days. Of course almanacs and bibles are still the most popular books, the bread and butter of the business, but there's no doubt small, informative volumes that fit into a pocket are in demand. I'm bringing some out. *Every Man's Pocket Guide to the Law*, for instance. *Every Man's Pocket Guide to Travel*. *Every Man's Pocket Guide to Books; or Building your own Library*. I'm writing that one myself. Mrs Cranch. May I call you Sarah? Sarah, I'd be glad if you could write *Every Man's Guide to the Coffee House in London and Philadelphia*. Would you do that, eh? I reckon there'd be a real interest. Your book could even help establish more coffee houses here. As it is we have not enough of them, and rather too many squalid taverns.'

*

'What luck!' Tom says to her that night. They keep each other warm in the freezing room, laugh at the sound of husks and straw crackling beneath them.

'What do you say to stealing out to the stable and spending the night in the hay loft?' Tom says. 'Hay makes its own heat and it's much softer than straw.'

But it's too cold to get out of bed. Dobson is jovial but mean with fuel. Lush ice leaves flourish inside the window.

Nor will he provide soap. 'The English do always demand soap,' he says. 'You have a towel: rub off the dirt with that.'

'What do you think of Robert?' Tom asks her.

'I like him well enough. How could I not when he's offering us work just like that! But do you think he really wants me to write the guide? I'm not sure that I trust him.'

'Of course he does! He's plain speaking, says what he means. A frank Scot, that's what I like about him. Dear Baldwyn. We have him to thank. I shall write to him immediately, not least so that he will put Cranch's up for sale with all that's in it. Then I shall have capital to put into Wilson's business.'

'Will you become partners?'

'We could, though I mustn't act too fast. Are you ambitious for me, Sarah?'

'Of course I am, my darling.'

'To be cautious goes right against my inclination. But I must let him suggest it. We may agree on many things: he's a republican after all, though he wasn't happy that I might be a Jacobin. He's also a respectable Presbyterian and I'm not. I don't know how significant that may be yet. Partners must agree a great deal.

'But dearest Sarah, look out, for I am ambitious for you. Once you've written your *Guide*, who knows what else you may turn your pen to! I won't have you running home with pies all wrapped in cloths for me, like you did for Wintrige.'

'You won't have it!' She laughs too loudly: his face falls. She kisses his brow. 'I'm teasing you. I think you really do believe in women. I've never met a man who thinks as you do.'

'If any country will let its women shine it's this one. Surely! It was too bad the Corresponding Society was nothing but men.'

'There were plenty of women at the big meetings.'

'Yes, but not on the committees, not in the debates. Not writing pamphlets. We'll write something together. We'll write a book together!'

They know no bounds.

*

Robert has a further proposition. One evening he invites them to his house in Zane Street where he lives alone, his wife having died three years earlier in the yellow fever epidemic of '93.

'I am lonely here. Martha cooks and washes for me but the house is too empty. I should like it greatly if you would live on the upper floor. It's unfurnished, so you must buy yourselves some sticks of furniture. I'll need rent but you can pay me in arrears.'

Sarah says, 'It is a good offer, Robert. I'd like it and I should think Tom would. Yes?'

'Yes, an excellent idea.'

'Let me loan you a few dollars today as an advance against production of pamphlets and the book. You'll be wanting a few more clothes no doubt, though we've only two tailors to choose from here. Try Watson's, off Water Street.'

'I don't intend to abandon my scarlet neckerchief,' says Tom.

'Och Lord, no! How would anyone recognise you else, eh? Now, until you've bought a bed, you should move to Moore's hotel. Much nearer here than the Bell.'

In Robert's house they will share the services of Martha, who can certainly cook for three as easily as for one, he says. Indeed, she'll probably prefer to do so.

That same evening Martha is visiting her sisters somewhere in the city and has left a chicken pie and a baked pudding.

'There are apples in this pudding,' Sarah says, 'but something else I don't recognise.'

'Crookneck,' Robert explains. 'Winter squash. It's my favourite dish, for enough of it reminds me of home and yet it tastes of Pennsylvania too. Whoever heard of crookneck squash in Scotland, eh? Martha knows what I like.'

The men smoke and make their way through a bottle of peach brandy. Robert quizzes them about London.

'It's Pitt's terror,' Tom says. 'The government fears the people, not just in London but all over the country, especially in the cities.'

'I read the Tricolour was raised on the Tower.' Robert puffs and drinks, puffs and drinks.

'That was nothing. The chaplain's son! No doubt he got a thrashing, nothing worse.'

'Poor boy,' says Sarah. 'Yet the people will never turn to blood like in Paris. I'm sure of it. They meet in huge numbers and cheer and weep and listen in silence. Thousands of people. I was there. I'll never forget that silence in St George's Fields.'

Robert stares at her as she speaks. It makes her uneasy.

'It's reasonable that you should think so, my dearest,' Tom says quietly. 'But I'll tell you what I heard the night of the attack on the King's coach when he went to open Parliament.'

'I read something of that,' says Robert. 'Were you there, eh? Vast mobs, according to the report.'

'Not in the crowd, but I have friends who were and they told me about it, the hissing, hooting, groaning. Down with George! No King! No Pitt! No War! Peace, Peace. Bread! Bread!'

'Did someone fire a gun?'

'Perhaps. Perhaps not. It may have been a marble thrown or a pebble. But the carriage was damaged and a door forced open.' He's standing now, holds them with his telling.

'That night a man in a green coat claimed to have seized the King by the collar. I was in the Green Dragon, Moorfield and heard him speak of it. I don't believe he made it up. After the supposed shot, the King ducked onto the floor of the coach, you see. Just as the man would pull him out, collar in both hands, guards rode up and he made his escape as fast as he could.

'Now, think of this. What would have happened if the man in green had succeeded in dragging the King out onto the ground? The monarch would have been trampled to death and his ministers with him. George the Last! The British Republic might have begun last year!'

He sits and they all shift on their hard chairs, thinking. Sarah stares into the fire.

'What happened to the man in green?' she asks.

'Nothing that I know of. There was a reward of one thousand pounds that no one ever claimed. If he'd any sense he took the first boat out of the country.'

'Well, over here, my friends,' Robert says, 'we got rid of the King as you know. Without any trampling; without removing a hair from his neck! That task is done, thank the Lord. Let's drink a toast, eh!'

'To the Republic of America!' says Tom, leaping to his feet. They raise their glasses.

'But,' continues Robert, 'there's work to do yet on our democracy.'

'Then, here's to democracy!' Tom holds up his glass.

Robert raises his: 'Universal suffrage! A vote for all men.'

'Universal suffrage!' Tom and Sarah say together. Tom adds: 'A vote for all men and women,' and winks at Sarah.

'Och, women have not the head for it. They should do what's natural to their sex.'

'Let's not debate it now, Robert. Here's to democracy!'

*

Moore's hotel is a four-storey, weather-boarded house built of logs, the entrance outside at the top of a wooden staircase. Bigger, warmer than the Bell.

Tom says: 'Warmth is good, but I think I miss the husks.'

Later Sarah asks him if he thinks Martha is Robert's slave. 'We still haven't seen her, Tom.'

They're lying in bed, reluctant to get up.

'Pennsylvania abolished slavery years ago, in 1780. Now there are bonded servants. That may be what she is.'

'Like those we saw outside the coffee house, waiting to be sold, you mean? We've seen plenty of black men and boys holding horses in the street, carrying loads, pushing barrows. Weren't they slaves?'

'May be, or bonded servants.'

'What's the difference?'

'I think bonded servants are freed at twenty-one, or is it twenty-eight? They're still the property of their masters under the bond of course.'

'To be bought and sold.'

'Yes. I'll ask Robert about Martha, though it may rile him. We don't even know if she's a black woman, Sarah.'

'I suspect it from the way he spoke about her. And I think she's something more than just a servant, too.'

'What makes you think so? There's no art to find the mind's construction in the face.' He leans on his elbow.

'*Macbeth*! I've read it, Tom. But I disagree with that. King Duncan died because he failed to fathom Macbeth's mind.'

'By God, yes. Still, how does one do it?'

'I don't know. Intuition I think, not art. There's something about Robert that makes me hesitate.'

'You mean women being too weak-headed to vote?'

'Not just that. Something doesn't fit.'

'Isn't it because his hands and feet are so huge? He trod on my toes the other day! Oh, I should learn to be suspicious. I take everyone as he presents himself: it's a failing in me. Yet I saw there was more to you than your high colour and pretty face, didn't I? And *you* didn't detect old Wintrige's wicked ways.'

'How stupid I was! Why didn't I see what he was like? Yet I was troubled by his look: thought his mouth resembled a frog's.'

'I like frogs!'

'You see, he disgusted me so much I tried not to think about him. But in any case nothing stays perfect for long, Tom.'

'You're wrong. Some things do. I will have it so!'

'I would have it so, too.'

But she thinks of Newton: her first love destroyed.

*

Robert introduces them to the Indian Queen where men of republican inclination meet to debate and fortify themselves. The Indian Queen is a much bigger tavern that the Bell, with two kitchens and large rooms on the first floor for private meetings. As they arrive, doves flutter in and out of their cote in the apex of the roof. Inside, the air is ripe with pipe and cigar fumes.

'We began as a society,' Robert tells them, 'perhaps not unlike your Corresponding Society, but with more hope. Much more. Now, with the formation of the Democratic Republicans, we have eased our rules and absorbed ourselves into that party. Sit in tonight as visitors; see what you think of us, eh?'

'We welcome two friends of Robert Wilson,' announces Daniel Eckfeldt, the chairman of the meeting, in a German accent. A large man, grey hair carefully combed over his forehead, his rough-cut bones belie kindliness. 'They flee the British despotism that they may live in liberty in our city.' Applause.

'Tonight we have urgent business. The election presses us. It is for us to ensure the defeat of the Federalists.' Loud cheer of agreement. 'Have you explained already to your friends, Robert?'

'Federalists are like Tories,' Robert says, taking the opportunity to address the room, 'aristocrats; some of us call them monocrats. They do their damnedest to climb back into bed with those pirates the British and claim all the while that we republicans do nothing but sharpen our guillotines.' Roar of delight and thumping of tables at this description.

The chairman takes over. 'Here is the plan. We shall hand out thirty thousand tickets all over Pennsylvania upon which it is written with pen the names of all the fifteen electors. You know printed tickets in the election are not allowed. This will require many agents to take each a bundle of tickets and disperse them to households. And first we shall write the tickets!'

Sarah knows Tom is thinking of the Corresponding Society,

comparing these cheerful Americans to his fellows in London, who moved on in fear from one tavern to another as the landlords fell foul of magistrates, or as volunteer militia harassed them. Of discussions and pipe smoke, of fighting a war with pamphlets, tracts and strong feeling against corrupt government and well-paid spies, like her own husband. The shame of that revelation! Tom had helped assuage her sense of guilt. Told her of the hopes and beliefs of the artisan radicals like those she'd encountered in St George's Fields. Of the stalwarts Hadfield, Harley and Pyke. Told it against the creak of ship timbers and constant blast of sea and wind.

She'd drunk in his words like life-giving nectar.

It's the first of many occasions at the Indian Queen. The core of the Democratic Republicans' belief is the equal rights of man. They want freedom of speech, of press, of assembly; freedom to criticise the government, to demand explanation from it. They are deists, Unitarians, a few atheists, Quakers, Presbyterians. Handfuls of Irishmen, Frenchmen, Scots. Americans with Dutch and German names. Men born in and fled from England. Balding, thick-haired, pale faced, ruddy-nosed, united by sober dress and well-washed linen stocks, by degrees of wealth, determined mouths.

They discuss everything: the existence of God, the inevitable degeneration of all governments into despotism; universal suffrage, the laughable English Constitution, how to fund education, the moral character of the labouring class, whether slavery causes vice.

Tom takes an extreme line on equality, especially in the face of reasonableness. Someone accuses him of being a Leveller and he proudly agrees.

'You Democratic Republicans suffer the disease of moderation,' he tells them one evening. His tone is friendly while yet the vigour of his speech demands they attend. 'You promote equality but you will not carry it through. What will you do with property; what will you do with land? You can destroy poverty and injustice with one stroke if you abolish ownership and distribute all land.'

'Even Tom Paine pulls back from that,' Willet Folwell, a Quaker, speaks up. 'Have you read *Agrarian Justice*, my friend? Paine tells us that we can rectify the violation of humankind's natural rights by taxing estates.'

'Most certainly I have read it,' Tom replies, 'and believe the great man has not gone far enough. All land, rivers, lakes, forests, mines, houses, all must be bought back. If you continuously tax the rich they will resent it. We shall not resort to guillotines. Must not. Let us pay out the landowners and return everything to the people to be administered in a beautiful New Republic!' Those caught by his enthusiasm applaud.

He's standing, flushed with fervour in which Sarah, too, feels a part. His ideas fly so freely!

'And how will you administer it?' asks Folwell.

'The Republic will consist of parishes. All land and buildings in each will belong to all those who live in each parish.'

'But how will that be *administered*?'

'By elected men and women in each parish.'

'Our friend would carry through the righting of inequality to the bitter end.' This from a stout man sitting at the side of the room, tapping his foot with impatience. 'Why stop at redistributing land?'

'Because that is where the greatest injustices thrive,' Tom retorts.

'Probably our friend owns no land, so he is untroubled.'

Murmurs of agreement. 'But once we've dealt out land and houses and streams and ponds and all the rest, what else counts as property? Will our friend agree to the distribution of his chattels, for instance?'

'Will everyone's chattels belong to everyone in the parish? And his wife. Will he agree to share his wife?'

There's a silence. A thin, garbled splutter from Eckfeldt. People stare at the man and turn away.

'I'm sure no one will expect me to respond to that,' says Tom. 'The speaker is evidently a lawyer!' Muted laughter.

On their way home Tom asks Robert what he knows about the questioner.

'He's British.'

'I thought so.'

'Recently moved here. Arrived all of a sudden. And you guessed correctly: he's a lawyer somewhere on Second. Not far from the shop, I'm afraid. Leopard, he's called. A memorable name. William Leopard.'

*

The rooms on the second floor of Zane Street are not large but there are four of them: space indeed. Robert's house is one of two in plain Georgian style and spanking brick with green-painted shutters to each window and three steps up to the front door. He himself occupies the first floor; the three of them eat together and spend evenings in an uncomfortable living room on the ground floor.

It's certainly not grand. The gradualness of Robert's success is evident in sparse furniture and few carpets. But there is no shortage of fuel for any of the fireplaces and Tom and Sarah buy themselves a feather-filled mattress.

With neither curtains nor inside shutters, they grow to love moonlight. And the lesser silence of dawn.

A tree grows near their window. They stand together looking out. A bird like a thrush with a red breast sings an unknown song.

'When I was a girl I often watched birds from my window. Kneeling on my bed.'

'Now you're Mrs Cranch I'll watch with you.'

They never tire of one another.

Although it is hard not to wake at first light, Robert rises so very early that he's always breakfasted before them. On Sundays he attends the Second Presbyterian Church in Arch Street with its elegant, slender steeple.

'It can help a man's path in life to belong to one of our well-established churches, Tom. You should consider that. We Presbyterians are not abstemious like the Baptists.'

'So I noticed!' They're drinking Robert's favourite peach brandy. 'I was raised a Quaker,' Tom adds.

'Och, you, a broadbrim? You've been keeping it dark, man. But you've come to the right place: Penn's city. You'll have noticed Quakers are still the main men. So that's why you chose to come here, eh?'

'No, it's not, and I've not been a follower for some time.'

'I've been thinking you're one of The Atheist crew.'

'I am. But Sarah …'

'When I was a girl I went to St Mary-le-Bow with my mother. My father wouldn't let her worship as a Methodist.'

'And now?' The ice-blue eyes will not let her escape. 'All women belong to one church or other. Outnumber the men.'

'I have not attended a church for some time.'

'That won't do here, young woman. You must find one if you're to be accepted.'

She says nothing. To join pews of stiff-bonneted women dulled by complaisance – no! For she is yet like a child entering the world, or a bird making its first flight.

Once, she'd detached a broken nest from above her window at Battle's and was amazed at the tiny space, jumping with insects, in which the young birds lived before they flew. Mud-solid, but cracked. Her life, too, was enclosed, dark.

Love has opened everything for her. She won't be confined again.

Before long, she tells Tom that Martha is free.

'I asked her straight out: she didn't mind. She said she was Robert's slave once. He bought her when he arrived, but freed her. Manumitted her.'

'Ah, that's a relief. I found out that the Pennsylvania law was not for total abolition of slavery. Those who were slaves before 1780 are slaves for life.'

'You see it's not the land of liberty, Tom.'

They are sitting at their table in fading light.

'Come now, they try their best. There are many good men here.'

'Mmm.'

'Sarah, there will come a time when all men and women in the world will be virtuous, wise and happy, I'm sure of it. When we've removed inequality. Life will be gentle, there'll be no war, no crime, no superstition.' He is unusually still.

'How can you think so? That's a description of heaven.'

'I've known many good people. Haven't you?'

She sifts memories. Tells him about Ben Newton. 'I loved being with him when he drew.'

'Would it had been me!'

'You can't draw!'

'Was he a good man, Sarah?'

'I don't know. I was just a child, I couldn't tell. Sometimes I thought he was sad, preoccupied. Now I think he was certainly a radical, though of course he wouldn't say so to me. We used to laugh at people in the coffee house, especially the odd ones, comical ones. His drawings were so funny.'

She says to him: 'After Newton was killed I was never happy again until I met you. You were blithe like the birds I saw through my window or on my way to the coffee house when I was married and left so early in the morning. Tom, you're like a blackbird singing from the roof.'

'My Quaker father thought it wrong to sing and dance, you know. My mother went along with his views, but as soon as he was in the shop, then she'd sing.'

'What was your father?'

'A bookseller. In a very small way. He was not a success.'

'Are they alive?'

'Both dead. Worn out. They worked hard. Yet they were happy with each other and somehow I understood that, even as a boy.'

'Why aren't you a Quaker any more?'

'I realised that I could not believe in a god who demanded worship while allowing so much injustice. I was strongly influenced by Tom Paine of course. And I went to Newington Green and heard Dr Price. It's from him that I've taken the belief that human nature improves. But let me tell you that Quakers believe men and women have equality of soul.'

She says: 'Is that why you're so good to me?'

'If I'm good to you it's because I love you, my dearest. Though, yes, of course men and women are equal. In Quaker marriages, you know, husbands and wives strive to recreate the equality of Adam and Eve in Paradise.'

'Ah, Tom. I think we are living life before the Fall.'

*

Spring comes suddenly, overnight.

Tom and Robert are in the shop planning a round of pamphlets. Tom is to hand them out at building sites. It's no good distributing them to the well heeled in the Indian Queen who don't need to be informed. He'll sell them, even give them to labourers and craftsmen, men, women whose lives must be changed for the better.

Sarah's *Guide* is progressing. She's almost finished the section on coffee houses in London; knows that soon she'll have to visit coffee houses in Philadelphia and dreads the reception she'll get. They are not places where women often go, especially on their own. She will be treated with suspicion from the start. That she comes from London might further antagonise the owners and in any case when would they have time to answer her questions?

Martha knocks.

'Mrs Cranch, a visitor. I put him in the big room.'

'Thank you, Martha. Call me Sarah. Please. I'm not the mistress of the house.'

'Mr Wilson, he like to keep the forms, he say.' She laughs.

'Who is it?' Sarah asks as they go down stairs.

'He say he tell you himself.'

'Oh. It isn't my father is it?' Entirely unlikely, this is a fear that occasionally surfaces.

'No! He not old.'

Sarah recognises the man immediately: the aggressive

lawyer from the Indian Queen. Who suggested Tom share his wife.

'William Leopard, Mrs Cranch.' He offers a hand. What can she do but take it?

He's stout, pocked, his black hair lank. His clothes are of good cloth, his hand hot, his glance sharp as broken glass. She wishes Tom were there.

'I hope you will accept my apology, Mrs Cranch. One night in the Indian Queen soon after you and your husband arrived, I asked some impertinent questions.'

'You should apologise to him.'

'Indeed.' He waves his hand, dismissing Tom. 'But you were offended perhaps.'

She feels strong irritation, refuses to return his persistent smile.

'If you wish to make an apology I insist it be made to Mr Cranch.'

'But your husband is not at home, I think.'

'No.'

'The republicans at the Indian Queen are respectable men, Mrs Cranch.'

'You hardly need tell me that.'

'They are men of substance, long-standing, have wives and children, are pillars of their churches.'

'Have you come to tell me what is obvious and known, Mr er... Leopard?'

'I merely set out the premises, Mrs Cranch. It is true that the moral reputation of Philadelphia is not wholly good. I heard of it soon after I arrived and have now observed it fully. Yet that is exactly why those with power and influence, the men of substance, those republicans whom you have met, believe so strongly in the necessity for public virtue. Reason, they believe, will always rule, and behaviour will be restrained.'

'Mr Leopard. I did not ask you to come here; I certainly did not ask to be lectured. I have work to do. Please make your point or leave.'

'Mrs Cranch, of course!' She sees the flash of charm as he strikes.

'I understand that you and Mr Cranch are not actually married. That in fact legally you are Mrs Wintrige. I am correct?'

'What business is it of yours?'

'The men of substance do not like adultery. Mrs Wintrige.'

Sarah sits down.

Leopard remains standing. 'The men of substance, our fine Democratic Republicans at the Indian Queen, are not merely not fond of adultery. Most of them do not practise it themselves. And they might be particularly displeased when two Britons, so recently arrived, popular and increasingly prominent, are found to practise it under the guise of marriage.'

Sarah feels her skin blaze, her stomach turn.

'Of course you will say that these men of substance contradict themselves. That they uphold liberty for all while condemning those who act freely, doing no harm to others, for no doubt no one is harmed by your action. That they uphold toleration and forget that in his *Rights of Man* Paine declared toleration as much a despotism as intolerance.

'You'd be quite right that they contradict themselves. As a lawyer I am alert to consistency and the lack of it.

'I am well acquainted with these men. What I know, Mrs Wintrige (or perhaps you'd rather I addressed you as Miss Battle?) is that these worthy republicans might prefer to exclude those Britons, currently so salient; might prefer not to buy their writings or anything published by them or their friend, Mr Wilson. That is, all those things might follow were they to hear of the adultery.'

'I must speak to Mr Cranch about this.'

'By the time he arrives here it could be too late. And by the time you have sought him at Wilson's shop and made your complaint to him, the news might be out.'

Oh surely Tom will know what to do! And Robert. Though, no! It will be useless telling Robert for she and Tom have not yet confided in him. He, too, might disapprove. Might even make them leave the house. She's never known fear like this; she wishes he'd go, go. His horrible smile, so grimy, so charming.

'What shall I give you to go away and not return?'

'You could give me thirty dollars today and the men of substance would not hear. And I shall go immediately. But I might come back on some occasion in the future. The new world is a tangle of inconsistency. As a republican myself it is my duty to point out contradictions.'

'But only to those who must pay you for it!'

'We need to make a living, we immigrants, as you know yourself.'

Pay him now, pay him, she thinks. Get him out. Talk to Tom soon, soon.

'Thank you, Mrs Cranch. I shouldn't tell Mr Cranch if I were you. He'll not have a solution to your difficulty even if you do. Good day.'

*

Tom is furious, Sarah tearful. It's the first time she's seen him angry: a detonation of loathing shoots through his whole being.

'Why did you give him any money? Why did you? Why? The man is no better than a rat, feeding off others. Or like those repulsive pigs gorging on filth in the streets here. He must be exposed and driven from the party, the country. Sent back to the pit of corruption – Pitt's corruption! – out of which he leaked. Foul effluent! That he goes under the name of republican is repugnant!'

His face contorts; a fierce ridge appears between his brows. 'To speak of his duty as a republican! Ach! What hideous hypocrisy!'

He rages about the room as if he would rid himself of his own body. Throws off his jacket, tears at his red neckerchief, beats his fists on the table, grabs chairs by their backs and bangs them up and down on the floorboards. Fortunately, Robert has yet to return, is not below.

The energy that she knows from his love for her, that fires his optimism for mankind, now drives a savage hatred. For a moment, she is afraid.

'What could I do? I had to get him out of the house. It was the only way. You were not there.'

'You should never have let him in! Why did you? Why? Did Martha let him in? Of course he came when he knew I wouldn't be there! Probably he even watched me leave the house. He approached you because he thought a weak woman could not resist him. And you didn't!'

'What could I do?' she repeats, but he ignores her question.

'It's intolerable! I'll not have it! I'll not be threatened by a criminal oozing out of the slime of the old country!'

By now he's at the window, thumping on the sill. 'A stupider man than I would challenge him. Shoot him like the vermin he is!'

He's not looked at her once. Will not.

'Tom, I'm sorry. But he's right: they have accepted us, they approve of us. We are doing so well. If they think we have deceived them they may indeed reject us. And we have deceived them!'

He stops pacing.

'But our love is greater than all the respectable marriages piled in a heap as high as the spire of Arch Street Church!' He looks at her at last. Rushes to her, holds her to him. 'Is that not so?'

'It is.'

The wild anger leaves him.

'Oh Sarah, Sarah! You had to pay, of course you did. I understand how you had to. I understand. But damn him! Damn the man! Damn him to hell! How dare he threaten you like that! Ah, my dearest Sarah, if only I'd been there.'

'What would you have done?'

'I'd have faced him down.'

'But if malice drives him he would not have cared.'

'Yes, it's true we don't know if he merely wants money or wants to destroy us. He was profoundly hostile at the Indian Queen. I'll talk to Robert. But no, I can't! Robert is a well-dressed widower who attends his church each Sunday. And we've been deceiving him all this time. We still haven't told him.'

'It's too late for us to live separately.'

'Oh, dearest, no! Don't speak of it. No.'

His face suddenly shines. He finds strength when she can only despair. It is a great virtue in him.

'Look. We have paid the sum, so let us now forget as far as we can. I concede that no joy comes without alloy. To that extent I allow you your view! But we shall not let it harm us. And if we must pay again, let's regard it as a negligible penalty. A penalty for our happiness.

'We'll find the money, we'll pay it. It will not break us. If it is only money he wants, he'll not ask too much: no blackmailer would ruin his source of revenue. Sarah, compared to everything we have in our life, it is small. Compared to what we have, thirty dollars is nothing. Nothing! Let's forget it. We shall not be intimidated. Our life will not change.

'In time I may be able to speak to Robert about it. In time we may find a way to remove the wretch, though police here are useless. Meanwhile, let's continue as we began, with our life, our married life, the best thing in the world.'

3

The century has little time left to run and in London threat of French invasion is back once more. Sam Battle skims the first page of the pile of eight newly delivered newspapers for a report of yesterday's meeting.

9 February 1798

The merchants, bankers and traders of the city of London met in the square at the Royal Exchange, where a hustings was erected for their accommodation, for the purpose of promoting the voluntary subscription for the defence of the country.

The meeting was very numerous. Mr Bosanquet, alderman Curtis and some other gentlemen, addressed the meeting upon the subject of the present state of the country, urging the necessity of opposing vigorous exertions to the inveterate hostility of an implacable foe, and of patriotically coming forward, with our aid, in support of everything dear to us as Britons and as freemen.

The speeches were received with universal applause; and, on the meeting being dissolved, four books were opened, in which a great number of names were immediately subscribed. Mr Boyd annexed £3,000 to his name and the other contributions were proportionably liberal. Previous to meeting, the committee who were appointed to conduct the business of the day, met at the Mansion-house, where upwards of £20,000 were subscribed.

At the end of the meeting yesterday, as he'd expected, customers flooded down Change Alley to be greeted at Battle's by its morose proprietor. He approves of their views, of course, especially since his married daughter ran off with a *second* Jacobin. Secretly he thinks she's safer out of the country, but his resentment towards his wife for foolishly getting herself killed has also extended to his daughter. As if to underline his utter distrust of women he employs a surly replacement for Sarah behind the bar, competent and only slightly less bad-tempered than he.

Little is known about Sarah. It's believed she's not written to her father, though no one dares to ask him, for fear of an explosion. Out of Sam's hearing, a traveller returning from Hamburg assures his listeners that he saw an Englishwoman with blushing cheeks on the arm of a man in a revolutionary cap, presumably 'citizen' Cranch. Another man with a correspondent in Philadelphia says that the streets are full of Red Indians and that Sarah has definitely married one of them.

Around the main fireplace, within Sam's hearing, the talk is loud.

'They say Bonaparte's assembling his best troops at all the ports, ready to board.'

'Thinks he can outwit Nelson!'

'He declares he'll spread the flame of liberty to England as well as Greece and Egypt and the deserts of Arabia, eh, Thynne? Do you look forward to a good singeing?'

'You may laugh, Bullock. When the money's all gone on sailors and ships and troops and cannon and shot and feeding prisoners, it'll be more than just the industrious poor crowding the soup shops, you'll see!'

'I'll tell you how many meals are served in the soup shops every day.'

'No, Lyons, don't! We'll go there ourselves and watch Bullock and Thynne banging at each other when they're both waiting for their broth.' Laughter from listeners.

Bullock squeezes his lumpy nose with lumpy fingers.

'They'd save the expense of prisoners if they did what they ought to with the Irish.'

Someone chirps up: 'At least there's good use for the Tower.'

'We should learn from your libertarian French, Thynne,' Bullock continues slowly. 'Heads off quick as a blade; much the cheapest way. Decorate the walls with 'em, like we used to do on Temple Bar.'

'You always were a pig. Don't deserve the name Bullock: insulting to our great English beef,' counters Thynne, his sharp features straining to puncture his rival.

'Irish, French, let's clear our minds of foreigners,' a pink-gilled man steps in from the margins. 'Have you seen the new prints at Digham's in Paternoster? Shakespeare, our great Shakespeare, now there you have a man to unite us. Prints of all the women in his plays.'

'Oh yes?' The minds of the company wheel round.

'Desdemona, Cordelia, Imogen, Portia, Ophelia. Enough to bring a tear to the eye.'

'Whose are they?'

'You won't have heard of him. Engraves his own paintings. He sells the originals for more guineas than I can afford. Setting up his own shop now, I hear.'

'His name, Fellowes?'

'Joseph Young.'

'Oh I've heard of him. Not exactly for his Desdemonas I'd say!'

'Aha! Then Sopwith, tell us about those. Have you got some? Will you bring them here?'

'You don't buy them, you hire the portfolio by the night. Not sure if Sam'd have it.'

'Upstairs, maybe, in the auction room.'

'Get Sam over here, Fellowes. He'll not mind as long as we pay.'

*

Money flowing soon enables Joseph and Lucy to move to better premises. He rents a narrow house in Little Russell Street with a shop window big enough to display a print in every pane and installs a printing press on the first floor. Second and third floors house meagre domestic arrangements. There, too, Lucy has her painting table, in a room high above the printing press, though she must also listen out for the shop doorbell, run downstairs, smile, take money from buyers or their servants, note sums in the account book she's covered in offcuts of flowered wallpaper.

She worries constantly about Matthew. Three days after his sudden appearance in Albion Place a 'friend' came for him and that was the last they'd seen of him. Joseph takes a note with their new address to the George in St John Street and returns in black mood.

'Was he there?' She sees the answer on his face.

'No. Of course not. He is safe somewhere no doubt.'

'Did they say so?'

'No, of course not! They wouldn't tell me that. They don't trust me.'

'Oh.'

'Matthew was right, there are spies all over the place. I might be one for all they know. The man in the George will have to move to another alehouse now I'm sure of it.'

'Then I shan't know where to send letters.'

'No, you won't! Lucy, you must cease thinking about him. He has chosen a desperate way. These are men of violence. They are at war with the government. They are right to attack corruption, lies, injustice; for that I am on their side. But their methods are mad and they will come to grief.'

There is no comfort for her.

But he is happy with her work. She colours all his prints, exactly as he prescribes. He is meticulous about the Shakespeare scenes for which there is great demand. Customers are particularly pleased when they find they can buy one or more from the same young woman figured in them.

William Digham's promise of sporting and topographical prints evaporates – indeed they rarely see the little printer now that Joseph has his own press, his success. Here's another disappointment for Lucy who felt gladdened purely by his presence. It consoles her to keep in mind the possibility of fleeing to him, a safe house of kindness and understanding. It would take longer to get there of course; she'd need a hackney or a sedan.

She colours Joseph's engraved satires though not his 'Amorous Scenes', as they're entitled on the covers. Has no idea who limns the pink glut of limbs. As the portfolios, bound in brown morocco, are hired not bought, Joseph need not produce so many prints. In any case it's the follies of street life, tavern life, theatre life that pour from him in great variety. The sketches he makes are mere reminders, for at his bench he cuts straight into the copper as if the figures caper out of his head: pickpockets, labourers, sellers, harlots. Two half-naked women wrestling in Murphy's in Little Russell Street itself. In that engraving Joseph surrounds the women with a jovial, drinking crowd, cheering on the fighters. On the left a small, unexpected figure in black, turns an eager gaze at the flying breasts, plump, tangled arms and thighs. Disturbed though unprotesting, Lucy reddens the unmistakeable cheeks of lascivious, gawping Rev. Mr Dale.

*

Come August end Joseph takes her to Bartholomew Fair, exuberant with life in the face of loud demands to close it down. Before, they'd have walked from Albion Place. She feels an odd sense of return when the hackney drops them into what at all other times is Smithfield, now pulsing with people rather than heaving with penned animals.

Laughs, shrieks, drumbeats, bugles, blind fiddlers, perpetual hurdy-gurdies. Acrobats and traders call out their skills and wares, and there's a constant blast of Sausages! and Pies! Hot Mutton Trumpery! Stinkin' Shrimps! Teeth Ache!

Joseph is elated, a drunken man in full control of his wits. He pulls Lucy through the crowd; they buy cheesecakes and ices, drink saloop, laugh like the happiest lovers in the world. Tossed on the waves of anarchy, Lucy darts excitedly from booth to booth, plays like the child she never was.

They are both children with money to spend. They watch harlequins cavort on wooden boards, buy tickets for Synget's Grand Medley on a precarious stage, the audience booing and clapping according to each performer's dress: dancer showing her legs: applause! singer with too many ostrich feathers on her head: boo!

'I went to a theatre when I was a boy,' Joseph says. '*The Destruction of the Bastille*, it was. It wasn't a play at all but a representation. I loved it. Someone took me, I don't remember who, to distract me from my mother's death.'

They gaze at an elephant and monkeys cooped in Miles's Menagerie, ride in a swing boat, watch a man eating fire, pierrots treading a taught rope, a parade of painted Indians, severe and sad. Give pennies to one-legged, no-legged, one-eyed sailors; a whole fist of pennies to the armless, legless man who fills a pipe, lights and smokes it; peep behind curtains at an albino lady; peer down a microscope at the smallest bible in the world.

Again and again Joseph stops to sketch on his pocket pad, picks up the comments about his pretty companion.

'Hear what they say about you Lucy!' He puts his arm round her, plants a public kiss on her flushed cheek.

In hastily erected booths, whose starred and mooned sacking flaps on crude poles, sit fortune tellers and sly sellers of simples promising eternal youth and cures for every ill. A necromancer predicts for pennies in a dark alley.

Someone runs past, there's a hue and cry, dogs join in, a child is knocked to the ground. Joseph and Lucy become separated and when at last he finds her she is surrounded by beggars wheedling for money, pawing her clothes. A fascinated crowd watches as Lucy, shaking, unable to escape, hands over her purse.

'Don't mind 'em, miss.'

'Nah! Don't give it 'em!'

'Go on, give 'em some'at.'

'Give 'em your shawl! That's worth a bit.'

'No, don't, miss. I'll get a Runner.'

A set-to, punches, hair-pulling, bodies knock into Lucy – their forgotten cause.

Joseph strides through the onlookers and suddenly no one's there.

'Lucy! What's this? Frightened by a few beggars? They would never do you any harm. They just want your money.'

'They were pulling me, mauling me. They would have taken my clothes if you had not arrived.' She is white. Weeping.

Three musicians appear with a crowd of hangers-on. One plays an organ strapped to his shoulders, another a reed pipe, the third a tambourine he tosses into the air, catches on the tip of one finger and resumes playing without the music having missed a note or a beat.

Joseph sketches rapidly and shouts at Lucy.

'That's nonsense. What a chaplain's daughter you are! Protected from the world. But you don't live in your tower any more. These are our poor.' He gestures all about him. 'All these are poor, not just the beggars.' He throws a coin into a bag attached by a stick to the tambourinist's hat, forcing the musician to bow his head in thanks and mockery.

A girl, sweating with effort, pushes a barrow past them loaded with baskets of pears. 'Look at her. These are the people Matthew is fighting for. For whom he's hatching vain Empires. These are the people for whom he'll start a revolution. For whom he'll kill.'

'Kill?'

'We'll go home, Lucy. Come on, my flower. I have sketches for a whole new series here. Worth every penny I've spent.'

He buys her a stick of cherries. She reminds him that he did this once before when they first met, but he cannot remember.

4

Robert Wilson, Bookseller and Publisher, Chestnut Street, Philadelphia, is thriving. A year after arriving in the city, Tom contributes a substantial sum from the sale of Cranch's in Berwick Street for a share in the business, and while he's not yet a partner, his say in major decisions becomes increasingly important. He takes specific responsibility for the pamphlet war which, together with certain newspapers in the city, keeps up opposition to the Federalists, with an eye to winning the presidency at the end of the century.

For the Democratic Republicans lost the election of 1796 and now have to endure four years of Federalist president 'His Rotundity' John Adams.

'Before we know it, there'll be a hereditary aristocracy, just you watch, eh?' says Robert. 'And they'll restore the monarchy to boot!'

As usual Tom is keen to hand out his pamphlets himself. That way he can read bits out to people and help bring reason to those who cannot read themselves. He walks the muddy, unpaved streets all day, encountering carters and market traders, fishermen and medical students, carpenters, masons, plasterers. Shaking hands, breathing the air of the unrepresented. Returns greatly excited, cannot stop talking throughout supper, relating stories of singular lives.

'You've no need to do this,' Robert says. 'Peddlers will take your pamphlets out of the city along with the chapbooks and almanacs, catechisms and primers.'

'Yes, but *in* the city, Robert, people must hear, must know.'

'Och, you're such an innocent, Tom. Do you think they really listen, all those grimy men with their adzes and hammers, eh?'

'Of course they do!'

'Don't get too close, will you? We don't want the yellow disease in Zane Street.'

Sarah has persuaded Robert to reduce the subject of her book and rename it merely *Guide to Coffee Houses of London*. It has come out sooner and sold fewer copies, but, the work complete, she is able to spend time in the shop. She shelves new books, gathers together the publications Robert will swap with other publishers. Occasionally stands still in quiet dampness to recall the loud smells and smoke of Battle's, enjoy astonished relief that she really has left all that behind.

Her education was adequate but barely matched the ambition that hatched in her as a girl. It began with Ben Newton tutoring her in her letters, then telling her about the world outside Battle's, outside England. James Wintrige, for all the blankness of her marriage to him, spilled dried twigs that, against his intentions, caught fire. Only Tom Cranch recognised the seriousness hidden by pink cheeks and womanly charms, the only attributes Wintrige and the coffee house customers ever noticed. He saw the look in her eyes as she observed, doubted, commented to herself. Saw intelligent scepticism, born of amusement and grief.

The shop is well stocked with books, pamphlets, newspapers and magazines. Robert keeps all the newest writing, however extreme by his standards, for there are buyers he doesn't want to lose. Tom shows Sarah works that would never have come her way trapped in Battle's: the new volume of Blake whose 'Echoing Green' he copied out for her in London. His favourite Milton. Sarah pays one dollar for the latest reprinting of Mary Wollstonecraft's *Vindication of the Rights of Woman* and takes it back to Zane Street, a piece of unexpected treasure.

Education is the key to better women's lives, she reads. Remembers that it was her mother who'd wanted her to go to school, while Sam saw no point in it. For him it was enough that she could count. Now she has time to read and read. Not that her life has ever resembled those women Wollstonecraft decries, pursuing beauty and the flattering worship of men, shopping, reading frivolous novels. But nor does she ever want to be without Tom.

'Mary Wollstonecraft says that Milton's Adam worships God, but Eve worships Adam,' she says to Tom.

'Oh, she's right. Milton conforms to his time in that. But his Adam and Eve have a wonderful love for one another. I recognise it and cherish it in him. My fairest!

'Look at these two essays I've found in the *Massachusetts Magazine*,' he says. 'A writer called Constantia. She wrote them seven years ago, before Mary Wollstonecraft. I asked Robert who she was and he told me not to waste my time with women's words.'

'Robert likes women to be quietly occupied. Sometimes he stares with those ice-blue eyes as if he'd silence me for good.'

'I think he's about to ask you to write a book on a domestic matter. You'd better be prepared, my love.'

'Why does he never speak of his wife?'

'I suppose because she's dead he can't bear to. If you were to die I'm not sure how I'd live.'

'Ah, Tom. But Robert is not a sad man.'

'True. Or he's decided not to reveal his sadness to others.'

'Mmm.'

'I admire how firmly he holds his views, yet at times it's stiffness, pig-headedness. I'd like to shake him out of it. But I'm not tall enough! He might whack me with his paddle hands, stamp me into a pancake!'

'You'll like Constantia, Sarah. She thinks Adam more to blame than Eve; says that Eve, after all, sought knowledge in good faith, sought to improve her mind. It's a nice point.'

*

'Sarah, what do you think to speaking at the Indian Queen?' Tom asks her. 'They need to hear the voice of an intelligent woman.'

'It's hard being the sole woman there. I'm sure they only tolerate me because of Robert and you.'

'No doubt. But it will do them good. Presumably they do talk to their wives, though only about the qualities of the new preacher and whom to invite to dinner.'

'To complete our meeting,' says Daniel Eckfeldt, 'Mrs Thomas Cranch will address us.'

By now, late in the evening, the men are somnolent with tobacco and rum punch, but they rouse themselves in the room's choke-thick air to listen to the fair Englishwoman with the pleasantly polite demeanour. Not a bluestocking. Surely not fiery.

'Mr Eckfeldt and Gentlemen, I speak as a woman, perhaps the first to address you in the Indian Queen.'

'Well said!' someone calls out and is immediately hushed.

'As you know, I come from the old country where both men and women endure gross repression. Here I am, proud to be in a land freed from its yoke. In the city of brotherly and sisterly love, where all is promise. A city in which recently it has become possible for a girl to attend a Young Ladies Academy and learn mathematics, geography, chemistry and natural philosophy.' She can't remember what comes next. Looks down at her notes.

'I shall allude to ideas already afloat; I have originated nothing. I don't mean to lecture you; I mean to ask more questions than make assertions.'

The assembly shifts slightly. She is going to bore them after all.

'Let us hear your questions, Mrs Cranch,' says Eckfeldt.

'That men have physical superiority to women is obviously true.'

Breasts swell; she almost gives up.

'Does it follow that because their bodies are stronger than those of women, so are their minds? A lion is stronger than a man. Is his mind superior to that of a man?

'Of course there are differences between people. Within the sexes, one man may be more quick-witted than another, one woman more quick-witted than her sister. But why should all men be more quick-witted than all women?'

Someone rises to his feet and waves but Eckfeldt holds up his hand.

'We shall hear Mrs Cranch. We shall not interrupt.'

'For the moment then, I should like you to concede that God made differences in mental strength between individuals, not between one sex and the other. That being so, we must ask: if women have reason, imagination and judgment as men do, how will they employ these mental faculties?'

'It is an intriguing question,' Eckfeldt says in his heavy way, breaking his own injunction. Sarah pauses, uncertain whether he will continue. She wants to complete what she's dared begin.

'Can it be sufficient for a woman to exercise these faculties on the needle and the making of pies?' She hears her inner voice ask her who then will sew and cook? She hastens on. 'Can it be sufficient that women occupy their days in efforts to retain and enhance their physical attributes for the pleasure of men?'

Chairs scrape. Men puff on their cigars. Chaw. Yawn. One man, wide awake, stares at her intently. She sees, suddenly, William Leopard.

'If, as I imply, education must be provided for the better use of all women's minds, it is reasonable to ask how then they would employ their improved mental faculties. It is nonsense to claim, as some do, that they will become mannish.'

She herself proves her point, they see, having not yet lost her charms.

'Instead, they will make better mothers, wives who are companions, not idols, and in the world they will make better teachers and why not chemists and natural philosophers?'

Throat-clearing. They look out of the corners of their eyes.

'I finish with this question for you, you who believe in democracy. If you do concede that God made all people equal in their ability to use reason, imagination and judgment, though he also made differences in the strength of these, surely you will grant liberty and rights to all people, to women as well as men, whether they be married, unmarried or widowed?'

The audience applauds politely. Puffs and coughs. There's loud clapping from Tom and one or two others.

'You are giving us much about which to think, Mrs Cranch,' Daniel Eckfeldt says kindly. 'Of course, often we are talking about equality and liberty. Not often are we talking about women. The meeting is ended, gentlemen.'

'Your rational, equal women, Sarah, what will they do with their freedom, apart from becoming chemists? Will they go to war?' Robert asks her when the three of them eat supper later. 'And who will stew our meat? You'll not want to eat food cooked by Tom and me, eh?'

Sarah is flushed. She'd been terribly nervous, had almost abandoned the project. She'd written out what to say over and over, but Tom would not look at it.

'Speak from the heart, my dearest. You have no need of my comments.'

That she'd conveyed her thoughts without stumbling, thoughts that engross her now as they never had before, seems an immense achievement.

Martha is not present again, is visiting her sisters, something she does frequently and often with a sense of inexplicable urgency.

'Barbed questions,' says Tom, protective.

'I doubt women would go to war. As I said, they will work. Make better wives and mothers. Of course some will cook.'

'Desert their marriages if they so wish?' Robert persists.

'Men should not be freer to desert their marriages than women, Robert.' Has he discovered, at last, that she deserted hers? She lives with that dread like a deep, embedded splinter. 'If there were a law of divorce, based on equality, no one would desert a marriage.'

'Hmm. And children? Your free women will have children here, there and everywhere?'

She reddens. Robert can't know that her great wish is to

bear Tom's child, that twice already since their arrival she has miscarried at an early stage. Only she and Tom know, for there'd been no obvious outer sign of pregnancy.

'Few women would want that. They would be even less likely to want it if they were treated equally in marriage.'

Robert grunts. 'Och, you've not been married long enough yet. You two still have the dazed look of a much younger couple.'

Sarah smiles wanly at Tom. The subject of marriage worries them whenever it occurs, however rarely.

'From my Quaker upbringing,' Tom says. 'I believe in the equality of husband and wife.'

'But now you're an atheist, eh?'

'Atheism doesn't prevent me from believing in a marriage of equals.'

'Let's bring about equality for men first, I say. Can't have women straying from their proper place, their natural sphere. Which reminds me. And now you'll think I'm contradicting myself. On the contrary, my project should please us all, eh? Sarah, I should like you to write another book.'

'I'm honoured that you ask me, Robert. What have you in mind?'

'Have you heard of Amelia Simmons?'

'No. Is she a poet?'

'Hah! No. Women poets! No. Last year she published *American Cookery* and made a great success with it. Specially written for American women. There's an appetite for such books! Let *us* publish one, which we'll call *The New American Cookery*. Ours will be better because you have some education, Sarah. This Amelia Simmons describes herself as an orphan and the first edition was full of mistakes.'

'What does it matter that she's an orphan? The recipes may

be good, all the same. Why should I compete with her? Besides I know nothing of cooking in America.'

'Och! No need to be fiery! I have a copy for you. Please look it over: you'll soon see how to improve on it. And talk to Martha. Between the two of you you'll cook up an excellent book. And make us all a lot of money, eh?'

*

Tom says: 'I watched your face, dearest Sarah. I'm learning to fathom. You hid your thoughts well, but I read them all the same. You really don't want to write this book, do you?

'It's true, Robert is a milk-sop republican. No revolutionary. He's not even a fully ripe democrat. Disappointing, isn't it? But without him we would have had a hard beginning and we're still dependent upon him.'

'He wants to silence me with his *New American Cookery*.'

'You may be right.'

'What he says about women, the way he speaks of marriage tells me he was not happy in his own, you know.'

'Eventually we'll find out. But let's have our own plan: let's write a pamphlet together about the education of women.'

'I should love to do that! And written by a man as well as a woman, readers will take it more seriously.'

'Yes, I'm afraid that's so. And it'll make us little money. Isn't it time for another demand from that damned man? We've paid three lots, but it's been a while since the last.'

They decide Sarah will placate Robert by reading his book and talking to Martha and then they'll suggest something else. A book of essays. *Rights and Virtues in the New World* by Thomas and Sarah Cranch, perhaps.

'Martha,' Sarah calls, running down to the basement where

Robert has his primitive kitchen, with its earth floor, washtub, small open range, hanging pots and kettles. In the middle is a large table and surprisingly, along the wall near the range, a sofa, somewhat stained.

'Robert wants us to write a book, you and me! About cooking.' Martha stares at her for a moment, then bursts into loud laughter. Sarah joins in.

'Mr Wilson, he full o' funny idea!' Martha says eventually.

'To tell the truth, I'm not keen to write this book, though I'd like to know your recipes.'

'Mrs Cranch, Sarah, it cannot be. I don't know to write.'

'Oh, that wouldn't matter. I'd do the writing, you and I together would decide what to put in it and you'd provide all the recipes. I'm sure that's his idea.'

'Do he think I have all day? To write a book? When I cook his dinner?'

'Quite right. We both have other things to do. Still, I said I'd talk to you. And I told him I'd look at a book he wants us to use as a model. Would you have a look at it, too?' She held out *American Cookery*, put it on the table.

'I don't know to read, Sarah, Mrs Cranch!'

'Oh.'

'My sister, she know. Her master learned her. She like to read. She always tellin' me how she like to read.'

'Martha, would you take the book to your sister? Ask her to read some of it to you. Then I can tell Robert honestly that we've both looked at it and we've both decided we don't want to write his cookery book. Your sister can keep the book if she likes. And I'll teach you to read. Isn't that a good idea?'

'Oh, listen to that! It strike two!' Martha pulls on a straw bonnet and light shawl. 'I go to my sister now. Come back later, make supper tonight.'

She rushes off and shortly after, Sarah sees she's not taken the book and runs out after her. Catches sight of her at the end of the street, begins to run, but it's too hot. Then suddenly she wants to see where Martha's family live. She'll follow, not try to catch up, hand over *American Cookery* when Martha arrives.

She's never known such heat. Unlike any London summer, it's a powerful heat that doesn't vary for months once it's begun. Masts sprout beyond the brow of Market Street, yet there's no sensation of sea breeze. The market is small compared to Covent Garden, and as Martha is tall Sarah can keep her in view, though she has to concentrate hard when Martha takes a winding path between stalls, wanting to look, trying not to stop. Buckets of cabbages, tomatoes, onions, squashes like gargoyles, meat dangling, dripping, baskets of bread, a man sawing a sheep's carcase on a bench. Insects skirr incessantly. Dogs run everywhere, pigs forage noisily among the rotting fruit and abandoned boxes that surge out of gutters.

Martha turns down a side street, another, weaving away from brick buildings. Pavements narrow, stop. Streets lose their cobbles, houses shrink. Bushes clump on scrubland. Sarah spots brown birds she now knows to be American sparrows, flitting among the vegetation, pumping their tails, singing their sweet, trilling song.

Martha opens a gate into a yard of hens scratching drily before a low wooden house. Out of which burst children, barefoot, clad in little for the heat. A boy about ten flings his arms round her waist and she hugs him to her.

Sarah's position along the street is exposed. She cannot slink away, nor will she, for the embrace has moved her. She has to know.

'Martha!'

141

'Mrs Cranch, Sarah, what you doin' here?'

'You left this behind.' Sarah waves the book.

'You come all the way, Sarah, Mrs Cranch,' her arm still hugging the boy to her side. 'This is Willie. My boy. Shoo children!' she says to the others. 'They my brother's.'

Sarah holds out her hand. 'Pleased to meet you, Willie.' The boy shakes it, watches her solemnly. 'Here's the book, Martha. Now I must go back.'

'Willie, take it to Mary. My sister in the house,' she explains to Sarah. 'Tell her I comin' directly.' She walks through the gate with Sarah out into the street.

'A beautiful boy, Martha.'

Martha beams. 'He bring me joy. But Sarah, Mrs Cranch, you not tell Mr Wilson you see him. Not tell him you come here. Please. Swear by Almighty God!'

'Oh Martha I swear. Of course I won't say anything. You can trust me.'

'Nobody know about Willie 'cept Mr Wilson. No white people. He pay me, you see. Nobody know. He very angry if he think you know.'

'Martha, I promise. Goodbye now.'

He is indeed a beautiful child. Half-caste, his smile like Martha's, his eyes a piercing blue.

*

It's July 4th. Robert, Tom and Sarah buy tickets for the celebration at Gray's Tavern over the Schuylkill.

'After the processions, there'll be nothing here but bonfires on street corners, rum-swilling and disorder. I want you to see something better, eh? We have pleasure gardens, too. They're not all confined to London,' Robert says.

'What a patriot you are, Robert!'

'It won't be long before you are, Tom. The both of you. Och, I can see it coming.'

They walk over the floating ferry bridge draped with flowers and flags of the thirteen states, towards banks on which great trees rise up and dip down into the river. Watch a scow take across a horse and its rider. Skimming swallows. Stroll through the grounds newly landscaped in the Romantic style. Hear a woodpecker's rapid drill and melancholy hooting at the edge of the woods.

'Mourning doves,' Robert tells them.

From the top of a steep hill they look into a deep shaded valley through which an unseen force pours between rocks. In the distance, partly concealed by trees stands a series of three high-arched Chinese bridges painted with quaint figures. They come across a 'federal temple' and a bathing house disguised as an antique hermitage, grottoes, bowers, arbours, a Chinese summer house.

'Beats Vauxhall,' Tom says. 'Perhaps not for originality, but the grounds even without the artifice are infinitely more lovely than any land along the Thames in the city.'

They take lunch. One half of the tavern is a large greenhouse grand with trees and plants, their flowers unlit lamps. Visitors gaze down from a gallery.

Robert says: 'I shall go and make the arrangements for our Tammany feast. Tom, it's the first time a foreigner has addressed the Sons of St Tammany, you know.'

'Must I wear Indian dress?'

'Och no, though most of the Order will. White Indians. It's a strange sight. Maybe you should consider a few feathers.'

'And my neckerchief?'

'Tom, the members gather for the purpose of patriotic

143

friendship. They won't give a damn about your neckerchief. In fact there's a move to supplant Tammany with Columbus, though don't say I said so!'

'I'd love to live among hills and trees,' Sarah says when Robert has gone. They are sitting at a table in a corner. The tavern is arranged for small and private meetings as well as large and public ones.

'You might find it hard, dearest Sarah. You can't ever have encountered silence in Change Alley.'

'That's true. And I know this is not real country either. It's like walking into a painting.'

'Exactly. The Gray brothers paid an English gardener to design it.'

'Not the river, though, and those huge trees we saw growing along the banks.'

'No, you're right. Tom Paine says that the ordered beauty of the natural world confirms the existence of God.'

'Mmm. But what about earthquakes? Natural disorder? I thought you were an atheist, Tom?'

'Sometimes I think I agree with the deists, that God is a first cause, nothing more. We admire his works, but he cares for us as little as a captain cares for the mice on his ship.'

'That's wise.'

Listening, talking to Tom like this. It's what she's always wanted all her life, she realises in sudden delight.

Tom says: 'Tell Robert you're a deist next time he reprimands you for not attending church!'

'I'd rather say nothing to him.'

'No. I can understand that. You know, I remember a girl I met who ran away from her poor, wretched life in Norfolk. She made it clear that rural life is hard, not beautiful.'

'How did you meet her? When was it?'

'Oh it was years ago. I found her in the street.'

'Found her! Was she pretty? Did you want to marry her?'

'She was remarkably pretty. But certainly not! You are the only woman I've ever wanted to marry.'

'She told you all about herself?'

'I wanted to know why she was begging so I questioned her. She was barely articulate. Came from a huge family that scratched the land. The father beat them, all of them: mother, boys, girls. I took her back to my rooms, gave her food, introduced her to someone who needed a scullery maid. Of course she offered herself to me, but I couldn't. How could I?'

'What happened to her? Did you find out?'

'She worked for the man I knew and later died in childbirth. Her story is common. Her picture of life in the country, halting, fragmentary though it was, showed me it's not to be wished for.'

'I know little about your life, Tom. We've talked so much that I think I know you. Yet perhaps I don't at all.' She feels a sudden terror. Intimation of aloneness.

'No, no! You know everything about me! What is there to say about my past? Nothing. Of course there were a few women to whom I took a passing fancy. Or they to me. I picked flowers which withered. Nothing more.'

'How can you have been so heartless?'

'It wasn't heartless at all, for there was no love, no heart involved. I paid when it was a transaction. I fathered no children, never made false promises.'

'If only I'd known you back then!'

'Yes! But I was skulking in Soho, grimy with printing ink and you were getting ever redder in Change Alley.'

He lays both his hands on hers. 'This is the place for us, Sarah. Remember how you once said you couldn't breathe in

Battle's? Here, in America, the air is good: we have the freedom to love, to grow. Our life is here, in this new land. Now and in the future. And listen, my dearest. There's a painter in Philadelphia called Birch. In fact he's English, arrived not long before we did, but he's already making a name for himself. A portrait painter and miniaturist. I want him to paint a miniature of you to keep in my pocket always.'

Robert rejoins them and they move with the crowd to the federal temple, on the steps of which thirteen girls and youths dressed as shepherdesses and shepherds sing an ode to Liberty. A band strikes up from within and as dusk falls, fireworks explode, illuminating the waterfall and river. Then comes supper: the three take plates of poached salmon and egg sauce to a stone bench and table within sight of the Schuylkill. All about, people toast the day of deliverance.

*

In September Sarah is expecting again. She and Tom, in their increasing closeness, begin to write the pamphlet on women's education, but Sarah feels tired, her concentration thins and while Tom works on other pamphlets (there are only two more years to go till the election, till the new century indeed), she looks through *American Cookery*, searching for clues about Amelia Simmons, a woman with neither education nor position who nevertheless published a book. A woman who finds it necessary in the second edition, which followed fast upon the first, to apologise for 'egregious blunders' and 'very erroneous' recipes in the first, to blame her 'transcriber', to remind her readers of the disadvantages of being an orphan. In London, she thinks, the book would never have been published. Here, a woman can dare and succeed.

When Martha returns the book to her, Sarah begins teaching her to read, but it's hard to find a regular time. This is understandable. When not working for Robert's household, Martha wants to be with Willie. Besides, there's rivalry with her sister and Martha refuses even to try to be like her. Mary can read but Mary has no children and is very religious, spends a lot of time at the Rev. Allen's Bethel African Methodist Episcopal Church. That's how it is. Sarah is disappointed. Friendship with Martha is a new experience. Here is affection quite different from the love of a man, a fondness she's not known with her own mother, let alone any other woman.

'Sarah, Mrs Cranch,' Martha says one day, 'that man come again.' She refuses to give him a name. Sarah has not told her why William Leopard calls, but Martha knows.

'Mrs Cranch, I thought it wise to visit you before the onset of winter.'

'I knew you were about to appear again, having seen you outside the house two days ago.' It's a feeble attempt to trip him up.

'Oh yes? Perhaps you did.'

'But you didn't call.'

'Indeed.'

He always comes when Tom is out, always looks the same: disreputable, panting slightly, smiling, sure of himself.

'What amazes me, Mrs Cranch, is that you should actually want the status of married woman.' Sarah says nothing; will not be drawn. 'For in the married state you have even less freedom than if you'd continued under your unmarried name. And of course I've heard you speak of the need for liberty for married women at the Indian Queen.'

She will not indulge him with a reply.

'I wonder why any woman ever desires marriage. The legal position is one of complete dependence. Blackstone put it most succinctly: "the husband and wife are one, and the husband is the one". Hah!'

'But as you remind me periodically, I am not married to Mr Cranch!' She can't stop herself. 'And I have discarded my previous marriage.' A sense of worthless triumph wells.

'Ah, and there I have some information for you which you should not ignore. Some ten years or so ago a law was passed in Pennsylvania allowing the termination of certain marriages.'

Sarah looks at him.

'Of course I refer to your marriage to Mr James Wintrige. Shall I tell you more?'

'Yes. Please.' Leopard grins.

'Under the 1785 Pennsylvania law, divorce is allowed when either spouse has deserted the marriage for at least four years. It is not necessary to provide evidence of anything else, such as adultery. You deserted your marriage in 1796, I believe?'

'Yes.'

'Therefore you could sue for divorce in 1800.'

'But surely he would sue for divorce. And he is in England and neither of us is an American citizen.'

'So advanced is this law, Mrs Cranch, that only one year of residence is necessary for filing. All that is needed is to persuade Mr Wintrige to dwell here for a year. There are only two more years to wait. And though I say so myself, only two more years of my visits to you, if he should decide to do that.'

As if to account for this free advice Leopard raises the payment to fifty dollars and Sarah does not protest.

Later, as she begins to tell Tom, she realises the corollary of the welcome relief from blackmail.

'James would refuse to sue for divorce, I'm sure of it, let alone sail to America. And even if he did then oh, it would all come out would it not?'

Tom puts his arms round her. Studies her face with his deep, bright eyes.

'We need Mr Leopard to keep things quiet for us, don't we?'

*

Sarah sits in Martha's kitchen talking about a dinner that Robert and Tom want to give for Daniel Eckfeldt. Ever since she's met Willie, Sarah has wondered helplessly how Robert can be persuaded to admit his paternity. She's decided to ask Tom, but first, having promised Martha not to tell, she must ask her permission to speak to him about it.

Martha is making pastry, Sarah peels and chops apples.

'Martha, I've kept my promise not to mention Willie to Robert.'

'You have.'

'Will you let me tell Tom? We talk to each other about everything. He'll understand the situation, the need for silence. And he'll have a good idea.'

'What idea, Sarah?'

'Robert must cease treating you as a servant.'

'Oh he like it that way!'

'But surely you mind it, Martha?'

'I not mind.'

'He should marry you! I'm sure Tom would say so, too.'

'Mr Cranch he really wise.'

'Yes, he is.' Sarah blushes.

'There, look at you! You two! Mr Wilson he never like that with Mrs Wilson.'

'But she's dead, Martha. I'm sorry for him. How terrible to be widowed. And yellow fever, too!'

'She not dead.'

'Really?'

'She leave him.'

'Oh?'

'She take other man.'

'Oh!'

'She like other men, Mrs Wilson. Like plenty other men. And he like me. There, now I tell you!'

'Did Mrs Wilson leave him because of Robert and you?'

'She say so. But she already have favourite lover, she leave the city with him, take furniture, too, go some place south. They send message she die of yellow fever, but it not true. Folk see her there.'

'That explains everything about his attitude to women, Martha.'

'Oh but he kind to me. He like me still.'

The stained sofa. It's what Sarah always suspected, though of course up on the second floor neither she nor Tom would hear what goes on in the basement kitchen at night.

'And he knows Mrs Wilson's not dead, so he can't marry you? If his wife's alive it would be bigamy marrying you.'

'Oh he not want marry me! The big men in the church not like it. White man. Black woman.'

'And he keeps Willie in secret, too.'

'He give me money, food for Willie, clothes. So I no need to go to the Guardians. And he pay that man. He have no money left!'

'That man? You mean Leopard is also blackmailing Robert? No wonder Robert needs our rent. And that's why Leopard was here the other day. I saw him hanging around. Oh, Martha, Oh!' She held her stomach. 'It's happening again!'

150

'My poor Sarah. I get towels. I help you right away.'

She supports Sarah onto the sofa, to be stained yet further, Sarah thinks wryly, and Martha, with towels, warm water and kindness, helps her through what is, after all, a small event compared to birth itself. But it depresses Sarah greatly. Martha holds her to herself like a child.

5

At the Seven Stars, on Bethnal Green before it splits into Dog Row and Red Cow Lane, the men nod a good evening to the publican, step down into the tap-room. An upholsterer, two shoemakers, a bookbinder, dwarf tailor, soap-boiler, boot-closer, gardener, silversmith, baker. Ten in all. They pass round the jug, fill pipes with screws of tobacco. They are not poor; their clothes not ragged, not stiffened by brick dust, lime wash. Fustian, flannel, serge, the colours are dour. Their only badge is the shortness of their hair, though that's a spreading fashion anyway. They're middle-aged or more, have wives, walked well over an hour to reach the remote fields north-east of the city.

'Citizens,' says Thomas Jones, silversmith of quick intelligence, 'our meeting opens with the swearing in of our new member Matthew Dale. Citizen, step forward. You need not place your hand on a bible if you do not believe.'

The others watch him sceptically, this boy yearning to be a man.

He begins reading the sheet too fast: 'I, Matthew Dale, do sincerely promise and swear that I will persevere in endeavouring to form a Brotherhood of affection among Englishmen of every religious Persuasion and that I will also persevere in my endeavours to obtain a full equal and adequate representation of all the People of England in Parliament.' Gasps for breath. Sets off again, more slowly.

'I do further declare that neither Hopes Fears Rewards or Punishments shall ever induce me directly or indirectly to inform or give Evidence against any Member or Members of this or similar societies for any Act or Expression of theirs collectively or individually in or out of this Society, in Pursuance of the Spirit of this Obligation. So help me God.'

The last four words come out as a confused mutter, he having refused a bible. There is a general murmur of approval and Jones leads him to each man to shake hands. Left hand to left hand, thumb to forefinger's first joint.

'Unity,' says the first man.

'Answer "Truth", Matthew,' Jones instructs him.

'Truth.'

'Liberty,' the next man says, his grip hard, a painful press on Matthew's finger joint.

'Answer "Death".'

'Death.'

'Citizens, our meeting continues as usual with a debate. Citizen Dale has volunteered to take notes. (Matthew – remember, names in the secret script I showed you.) Our subject, sent to us by the committee, is national schools.'

An aggressive yawn from one corner of the room.

'No, Citizen Clark, this is a vital matter. The question is: how shall the republic educate its children?'

'Gardeners, soap-boilers, we need no hedgecashun.'

'Citizen Jones, I agree with Citizen Clark,' pipes up Matthew. 'I say we have no need of schools at all. Destroy them! Our purpose is to work,' (he blushes, for he has none), 'to clean away corruption and lies and live a pure life.'

Silence. Reluctant applause from soap-boiler Clark.

'Citizen Dale. We well understand that you might wish to destroy a school such as that from which you recently escaped. But how are we to spread our word if the people cannot read?' The bookbinder's face contorts kindly. His skin seems sewn from his own off-cuts.

'The committee would have us agree to national schools in the republic,' says the upholsterer, the oldest man present. 'Let Citizen Dale record that we do agree and let us get on to more important matters, citizens.'

'Such as?'

'The business out of doors.'

'First, citizens, the committee would have us consider a new name.'

'I say we keep Sons of Liberty.'

'That was only ever a few of us. What's wrong with United Englishmen?'

'United Britons is more like United Irish. What's right for the Irish is right for us.'

'True Britons has been suggested,' says Jones. 'Citizens. Let us vote on United Britons or True Britons.'

The vote is unclear, duly noted. The men begin to empty their mugs and stand ready for the evening's main activity. A huddle of Jones and two others speak in low voices. Matthew hovers.

'No notes for this, Matthew.'

Arthur Heron the bookbinder asks Jones: 'Thomas, are we driving on again?'

'I've been talking with the Captain,' Jones speaks in low-voiced urgency. 'This morning. He is for going ahead; says fifteen hundred men might take London. But it'd be no less than five thousand could keep it, he thinks.'

'Look what they achieve in Ireland! Look at it!' The voice of upholsterer John Boxer, grates between breaths from poisoned lungs.

'John, I think more of us should meet with the Captain and the committee.'

'But have they any plan? A plan for acting upon not debating. That is what we need, a Plan of Insurrection. Tonight I'll go to see a person I know in the Tower' (Matthew's ears prick up), 'to consult whether if we can make a Hubbub that cannot be delivered up.'

'That's good, John. Once begun we might sweep through the Nation. The committee surely know how many divisions will join us, how many have organised in the rest of the country.'

Even as he glows in the light of this language, is flattered by Jones's treatment of him as an equal, Matthew feels the wash of vagueness lap about them. He has been welcomed, protected in Thomas Jones's house in Plough Court, Fetter Lane, ostensibly learning the work of silversmithing, in fact helping Jones write pamphlets, sometimes minding the baby. Occasionally he thinks of William Leopard. Wishes he could see him now.

The main activity of the evening assures him somewhat even if there are only ten men to drill together in the garden of the Seven Stars. They have weapons, well a few, which they pass from hand to hand like priceless contraband. Lit only by the alehouse windows, they learn to march in step, to halt at command, to hold still for testing amounts of time, above all to obey without argument; not to think, rather to listen even when commands are whispered, and to act.

They drill for an hour, dare not shoot for fear of raising villagers, stop suddenly at heavy breathing behind the hedge, resume when they hear the slow tread of cows. Troop back into the tap-room, fetch more jugs, tobacco, open the door and sing loudly, as proof to spies or casual sneaks that they really are a convivial debating club rounding off the evening in their cups.

A good-natured nice king
But hope we ne'er shall have a-nother!

Pause while they listen for the clink of hostility. Then louder than ever the songs they've learned from the Irish, 'Erin go Bragh', 'Croppies Rise Up' and, from the heart of the Revolution, 'Dansons la Carmagnole'. Best of all:

Ah! ça ira, ça ira, ça ira
Les aristocrates à la lanterne!
Ah! ça ira, ça ira, ça ira
Les aristocrates on les pendra!

And all the rest of the verses, every word.

*

Although Joseph sometimes speaks of Lucy as his wife, of course she's not. He tells her she's his wife by common law, for haven't they lived together now for more than three years?

He hasn't brought Fanny Lobb to the new house in Little Russell Street. Yet Lucy now knows when he visits her, for she has learned the signs that must precede it. First his ebullience dulls, he becomes morose, still occasionally weeps at the worthlessness of his work. Something distils within him, drip by drip. He barely speaks, nor will she risk abuse by speaking to him. He looks up from his work only to stare, listening to an inner violence. Sits all night without moving, as though suddenly he might crumble to dust.

She is relieved when at last he goes. Shutters out intermittent bawling from the street; tries less easily to shut away her worries about Matthew. The Watch proclaims each half hour. She reads the poet of consoling gloom.

'How have you the patience for such melancholic stuff? Nothing but dying trees and dead rabbits,' Joseph has said to her. Though he approves of Cowper's poem against slavery, he abjures all writers except Milton and Paine. And Shakespeare of course.

Alone, her feet warm before the grate, Lucy reads Cowper undisturbed.

> *But me, perhaps,*
> *The glowing hearth may satisfy awhile*
> *With faint illumination, that uplifts*
> *The shadow to the ceiling, there by fits*
> *Dancing uncouthly to the quiv'ring flame.*
> *Not undelightful is an hour to me*
> *So spent in parlour twilight: such a gloom*
> *Suits well the thoughtful or unthinking mind,*
> *The mind contemplative, with some new theme*
> *Pregnant, or indisposed alike to all.*

She is suffused by gentleness. The poet is a mother to her, a father, kinder by far than they who brought her into the world; than her brilliant, erratic, heartless, common-law husband.

His return, exhausted, his pupils glittering pinpoints, is

always merely a confirmation. He plunges into sleep and she must wait until he wakes.

Fanny did sit for him as Emilia. The print sold well, Lucy's distress as Desdemona all too real. He abandoned a scene with Fan as Lady Macbeth and another with her as Gertrude for which she might have been suitable. But he brought along his black Othello before the move from Albion Place.

'Lucy, meet a friend of mine, Gilbert Downs. He's agreed to sit for Othello to your Desdemona. He knows the play.'

A big man, taller than Joseph, Gilbert, curious, genial, shakes hands with Lucy.

'I've read the play and I'm pleased to be your husband, ma'am!'

'Yes.' Lucy nods politely. Gilbert cannot know how his joking declaration pains her, for, of course, he could be, she not being married in law.

Something in her face alerts him. 'Your play-husband, Mrs Young, for I am myself married and my wife, Ann, would not tolerate bigamy.'

'Indeed, Gil, you are a good husband.' Lucy is unsure whether irony or guilt or neither flit over Joseph's face.

'Well, I'm glad not to have to remember all the lines,' Gilbert says. 'What memories these actors have!'

'Valets surely must remember what their masters want, Gil? Gilbert is valet to Lord Whoever-he-is with a vast wardrobe, Lucy. Will he buy a print of you as Othello?'

Gilbert laughs. 'No, no! He mustn't know of it.'

'The valet as general!' says Joseph. 'You may develop some airs, Gil.' More laughter.

First Joseph paints the half-completed scene in which Desdemona presses Othello on Cassio's behalf. Gilbert is swathed in a fine white cloak with braided edges. It emphasises his height, his upright bearing, his blackness. Lucy watches.

Then comes the first scene of the play's final act. Desdemona in bed asleep. Othello standing over her with a lamp contemplating the wife he'll shortly kill.

'And shall I sleep all day?' she asks, half-jokingly.

'When I've painted you, Lucy, you can get on with your work.'

'No, Joe. That won't do at all,' says Gilbert. 'How can I think that whole soliloquy with only a bed before me? My face will express nothing but thoughts about your sheets!' They shout with laughter. Lucy, unsmiling, closes her eyes, knows she'll never make him laugh like that.

It is the strangest thing she's done in her life, though sewing a Tricolour for the King's Birthday in the middle of the night was odd enough. Desdemona's story is hard to bear. How awful to be an actress, to act your own death on stage! Yet here she is, feigning sleep on her bed, contemplated by a man who is not her husband, who is making himself think Othello's jealous, murderous, loving thoughts while looking down upon her.

She wonders about Gilbert: is he a freed slave? She's seen black musicians in the street, black servants in livery. One comes regularly to hire the amorous portfolios for his master. Gilbert has been educated, speaks easily. He and Joseph are friends; no doubt he knows of Joseph's other life. Of Fanny Lobb.

She dozes. Is Gilbert's wife black too? He is a handsome man. Does he, like Joseph, have another woman from whom he cannot keep away, despite what he says about bigamy? What is he thinking about as he stands there? Can he look at her lying on a bed without wanting...?

ALIX NATHAN

She closes her eyes more tightly. Gilbert notices a delicate erubescence rise from her neck to her face.

*

Thomas Jones, revolutionary silversmith, has a second wife, Lizzie, several years younger than him. When his first wife died in childbirth along with the baby, Thomas transferred much of his distress to the cause of revolution. He met Lizzie in a tavern whose landlord was friendly to democracy; saw the sense in distraction from his widower's grief.

Matthew is happy minding Lizzie's first child when, some days, feeling the need for society and pocket money she returns to the tavern to work. Thomas's silversmithing is a success and in the Jones home in Plough Court there are mats on the floors, there's more than one upholstered chair and plenty of bedding. The child, Edward, is lively, just walking and has begun to speak. Matthew observes a childhood quite unlike his own, the fond parents attentive to their offspring.

Thomas probes, for he must ensure the division has not been infiltrated. Questions Matthew about his father, his education, his beliefs. The boy, as he thinks of him, is painfully honest. Soon both find relief in the other's confidence.

'Matthew. You should know that there are government agents everywhere, paid well. We must always be alert for them.'

'Aren't the men sincere? They seem so to me.'

'Sincerity must ring like gold. The gleam of silver deludes – it is malleable in heat.'

'Do you suspect someone? The Snob?' This is the nickname of Jas Bacon, the shoemaker.

160

'No. That's just his manner. I tell nobody but you. Pole. The baker. We must watch him, cautiously. He is too quiet.'

Once in a while the United Britons dare to meet in Thomas Jones's house. A back way takes them through the court and into the cellar. There the threatened French invasion shakes their unity.

'We should think again. I am unhappy with this heavy dependence on the French that we have nourished for so long,' says Arthur Heron, his face basted remnants of leather.

'What? Where's your trust, Heron?' says John Boxer irritably, breathing harshly. Jones admonishes him: 'Citizen.'

'Where's your trust, *Citizen* Heron?'

'They have betrayed the revolutionary cause, *Citoyen* Boxer.' Heron can stand up for himself. 'They are more desirous of establishing an extensive military despotism, than of propagating republican principles.'

Matthew holds back, watches Thomas whose opinions are now his guide.

'Moreover,' Heron continues, 'they joyfully massacre priests.'

'Priests,' growls Boxer.

'And prisoners.'

'There's some justice in your view, Citizen Heron.'

'Thank you, Citizen Jones. We must effect change with our own hands. It would therefore be best we join the Volunteers and keep the French out of our country.'

Roar of disapproval from soap-boiler Clark and his companions. A murmur from Pole.

'We can't succeed without French arms,' Boxer rasps.

'But as Volunteers we shall be armed!'

'Citizens! We surely do not want to become a mere part of France,' says Thomas. 'We want our own English Republic.'

'Keep out Bonaparte with our own arms, citizens, then remove the King!' Heron's voice is rising.

Amid shouts, jeers, a stick appears through a hole in the ceiling, a sign from Lizzie that the men must disperse. Perhaps she's seen a gathering of Runners on the corner of the street. Or some known opponent pass by slowly, listening to the night.

*

Joseph makes his way to Change Alley with a large, flat cloth-wrapped parcel. His mood is circling down. Soon his mind, closing in, will catch itself and start to burn. He'll need Fan with her blinding drugs of raucousness, songs, sex, drink and pipes of opium and tobacco to stanch the fire.

He'd far rather go to Wych Street than Battle's Coffee House, yet he knows there's money promised, possibly a lot. The area makes him feel queasy; too close to the rich with their well-cut waistcoats and airs, and the rushing, jabbering jobbers and operators pumping the engines of revenue. Owner's daughter ran off with a Painite, they say. Good for her.

He makes his way to the central bar where a frowning woman apparently unaware of him takes orders from everyone else.

Infuriated by her inattention and the stench of coffee and chocolate he peers into her face.

'Yes?'

'I've come to see Mr Samuel Battle. Mr Sopwith brought a message.'

Instead of replying she clicks her fingers at a passing waiter, points at Joseph, turns her back.

In his dark office Sam Battle makes up for the sour welcome to which he guesses Joseph has just been treated, offers him a dish of coffee.

'Mr Young, I have a proposition.'

'So I understood.'

'Several men ask to use a private upstairs room for weekly meetings of... of ...' But Joseph won't help him. 'Of... ah yes, connissewers. Connissewers of art. I hear your work is for hire.'

'To hire out both portfolios so regularly would be to deprive others. I should prefer to sell them.' Was it the coffee that provoked this cunning move or a final burst of energy before his mood plunged? 'And if I sell them to you then I must draw or engrave a whole new supply.'

'How much do you ask?'

'Sixty guineas for two portfolios.'

Sam sits down. 'Sir, do you imagine I am a wealthy man?'

'No doubt you will charge your connoisseurs for hire of the room.' Joseph hears the voices of his friends Jack and Hugh: 'Show us your shiners!' they shout. 'I don't imagine you are poor, Mr Battle. I think you'd best see the work.'

He unwraps the parcel. 'Look, bound in morocco; beautifully done, the title in gold.' He opens up the first portfolio and Sam is defeated as Joseph knew he would be.

Licking his lips, his eyes darting wildly over the sheets Sam agrees to the price, urges Joseph to wrap them up again.

'Mr Sopwith also told me you have prints from Shakespeare.'

'Shakespeare's women.'

'Ah! Are they, are they like...?'

'They are nothing like these. They are entirely respectable and in high demand.'

Shivering with erotic sensation, in defiance of a dead wife's ghost, Sam has no memory of his daughter's longing to improve the coffee house with lectures and concerts. He'll recoup the cost of the *Amorous Scenes* before long and then make money. And if he has a few Shakespeare prints downstairs, too, won't that somehow make up for what'll take place above? Some of the merchants who go elsewhere today might change their minds once they know what's on offer, both downstairs and upstairs.

Joseph returns home empty-handed with his pockets full of shiners. For a few hours he's light-hearted.

*

Nine men assemble in the taproom of the Bleeding Heart, Hatton Garden. Eight division commanders and Matthew, assessed by Thomas Jones in his position as commander of the North City division as exceptional. Not just for his education and youth. Thomas has seen the hatred that propels Matthew, a hatred whose other side is the gentle playfulness of his relationship with Thomas's toddling son Edward.

Each man present uses a pseudonym or none; no notes are taken. They await 'Captain Evans' whose fame as a naval hero masks a landowning Irishman embittered, hardened. The organisation is military: companies of ten, each with a commander, groups of five a 'deputy division' commanded by a captain. The North City company is not typical, for most of the companies contain Irish dockers, soldiers, discharged sailors.

'Captain Evans' is mild and courteous, his manner deeper than a veneer. Superior in birth, education and naval experience, it is not hard for him to achieve discipline and loyalty.

'I am sure you understand the danger in our very existence; much worse here than for the companies now growing apace in Sheffield and Birmingham, Manchester, Leeds and Chatham.

'Yet it is here that we must begin. London is the head and the head must lead. I know the courage of all of you is without question.'

'We can assure you of that, Captain.' Matthew, silent, observing, longs for the details, the plans, to know his part.

'A coup d'état here in London, the capture of the King, will fire up the citizens, our fellows in the streets. Once the news is out, citizens will rise all over the country with our companies to the fore in every city and town.

'Tonight I want men with special knowledge. It is they who will help me put flesh onto the bones. And these are the bones: to storm the Tower and Bank, seize barracks from within, throw open the prisons. As these succeed so shall we capture the King and the Man-Eaters who surround him. At that point shall the people rise up, inspired, supported, for soldiers will turn in droves. Of that we can be sure. Then as a sign to the rest of the country we stop the mail-coaches in Piccadilly.'

Each man is allotted a place, given two weeks to find all necessary information. For Matthew it is the Tower. Of course he could draw plans here and now, he says, having lived there all his early life. But he well understands that more is needed: points of entry and exit, points of particular danger, numbers of soldiers, times of guard change.

'My intention is this, Captain,' he says to his leader. 'I shall supposedly be reconciled to my parents, claim complete renunciation, and so return to their apartments. From there I can ascertain everything necessary.'

'Will they not turn you in, Citizen? Such parents do exist.'

'They know nothing of my whereabouts and occupation for the last three years. I shall tell them tales, promise to go up to Oxford, and, above all, speak in such anti-Jacobin terms as will convince them well.'

'Don't convince yourself in the process, Citizen,' says Captain Evans, smiling mildly.

It is the greatest day of Matthew's life.

*

Early in 1800 a bill appears upon the Monument:

HOW LONG WILL YE QUIETLY AND COWARDLY SUFFER YOURSELVES TO BE HALF STARVED BY A SET OF MERCENARY SLAVES AND GOVERNMENT HIRELINGS? CAN YOU STILL SUFFER THEM TO PROCEED IN THEIR EXTENSIVE MONOPOLIES, WHILE YOUR CHILDREN ARE CRYING FOR BREAD? NO! LET THEM EXIST NOT A DAY LONGER. WE ARE THE SOVEREIGNTY, RISE THEN FROM YOUR STUPOR! FELLOW COUNTRYMEN! BE AT THE CORN MARKET ON MONDAY!

From Monday there is hissing, hustling, pelting with mud, the target meal men, corn factors, Quakers. The crowd shifts, disperses, forms again, mud becomes brickbats and stones and all week tumult pounds the streets for bread and revenge, the militia is called out, the Riot Act read.

The bill is pasted up by Joseph reluctantly resuming his radical beginnings. There's no Corresponding Society now to which he can belong, only furious groups that meet clandestinely to prick on chaos. Once an eruption occurs all rush to join. But a riot is hardly a coup. Only Captain Evans's United Britons plan for revolution and he'll have nothing to do with them.

It's not so much Joseph's new income that disturbs him enough to act once more, just once, as what he sees for himself on the streets: the starving poor, the very servants of the rich in wigs powdered with flour. Perhaps there's a shred of rivalry with Lucy's brother. Not that there's any information at all about Matthew. Still, Joseph has a good rough idea.

Once the crowds are moving like a tide, he makes for Fanny Lobb's, where mayhem galvanises the cock and hen club like an electric charge. Where Fanny's songs, her gyrating and gestures ignite a riot of sensuality.

Nowadays he often stays away from Little Russell Street for longer than one night and Lucy is not unhappy when he doesn't return for two or even three. She is pregnant. Knows for certain from the pricking of her breasts, her lethargy, desire to think of nothing but herself.

She's not told Joseph and has no one else to tell. She thinks vaguely of her mother but not for long. She fears Joseph will not be pleased. Wonders how to tell him. First she must wait till the right moment, when his mood is fond. Yet will she want to jeopardise such a moment, risk his anger? Why would he be angry? Would he not be glad to have a child? She knows him better than she did at first. Understands him not at all.

She hears the street door close, braces herself. Will she tell him tonight? Might she leave it till tomorrow? First she must wait until he's recovered from his excesses.

With remarkable discipline she refuses to allow herself to envisage that life of his. She cannot complain, being only his wife in common law. Besides, sometimes she loves him. And always she admires him: The movement of his hands when he sketches, when he paints, even more so when he cuts through copper still amazes her, so rapid, certain, almost not human at all.

She recalls the lions in the Tower menagerie. As children she and Matthew had often watched them, how the great beasts never moved unless they had to. Matthew would do his best to rouse them from sleep, rattling a stick up and down the bars. Mostly they ignored it, but occasionally they rose to their feet, stretching their hugeness, exposing massive teeth in enormous yawns. Joseph getting out of bed in the morning; yes, there was something of the bored lion about him. The lions never wasted a movement. Joseph is like that in his work: each action unwavering, absolute, even if in daily life he's more like a bear, clumsy and dangerous.

She sees immediately something is wrong. He comes over to her and takes her hand, a gesture he never makes when returning from Fanny.

'Lucy, there is trouble. Arrests. They have arrested men in Red Lion Passage and the Nag's Head in St John Street. I think it's Irish they've taken at the Royal Oak, but not at the Nag's Head.'

'Matthew,' she whispers.

'They've seized the house of one of the leaders called Thomas Jones. Confined his wife and child. I believe Matthew was living with them.'

'Then he is taken.'

'It seems he may have escaped. It was hard for me to find out. If he has, he'll surely try to get out of the country.'

'Where, where will he go?'

'He'd best sail to Hamburg. There are plenty there who

think like him. Tonight he may be in a safe house on his way. Or, well… Perhaps not.'

'Then, where? Where will he be?'

'Oh, I don't know. How can I know?'

'Where do boats to Hamburg sail from, Joseph?'

'Wapping, perhaps. Lucy, I'm tired out! I must sleep. I'll ask again, find out more in the morning.' As is his way, he collapses on the bed fully dressed. Will not rise till late tomorrow.

While her mind shrieks with anxiety she knows she can now act without interruption; that she must find Matthew while Joseph is unable to prevent her.

She drags her bag out from beneath the bed, the same bag she had when Joseph found her in the doorway. His clothes are too big for Matthew, yet she must take her brother something to disguise himself. Shirts, breeches, the smallest coat, stockings even, for will it not be cold in Hamburg? Where *is* Hamburg?

She wraps bread and cheese in a cloth, thrusts money also wrapped in cloth deep among the clothes.

Remembering the day she fled from Joseph, scrupulously leaving coins on his table, she buttons on her outdoor clothes and adds all the coins she can find to the money already in her purse.

Closes the door on the sleeping man, hurries to the end of Little Russell Street, narrowly avoids a contingent of the Bloomsbury Volunteer Corps and hails a hackney.

6

Only one more year before the new century. Only one more year till an election in which President Adams will be ousted and Vice-President Thomas Jefferson elected to the presidency. Or so the Democratic Republicans hope.

The Indian Queen rings with hostility to the national bank, the national debt, both of them forms of corruption, they say, with denouncements of Britain's shameful piracy in pressing American sailors to serve in the British Navy, and with the Jay Treaty.

'Damn John Jay! Damn everyone that won't damn John Jay! Damn everyone that won't put lights in his window and sit up all night damning John Jay!' they roar.

The Federalists are split and democratically inclined newspaper editors and pamphlet writers dig joyfully into the fissures. Robert and Tom discuss starting a newspaper. Eckfeldt urges it, as does Willet Folwell, and several other men of means from the Indian Queen promise to back the enterprise. There's a rumour that Jefferson himself would become a sponsor.

Tom is keen. Inspired by the prospect of Jefferson in power he is excited at the thought of writing newspaper columns as well as pamphlets.

'It's the best way to bring about the revolution of reason. I'm sure of it: newspapers, pamphlets for all to read.'

'Och, there are already so many newspapers, Tom. They grow like brambles, eh?' Robert says. Sarah watches the two of them, seeing, momentarily, a Newton cartoon, Robert with his huge, sledge-like feet, his ice-blue eyes trying to pierce Tom who, like an American robin with his red neckerchief, sings high up in a tree out of reach of Robert's darts. It's rare for her to think of Newton these days.

Robert says: 'We'll be swept up in the wash of scurrility, Tom, just you see. People will think we're purely political and no one will buy our books, except for a few political supporters. We'll make no more money! And we'll have to fill columns with reports of balloon flights and notices of runaway servants.'

'We'll refuse advertisements selling bonded labourers at half the usual price of a slave. It sickens me, that. But we could advertise ourselves, the shop, our publications!'

'Pah! A rag bag of scraps and political venom.'

'Is William Cobbett to blame for all the rhetorical duelling?' Tom asks.

'*Porcupine's Gazette* certainly stirred things up. Libel charges were filed in '97, you know, and he still hasn't come to trial. I don't want to get into that sort of thing, however much it might amuse you.'

'I thought frank Scotsmen always spoke their minds.'

'I'm an American now, Tom.'

Tom consoles himself by writing occasional columns for others. Pamphlets are his favourite form, however. Big enough to contain a whole argument and spiky details, small enough not to daunt the reader as a book might. Written to be read aloud. Print follows quickly upon writing. But writing for

Democratic Republicans in the Indian Queen cannot be the same as writing for navvies building roads and canals, or newly freed slaves with no education.

'I do believe you're becoming evangelical, Tom,' Robert says. 'All this wandering about among the people. You're a political Wesleyan.'

'People need to know, they need to have hope. And if they can't read then I can tell them myself.'

'Och, think who they are, with their disgusting, drunken ways.'

'The mutable rank-scented meinie, you mean.'

'Quote all you like, but don't forget we have epidemics here, man. Disease. I warn you. It's not wise to mingle with all and sundry.'

'Those measles which we disdain should tetter us! If you'd lived in London, Robert, you'd understand. We worked in the dark, sad owls hooting at night, flitting like bats. Here optimism is king. We can achieve everything the good men hoped for in France without shedding a drop of blood.'

First he must go down to the waterfront. Of course many of the sailors are foreign, unable to speak, let alone read English. But there are dock workers and builders, the shipyard men, fishermen, tavern owners, the women who live off the sailors. He'll soon sell pamphlets or at least get a hearing. He has a winning way. People see his honesty, enjoy his humour, trust him never to walk off before they've had their own say.

Sarah and he eat supper at which, Robert being out, they almost persuade Martha to join them.

'Mr Wilson not like it. He like the forms. You know he always say that, Sarah, Mrs Cranch.'

Tom now knows of Martha's relationship to Robert but has yet to confront him about the hypocrisy, the absurdity of continuing to treat his mistress, the mother of his child, as his servant. Of course men have done that for centuries. But surely now, here, where reason prevails, he should treat her with greater equality, even if the law forbade bigamy. It will mean Tom finally admitting to his and Sarah's 'marriage'. He's not at all sure the men's friendship will stand the revelation, though, who knows, it might just benefit from mutual admission.

'Martha, I'll talk to Robert.'

'He not want to hear it, Mr Cranch.'

'He should divorce his wife and marry you. There's a law in Pennsylvania that would enable him to do so. For his wife deserted him, did she not? We've heard about this law recently.' He winks at Sarah who frowns.

'I tell Sarah he not want to marry me.'

'Some men here are quite open about their mistresses, Martha. Governor Mifflin, for instance. And Rev. John Hay travels about the city with his mistress and child.'

'They're important men,' Sarah says, 'perhaps they can do as they like. It's more difficult for a lesser man to brazen it out.'

'Well, I'll talk to him all the same. Really I shall.'

Now they are preparing for bed. Their blissful bower, their shadie lodge. He'd shown her the lines in *Paradise Lost*. Living with him, he'd warned her much earlier, meant living with Milton.

'It's time for us to break up with Robert, Sarah. To set up on our own. There are too many differences between us, we disagree too much. What does he care about? Sometimes I think he just wants to make money. He's blinkered in his attitude, creeping along.'

'Shouldn't you heed his warnings?'

'Nothing would ever change if we all stayed at home! I must circulate more pamphlets. But I also want to publish a newspaper, and sell cheap reprints to pay unknown writers.'

'He'll see us as rivals, Tom.'

'Not necessarily. Our publishing will be more radical than his and we shan't take that many clients from him.'

'He'll resent any loss at all.'

'Well, I hope not. I'd rather not quarrel with him. Yet I'd also need the money back that I gave him, to buy premises.'

'Will you tell him soon? Shouldn't we wait until the election is over?'

'No. It must be soon; I'll take the first opportunity. Meanwhile, come with me to see the new ship. They're building a frigate called *Philadelphia* in Southwark, near the Old Swedes Church, which, by the way, is where the minister refuses to marry black and white couples, though fortunately it's not Robert's church. I gave out dozens of pamphlets to sailors on my way to the shipyard, so I heard about it. Goodness, they're a motley crowd, sailors! Men from everywhere. It's some distance along the river. We can ride some of it if you don't feel strong enough to walk, my dearest.'

'The ship's half built. It's for the infant American navy to protect merchant ships now that the French are hostile. Great poles of scaffolding like trees. A huge sloping gangway, ever more timbers to raise the height of the hull. Axing, sawing, hammering and the great bow like a mighty whale beached above the river.'

'How wonderful! Let's go at the end of the week.'

'I feel a strange attraction to it. As, though the ship were an emblem for our life here, that we're building so strongly, so stoutly.'

When they are in bed, she says surely Wollstonecraft is

174

wrong that a man and woman should no longer love each other with passion when they have children. 'She even says a neglected wife is the best mother, Tom.'

'She can't be right about everything, Sarah; she's not a goddess! She's certainly wrong about that. We'll prove it.'

*

At the end of the week they postpone their visit to the *Philadelphia* because Tom has a headache.

'Pain makes me impatient. I'd be vile company; let's go on Monday.'

But by Monday he's running a fever, shivering, aching all over and goes to bed. Sarah bathes his forehead, encourages him to take Martha's broth, works through the proofs of his latest pamphlet with him.

Robert comes and stands at the foot of the bed, observing Tom's restless doze. He takes Sarah out of the room.

'Send for a doctor immediately, Sarah. I shall go and stay with Groff in Chester.'

'Robert, why?'

'I've seen it before. You should consider leaving yourself. It's what everybody with the means did in '93.'

Tom calls out from within the room.

Robert says: 'Goodbye, Sarah. Tom may be an innocent, but this was folly. I told him not to get too close. Och, does he think he needs to be a martyr for the cause of democracy? Worse than folly!

'Here's my address. Say goodbye to him for me.' She hears him run down the stairs.

Tom is delirious, seems unaware of her, focusses on some invisible threat in the corner of the room.

'Get away, get away from me!' He struggles to sit up, back against the wall, his hands held out before him. 'Go! Go!' Clutches at and fights the air.

'Tom, it's all right. Nothing's there. It's all right. You're safe. I'm here.' She strokes his hand and his arms collapse onto the bedclothes. She takes a hand and holds it.

'Tom, I'm here. Nothing will hurt you.'

Shudders shake his body and again he rears up, thrashing his limbs so that she can hardly avoid being struck.

'Away! Hideous! Great wings. Great body rising from the burning lake. Away from me! Away!' He cowers, borne down by the huge, unseen weight, trembling with terror. Powerless. Not the man she knows.

Martha knocks and comes in.

'What I bring him, Sarah? More water, more broth?'

'Both please, Martha, though I doubt I'll get him to take any nourishment. He's keeps seeing horrors in the room.'

'He so tired, poor man; he sleep soon. You want me stay a while?'

'Thank you, but no, I must be with him.'

'Mr Wilson, he left. He think it yellow fever.'

'Will you leave, too, Martha?'

'No. I stay with you. Mr Cranch he maybe get better. Not all people die.'

Martha is right. Tom sleeps, though fitfully, and Sarah half rests at those times, lying next to him on the bed, ready to hold the bowl for him should he vomit again, to soothe him when he wakes. She bathes his head, fiery with fever, makes him sip water when she can. It is a long night, longer than when the men danced on the roof of Newgate aflame. She dulls her mind, considers nothing except the immediate.

In the morning Tom shakes her gently.

'Awake my fairest, my espous'd... Awake, the morning shines.'

She looks up into his face, unshaven, newly gaunt, its dear smile.

'Tom!'

'I'm well again. The fever's gone, I'm not aching and I feel extremely hungry. Let's have breakfast. I could eat a whole pan of eggs and ham.'

He's unsteady going down stairs but much strengthened by food and strong tea.

'And I was about to ask Martha to fetch a doctor! Robert has deserted us, you know. Gone to Chester in a fright.'

'What nonsense! We'd best write and haul him back. He can't just leave the business like that. I'll put on clean clothes and go to the shop. And the proofs need to go back to the printer.'

'They do. But, surely you should rest first? I'll return the proofs.'

'I feel perfectly well, my love. Come with me, though, won't you?'

*

They write to Robert but his reply says that he'll only return when Tom is certified well by a doctor. He's told the bookbinder to delay delivery of the latest *Guide* for a week. If Sarah can open the shop occasionally that would be good, but he expects they can absorb loss of revenue for a short while.

Because the shop has been shut for a couple of days there are not many customers. They draw up lists of titles to exchange with the other major booksellers and publishers.

Replace books on their right shelves. Tom sits down to draft a new pamphlet, but can't put his mind to it.

'When I was a boy I was mad for reading, Sarah. My mother taught me, as she taught us all before we went to school and sometimes I read to her when she was nursing a younger child: Hooke's *Roman History*, Hume's *England*, pieces from *The Spectator*, *The Rambler*. There were plenty of books in the house of course, though strangely enough Father thought meditation better than reading. Too much reading oppresses the mind, he said. Perhaps that's why he wasn't much good as a bookseller! But I always read in bed. Took a flat candle with me. My favourite was *Robinson Crusoe*. Now it's *Paradise Lost* as you know. I was sure I'd sell books in my own shop one day; was determined to do better than my father.'

They are in Robert's office. One end of the huge desk is Tom's. Sarah enjoys surveying the shelves of earthenware ink bottles that Robert still sells. She loves to listen to Tom talk even though it's strange to be idle in this place.

'You have your memories of Newton, my dearest. I never had one best friend, but a group of us boys would get together for the purposes of, well, experiment. Once, it must have been November as it is now which is why I think of it I suppose, we collected between us several crackers and squibs and a neat pile of gunpowder.

'We crept down to the kitchen. My father was at home that night and was in earnest conversation with his Quaker friends two floors above; my mother will havde been reading or dozing. We achieved a few pleasing bangs without discovery. But then came the gunpowder which, we were annoyed to find, was too damp to light. So I tipped it into a frying pan and held it over the fire to dry out.

'You can imagine what happened: an explosion that knocked us all down, blew out the candles and sent the adults running down the stairs to drag out the bodies. But not one of us was hurt!'

'You always acted on impulse, even in your boyhood.'

'Yes. But my impulses are usually right!'

She smiles. 'Yes, you changed my life.'

'And my own. Sarah, let us go back. I think I might rest a while.'

The fever returns that night. Sarah cools his forehead continuously, fearing delirium again and when he groans at fierce pain in his abdomen she calls down to Martha to fetch the doctor.

Hears with dread his horse on the dark street, his hearty knock, his approaching footsteps.

'Dr Kammerer, Mrs Cranch. Your husband?'

'Yes. He was well for three days,' she says as if to prove he's not ill.

When Kammerer sits on the side of the bed Tom opens his eyes. 'Heinrich Kammerer, Mr Cranch.' He touches Tom's head, holds his limp wrist, peers closely at his face.

'Do you work near the waterfront, Mr Cranch?'

'No. Chestnut Street.'

'But, Tom, you went to the docks and yards ten days ago. He was handing out the pamphlets he had written, doctor.'

'The waterfronts are not a good place. Not good for disease. Or rather, too good for disease. Dr Rush would have us bleed and purge the fever, but I am not happy with this treatment.

'Cool him as much as you can, Mrs Cranch, make him drink water as often as you can. Mr Cranch, I will call again in twenty-fours hours' time.'

He takes Sarah aside. 'The skin is yellow.'

'In candlelight all skin looks yellow.'

'Mrs Cranch, his skin is yellow. The whites of his eyes are yellow. You will need a bowl for vomit, many cloths and towels. You may send your woman sooner if necessary.'

*

'Where has he gone, Sarah? Where? Tell me! I mean Death. He was here just now, I know he was.'

'Tom, that was the doctor. Dr Kammerer. He has told me to keep you cool and make you drink.'

'No, no. I recognised him. He was Death.'

His face is burning. 'He will come back. He'll drag me into the deluge, the fiery deluge. Torture without end! He's coming back. Coming to drag me. Rising up from the flames!'

He's too weak to struggle against his imagined enemy and falls back.

But then he stirs and groans. 'Sarah. Oh Sarah I haven't done it! My promise to Martha. To confront Robert.'

'Dear Tom. It doesn't matter. It's not important. Rest now.'

'It is! Robert must...' For a moment a flash of that anger he'd shown when Leopard made his first appearance burst over his face. 'I promised! And now I cannot do it.'

She wants to tell him that in time he will. But she mustn't lie.

'Sarah, you talk to Robert. Promise me!'

Her promise is a farewell.

She holds a cup to his lips and then he retches into the basin. He's vomited all before: there's nothing now but blood, black clots of blood. She bends to place the basin on the floor.

'Sarah, you've gone! Where are you? Where have you gone?'

'Here, I'm here. I haven't gone. I shan't leave you. I'll never leave you.'

'Best of women, best of wives, best of friends.'

She can't speak. Takes his hands in both hers and kisses them.

'Is darkness flaking yet?'

'Flaking?'

'Flaking darkness: dawn.'

'Not yet.'

'Have I told you that I love you?'

'Yes. You have, often.'

'Heav'ns last best gift, I love you dearly!'

'Oh, I love you so dearly, too.'

'My ever new delight!' But here he vomits again and from his eyes comes blood like a mockery of tears.

She wipes them and the blood that gushes from his nose and mouth. He struggles as if to speak but only blood comes. She wants to plead with him to stay, not to go, please to stay, never to go, never, but knows it would make him suffer more.

She sponges his head with water, strokes his hand as he groans with pain.

He opens his blood-bleared eyes and looks at her with desperate longing. She can't smile, can't, turns to wipe away her tears from his sight and suddenly he cries out greatly and has gone.

*

'Sleep. Only sleep.' She closes his eyelids. 'Only sleep, my darling.'

She washes blood from his face. Slips down from the bed onto her knees, holding his hand still, pressing her head onto it until his knuckles hurt her but it's nothing for the howling in her head destroys all outer feeling. It was as if she bleeds, now, only there's no outward sign of wound, just tearing, pulling apart, bleeding within.

She loses consciousness and waking, sees what she already knows but sees as if afresh and sobs until all moisture has dried up and her brittle, cracked body might break if only it would break.

Again she wipes the blood caked in his black hair, from his face, climbs up next to him, his body still warm – he'd been so hot – kneels and touches his cheek, his shoulders, arms, as though she might remind him to wake, might see those eyes again, bright, deep, stroke his head as she remembers wanting suddenly to do one day in the coffee house, kisses his mouth before it should get cold. Keep him cool the doctor said! Is he cool enough now to live? I'm wrong, he lives! Her fingers touch his lips to feel the breath that isn't there.

She lies down, her arm across his chest, her face in his hair still damp, smelling of sweat, death.

How can she have slept? Yet she finds milk, a plate of bread and cheese nearby, which she can't eat. Nor can she call to Martha.

Dead. He is dead. Again it strikes anew like an outrageous fiction: only turn the page and know it is untrue.

Gone. He has gone. He has left me. I can never speak to him again, hear him, see him move, smile, feel his touch. Never. Never. Why has he done this? Why has he gone? Why did he not think of me?

She digs her nails into her face, tears at her clothes, the grimy gown she'd not changed for days. She knows what it is to heap ashes on one's head.

'Sarah, you must eat.' Martha stands by the door.

'I don't want it. It will not bring him back.' She bursts into tears. 'I'm sorry, Martha. Please let me be.'

Why did he ever go to the shipyards? Just to speak to sailors, to give out pamphlets. He might have lived! He needn't have done it. He should have remained here. Why didn't she make him stay here? If he hadn't gone he would never have become ill. Would have been here now.

The night is silent. Nothing moves on the street outside, not even the goldfinders' dripping cart. No owl flies; no night bird whistles or sings. Everything is dead. Except the great booming in her head. Her heart still there, its foolish, mindless, incessant booming. Refusing to die.

She denied him. Denied him the smile he wanted. How can she live?

Later, Martha knocks again.

'Sarah, we wash him. The doctor will come.'

'I'll do it. Thank you, but I shall do it.'

'They take him away.'

'No! They mustn't take him. Don't take him away! Please don't take him away!'

She doesn't sleep again. Night. The moonlight they had grown to love through unshuttered windows is absent, rightly. So should there be no dawn, the lesser silence they had also loved. She hates the creeping light, dreads day. Dare not sleep for fear of waking, innocent.

Martha brings clean water, cloths and towels and Sarah washes his body, his loved body, now so thin. Now cold.

He was never cold. Never motionless like this. It's wrong: I have imagined it! In a moment he will wake!

She dresses him in clean clothes. A spare red neckerchief, for she will never part from the other. Finds the miniature he'd had Birch paint in his coat pocket. No use to her. Why hasn't she one of him? She puts it back. Something of her close to him. He said he wanted to keep it in his pocket always.

All the while she talks to him as though he's come in from a day writing in the shop, talks, planning what they'll do tomorrow, talks low and lovingly, continuously so as not to hear no replies, as if by talking she'll somehow keep him always as he always was.

*

Martha helps her through the days. The terrible footfall as they carry him downstairs. The plain coffin painted black. Hurried burial in a burying yard on the edge of town, attended by Daniel Eckfeldt and a few others from the Indian Queen. Some Quaker prayers. He would have understood why. Robert sends a letter. Will not return until the house has been thoroughly cleansed.

Frosts bring winter. Black days. Days when sorrow stands, a cormorant, wings outstretched, unmoving. Days of unbearable longing. Days of remorse, terrible remorse for the smile she never gave him. Resentment, self-pity. Solitary nights of wild grief.

Martha makes her eat. Comforts her as no one ever had before.

She hates Robert, even obscurely blames him. He doesn't repeat his view that Tom brought about his own death, but though she will never accept it, she cannot forget it. She finds herself loathing the sight of his feet since she can't bring herself to look at his face; thinks of him attending his respectable Presbyterian God, coming away satisfied that all is in order.

There is no God that cares. How can there be? He'd be an infinity of tears.

In cold clarity she realises that soon she'll run out of money.

Her guide to London coffee houses made little; it was Tom's pamphlets and articles that paid their rent. Perhaps she should demand Tom's share of the business. But legally she has no right to it, though Robert does't know that, and of course, Tom would not have wanted any radical publisher to shrink.

There's her promise to Tom to confront Robert. She doubts she can do it to any effect, knows Tom might have achieved something. Martha, she's sure, expects no change. But Tom would have kept his promise, would want her to keep hers to him. She will do it. In time.

She thinks she should move out, away from Robert, to somewhere cheap but she hasn't the energy. Besides this is the room in which they'd lived, she and Tom. Their blissful bower, their shadie lodge. The chairs in which they'd sat together. The bed in which they'd slept.

One day Martha says: 'You so sad, Sarah. Maybe you go home to England?'

'Oh. Maybe I should, Martha. Would you come with me?'

'I cannot leave Willie.'

'No, of course. Or Robert.'

'He not let me go.'

'Oh Martha! I don't know if I can do it on my own.'

'God Almighty help you.'

'God Almighty and you, Martha. How like your name is to Mother!'

Martha laughs and they both cry.

The century is at an end. In December George Washington dies, the Father of his Country. It suits Sarah that all people mourn, that everywhere is hung with black.

There is little to mark Christmas, for most of the churches, including Robert's, ignore it. Daniel Eckfeldt invites Sarah to his house: as a Lutheran he's retained his old German traditions. Touched by his kindness, she politely declines.

On December 26th, eight days after Washington's funeral, a memorial procession and service take place in Philadelphia, still the nation's capital. Sarah stands near the Market Place in a silent crowd, the streets lined, every window of every house full of onlookers, and watches soldiers and clergy, the black-plumed riderless horse, the black-draped empty bier.

'Mrs Cranch.'

Astonished that he should approach her in her mourning gown, she turns her head away from the voice in disgust, but can't easily escape William Leopard through the press of people.

'A moment please, Mrs Cranch,' he speaks quietly.

She stares ahead, tears running over. Oh Tom! Tom!

'Do you think of returning to England, Mrs Cranch?'

She will not answer.

'It occurred to me that you might. In which case, please take this.'

He presses an envelope into her folded arms and shoves his way out through the crowd.

Though inclined to drop it on the ground and trample it in the dirt, she takes the envelope back to Zane Street and breaks the seal.

Unfolds a sheet of paper:

Received with thanks from:
Mr William Leopard
[sum carefully erased]
For Purchase of:
Fare for Voyage and
Reservation of Berth for: Mrs Thomas Cranch

On: *Fair American* (Capt. George Legge)
Sailing from: Philadelphia to
London
on January 18th, 1800.

PART III

PART III

1

'Will I take it all the way for you, Miss?' the porter at Wapping asks Sarah, tossing her box onto his shoulder as if it were a tea caddy. Irish, she thinks, like many were in Philadelphia.

'I'm going to Change Alley; you couldn't walk that far.'

'That I could. But I surely won't.' He smiles with jagged charm.

'I'll go by hackney. Please would you carry the box until we find one. Oh. But wait a moment!'

The pale girl she'd noticed minutes before, the girl searching so frantically for someone, has been met by a man who is remonstrating with her. Tall, his fair hair tied back, he tries to take the bag from her, puts his arm round her more to coerce than to console.

Sarah steps towards them, stops herself in time. No. It is not her concern. She doesn't know them. And here she is, staring like a child just as she did at the oddities and foibles in the coffee house.

'Let us go then,' she tells the porter.

Little has changed in London in three and a half years. She has become used to clean brick and painted wood, to straight roads on a numbered grid, the New World's rationality. Now she sees what was always here: ancient houses tumbled together, a pile of rubble where one has fallen, narrow roads jammed with carts, carriages, steaming horses. A few new warehouses stand by heaps of sodden ash. It's true there are blocks of neat-cut paving in a main street or two, but St Paul's is black as coal.

The hackney nears Change Alley, her anxiety sharpens. How will her father react? She hasn't warned him. No doubt he was disgusted when she fled, but it doesn't mean he'll welcome her return. Might he refuse to let her in? Where will she go then? Will he insist she move back with her husband? What has happened to *him*? James Wintrige, dissolved like a ghost into the past.

At the same time she is glad to carry her sorrow to a familiar place: a wounded bird seeking the thicket where once it nested. She knows there will be hazards.

She enters the coffee house at the back, her box left in the passage outside the kitchen. Her courage faltering, she opens the kitchen door rather than take herself to her father's office.

It's a bad time to intrude, late morning, food being prepared, cooking well under way. No one notices her till Dick, wiping his nose with his sleeve, looks up.

'Miss Battle. Oh Miss Battle!' He limps over to her, takes her hands in his knobbed fingers. 'You've returned! Oh, but Mr Battle will be pleased,' he says doubtfully.

The cook, Mrs Trunkett, who comforted Sarah with love and terror when her mother and Newton were killed, pushes the arthritic boy Dick out of the way.

'Sarah! Oh, how glad I am! Praise be to God!' She presses Sarah hard to her stoutness, holds her at arm's length, hugs her again, weeps copiously. 'Oh, so like her mother she do look, standin' here just like Mrs Battle. I did never think to see it! Is you returned for good now? Come, Dick, stir yourself, man, gawpin' there. Take Miss Battle's cloak and bonnet and things.'

This welcome dulls fear enough for Sarah to knock on her father's door at last and announce herself. The passage is dark, not unlike the ship from which she's just disembarked, where, of a sudden, light might cut down a hatchway. But his office is empty and having sent her box up to her old room in the attic, she cannot resist passing through the waiters' door into the main room. There, too, she remains unseen in the fume and din for some time, for who bothers to watch the door into the kitchen unless they're starving, and the starving don't resort to coffee houses. The street door is the one to keep an eye on if you've really nothing better to do.

She sees her replacement behind the bar, unsmiling face on a grumpy body that stiffens whenever it's approached. Despite this hostility the place is as full as ever it was, occupations entirely the same. And then a man who's taken his coffee and newspapers at Battle's for untold years catches sight of a new woman on the premises, looks again and alerts his companions to her presence. At which the entire table stands and raises its glasses and coffee bowls:

'The prodigal daughter returns! Miss Battle, we are delighted to see you. Hurrah!' The room rises and all join in the huzza until a hush falls and curious looks are directed to where, from a curtained snug, Sam Battle emerges. His face reddens, blackens. He walks out, disappears into the depths of the house.

*

Speech was never Sam Battle's *forte*.

'You've come back.'

'I have.'

'Shall you run off again?'

'Dick has taken my box to my old room, Father.'

'Oh. Well.'

He doesn't ask the reason for her return. The very name America, that treacherous, barbarous colony, is one he will not utter. And as to why she went in the first place, that is not to be thought of either.

Nor is mention made of James Wintrige. Sam ever disliked the man, a sponger who spouted revolution. He's not been seen for years. On Sam's principle Sarah should certainly go back to her husband. But Dick has heaved her box upstairs and Sam's well aware of the pleasure his old customers are expressing at her reappearance. Before the day is out he's sacked the bad-tempered woman from behind the bar.

Sarah's duty always was to replace her mother when she, against his wishes, damned stupid woman, went out and got herself killed. The girl tried to wriggle out of this duty through marriage, but her worthless husband knew which side his bread was buttered. Then she ran away, the hussy! Now she's back he'll make sure she stays.

In her childhood room Sarah goes straight to the window to scan the scene she knows so well. Gables, chimneys, tiles and broken lead guttering. Winter smoke aping snow clouds obscures the distance. Sparrows, whose freedom she once envied, furtive in the cold, hop into discarded nests of summer martins.

She unpacks her box: places clothes in drawers, arranges a packet of carefully wrapped papers and a dozen or so books on the chest. From her skirt she takes a red neckerchief. The pocket full of thrums went years ago.

She presses the neckerchief to her face with both hands and sobs in anguish.

*

Sam cannot refuse her an afternoon to collect her clothes from Winkworth Buildings. He's certain there's no danger she'll remain there.

It's getting late and no one answers her knock. She stands outside, envisaging the gloomy interior, leans up against the door as though to hear her youthful, uncomprehending self sink into the silence of her marriage. She and Tom had *run* down the stairs when they fled!

She brings a note for James, having anticipated, indeed hoped that he might not be at home:

James,

I am in England now and wish to collect my belongings.

I shall not return to live with you although we are still married, knowing, as I do, for whom you work. I read the letter that you wrote to R. Ford. You will say that it was not my property to read, to which I say that I had a right to know to whom I was married.

I now use my own name. I daresay you will not want me back in any case.

Please send to the coffee house to tell me when I may collect my trunk and clothes. If you prefer to pack and give them to the carrier to take I shall pay him when he arrives.

Sarah Battle

She walks back slowly, the familiar route, though then it was always dawn's ash light or late-night darkness, accompanied by Dick. There's no change in the streets except where houses have collapsed from age or been pulled down by mobs. She's heard something of recent times, of the disastrous last year of the old century: how in the spring great falls of snow buried mail coaches all round the country and mailmen rode or walked the post to London. How famished crows fell out of the sky, how lambs froze dropping from the womb. Preachers and madwomen threatened crowds with destruction of the world. Thousands left London. And while neither earthquakes nor pestilence appeared and the prophets were locked in the madhouse, in the summer rivers burst their banks, the ground flooded, harvests failed. Only the numbers of starving grew.

Men in their cups tell her this, pleased to find a woman who will listen. Once she disdained their attention. Now she hears them out, responds politely and escapes to her own thoughts. This they don't notice, content to talk at the pleasant woman, older, perhaps a little sober, but still comely.

Among themselves they fight over peace with France, whether to sign a petition insisting on negotiations. Most agree with the mayor, alderman and liverymen of the City who have already sent their own petition to the Commons.

Hovering before the fire, tamping tobacco in pipe bowls, they expend more spleen on the question of exactly when the new century began.

'We speak of it, but has it begun at all?' says a man looking up from his newspaper, shiny with the assurance of authority.

'Oh Lyons, how absurd!'

Lyons taps his source, blushes, smiles nervously.

'It says here that just because we've begun to count eighteen it doesn't follow that the century must be changed.'

'*Who* says, man? Whose nonsense is this?'

'Lalande. Lalande the astronomer says it.'

'But he's a *French*man, Lyons!'

'Rothersay, move away from the heat. Let Lyons tell us what he knows. Read it out, Lyons.'

'Lalande has published a pamphlet.'

'*Tell* us, then!'

'He says whatever calculation is to be made, we commence by one and finish by one hundred. Nobody has ever thought of commencing at nought and finishing at ninety-nine.'

'*Well*?'

'It follows that the present year, 1800, incontestably belongs to the eighteenth century.'

An explosion of guffaws compels Lyons to shrink back to his place on the settle.

Sarah, untouched, attends to the warming of punch. There are those who try to catch her eye, flirt with her, self-conscious now they're freed from wigs. Her position is ambiguous of course. She was married, but where's the husband? She ran off with a lover so she's a woman of the world. Are there babies somewhere? Are her opinions radical like the printer's with whom she eloped? Did she become bored with the man or was it homesickness that brought the handsome woman back all that way?

They don't ask, are all the more intrigued. But in any case her tasks are too many to allow much conversation. Without discussion, without even a spoken request she resumes the role she played before she fled. Every part of it: checking, ordering, supervising. The days caked with coffee grounds and alcohol, broiling meat and fish. Waiters, maids, Mrs Trunkett, Dick all look to her commands just as before.

Sam speaks only when he must. One day she's astonished to overhear him say with glee: 'My daughter has returned, you know!'

My daughter. My wife. Like her mother she has no existence of her own separate from Sam's, from Battle's. At night she hears her father's snores from his room below, his groans as he reaches down for the pot and hauls himself out of bed.

It is as though no time at all has passed. As though three years' sojourn in the New World has taken place entirely in her mind. Three years quickened by discovery, delight.

Those martins in whose nests the sparrows squat, do they remember their winter over the sea? They will return soon, come April, she realises with a momentary lightening of the heart. They will be here under the eaves, before the swifts come screaming in the dusk.

She remembers her twelve-year-old self; how no one spoke of her mother's death or Newton's. How strange that now she should repeat the pattern of her girlhood. Mourning at night with all the zeal of unextinguished love.

*

A handsome pump is erected in front of the Royal Exchange over a well, unearthed in Cornhill not long ago.

'Sam Battle, you must come with us to see the pump in its obelisk case,' says Bullock. 'Did you not contribute something towards it?'

Sam grunts. They don't know he didn't.

'It is your *duty* to see this fine monument so close to home. And think how useful it is were there to be a fire. Good God, this very house was rebuilt after a fire, was it not?'

'In '48.'

'Your father's day. Well, they'll put it out more quickly next time with this pump so close by.'

Sam cannot remember when he last left the coffee house. His wife's funeral? He has no need to go out. All arrangements with tradesmen were established years ago. There's Dick for errands. Mrs Trunkett at a pinch. Dick limps, but gets there.

For once Bullock and Thynne agree.

'You *must* come. The Exchange provides most of your custom, Sam. The monument and pump have been paid for by many of those who frequent Battle's. Besides it is an elegant thing.'

'*El*egant,' he growls.

'You need leave your house for twenty minutes only.'

'Damn, damn!' he mutters.

They edge him out, a group who've drunk at Battle's for years, who enjoy Sam's crabbedness. They remind the old snudge, as if he doesn't know it, of Sarah's capable hands. Shuffle him along Change Alley to the painted iron obelisk decorated with emblematic figures and an image of the house of correction that stood on the spot in 1282.

Sam gazes blankly, uneasy in the outer air. Smoke and fumes are his natural medium.

Thynne reads: '*This Well was discovered, much enlarged, and this Pump erected in the year 1799 by the contributions of the Bank of England, the East India Company, the neighbouring Fire Offices, together with the Bankers and Traders of the Ward of Cornhill*. There now! 1799. It's been standing since last century!'

'No, no. Lyons would have us believe we are still *in* that century.' They wag their fingers at each other and laugh.

Sam is agitated. What is happening in the house while he's not there? In his mind's eye the waiters lounge in the kitchen, pick bits out of pans, swig the residue from glasses. Mrs Trunkett sleeps in the corner. A maid drops the red-hot fruggin as she stirs the fuel in the oven. Dick is entertaining his cronies in the yard. Men call for their drinks to deaf ears; someone's dog shits all over the floor; a brawl erupts; someone else knocks out a plug of burning tobacco on a table. His heart begins to race, his skin goes cold.

The table smoulders, smokes, a flame darts to the settle, leaps to the ceiling beams; snow falls, the yard ices over; gales howl round the chimneys, the sound of mobs smashing all the windows fills his ear, there's heavy hammering on the door. *Sarah is running away again*!

He pitches forward, strikes his head on the iron, slumps.

Later they learn from the surgeon that the obelisk is not to blame. It caused a mighty contusion on Sam's forehead but it was his heart that failed. An opinion is expressed that had he known, he would have regretted not dying on his own premises. This is countered by the argument that there's far greater fame in death at the feet of a fine new monument than fizzling out, hugger-mugger at home.

*

Sarah has no time to mourn her father, even if she wanted to. Condoling takes place over coffee dishes, maudlin memories over punch bowls, funerary toasts to the clink of bumpers. She nods to all comments, assures older customers of continuation, gradually warms to a sense of freedom, not as great as when she ran away with Tom, but good all the same, definitely good.

A complex freedom, for she is now quite sure that she is expecting a child and may yet not miscarry. That she didn't bleed for months after Tom's death she'd put down to the shock of losing him and the timelessness that ensued. All days thereafter were the same, meaningless, without form, blurred by grief. The world was empty. Her body mourned him by drying up.

Now she begins to hope. Is relieved she will not need to explain to her father, but as yet tells no one. As her body changes shape, they'll just decide she's getting fat, she thinks.

There is more than ever to do in the coffee house. Sam kept the accounts, paid the waiters, Dick, Mrs Trunkett and the kitchen maid, looked out for holes in the waiters' striped stockings, stains on their waistcoats, admonished impertinence, ordered newspapers, tobacco, replenished drawers of pipes. Sarah absorbs these tasks, hires a girl to take her place behind the bar and feels the prick of reform. The newspapers can stay, she thinks, but she always wanted books in the coffee house, wanted the presence of intellectual matter beyond mere deals, politics and scurrility. She buys volumes for lending out, even hopes they might effect change to some of the more loathsome views she overhears. Tom certainly would have planted pamphlets and books. Oh Tom!

She consigns Rowlandson's *Wonderful Pig* engraving to one of the snugs, out of her sight; hands the beautifully bound *Amorous Scenes* to Dick to burn.

'Oh, but Miss Battle, there's *money* in 'em. You can't *burn* em! '

'I certainly can, Dick. Please do it.'

'The men paid good money.'

'What do you mean? Didn't my father buy them?'

''E did so. But them there as wanted paid to look.'

'I see. And did he get all his money back?'

'I don't know, Miss Battle.' Dick's firm allegiance to Sarah is not so strong that he can't lie in Sam's memory. *Amorous Scenes* had been a quickly profitable purchase. 'But them there'd buy 'em like a shot.'

'If I agree, they must be removed for good, Dick. Taken right away. Never again brought into Battle's.'

'I promise, Miss Battle.'

Later she's aware of a turmoil in one corner of the big room, low voices, raised voices, thumping on the table, the passing of coins, Dick placing a large wrapped parcel in front of men pink with pleasure. Dick pink with pleasure.

He offers her a handful of money.

'They says for me to thank you, Miss Battle.'

'Keep it, Dick, and put it somewhere safe. I hope you'll not retire from Battle's with it.'

There's plenty of money in Sam's locked boxes. She buys *The Task*, *Lyrical Ballads*, *Songs of Innocence and of Experience* and the most beautiful copy of *Paradise Lost* she can find.

2

James Wintrige drinks coffee one morning.

'I see you have a new wench at the bar,' he says. 'You have replaced yourself.'

'I cannot do it all. Now that Father is dead.'

'I heard.' He looks at her with half a grin.

'You did not reply to my letter. There are clothes and things of mine in Winkworth Buildings.'

'You deserted me, Sarah. By law you can take nothing with you: everything there is mine. Come back and live with me. Remember, we are husband and wife.'

'I don't care to be married to a spy.'

'And if I deny it?' His eyes lurk in their shadows.

'I read your letter to Richard Ford.'

'You stole it.'

'I found it. Of course it was not mine to read. But I did. You deceived me and all the men in the Society. I believed you when you spoke of reform, when you quoted Thelwall and Paine. It was all lies! Everything you did was for the government!'

'Do you think I would leave incriminating evidence lying about? The letter was false, left to confuse in case they came for me.' His frog mouth stretches as if into a smile.

'I cannot live with you. I want nothing to do with you.'

'You have committed adultery, Sarah. You are not the one to choose.'

But our love is greater than all the respectable marriages piled in a heap as high as the spire of Arch Street Church! Tom said in Philadelphia. Her eyes fill.

To cut short the conversation, to banish the sight of his fingers, anything to shift his greedy stare from her mouth, she agrees to let him bring her belongings, which he does one night as she's about to close the coffee house. She pays the carrier, waits by the door with the key, longing for him to leave.

He stands close. Words slip through thin lips.

'If you will not live with me in Winkworth Buildings, then I shall live with you here. I am your husband. As I said, *everything* of yours belongs to me by law. Battle's is mine.'

Here's a blow: she's had no time to anticipate it. Weary from the day's toil, she makes no reply; locks the door with relief when he stalks out.

The next day a cart arrives with his books and writing table, boxes of scribbled foolscap, a trunk, more possessions than she'd ever seen when she lived with him. She hastens him to her father's old room for she'll not have him in hers; then, too late, regrets it, for Sam's snores, the floor below, will now be replaced by *his*.

Parsimony. That's why he's here. Ostensibly, they'd always lacked money, always depended for sustenance on what she brought back from the coffee house. Yet he was paid well by the government, Tom said. What had he done with that money while she returned each night with pies and meat and drink?

Now, of course, with the Corresponding Society defunct he can no longer draw government pay spying on it. He has killed his golden goose, she tells herself. (Oh Newton, what a lovely satire it would make! Wintrige, wintry, thin, white, eyes sunk near to oblivion yet recognisably amphibian, studiously stabbing a great shining Corresponding Society goose to death with his pen and portable inkwell.) His work in the Customs Office only ever paid a very modest amount, whereas here at Battle's he'll have both board and bed. Even without her in it. She has a bolt fitted to her bedroom door.

For a while the place buzzes with gossip and disgust. Dick, Mrs Trunkett, the maids and waiters refuse to come at Wintrige's call; he enters the kitchen, looms over the stove or the huge preparing table, helps himself to whatever he can snaffle with long fingers, can gulp down frog-like. Sarah instructs them to serve him; for all her antipathy she doesn't relish strife, and she can hardly let him starve.

The customers are wary of a man with a reputation fuliginous as a smoke-house. They watch him when he's visible but mostly he lurks in one of the half-curtained booths, puffing screw after screw of tobacco, drumming on newspaper pages, not speaking. For days.

They try to winkle him out.

'Will you give us a toast, Wintrige?'

He mumbles, raises his glass.

'What's that you say?'

'The King!' They raise their glasses. Most of them. 'Now *you* give a toast,' he calls over to Thynne.

'I will give you Jack Ketch.'

A pause. Heavy breathing. Muffled titters.

'Fribbling,' mutters Wintrige. 'Stupid, fribbling toast.'

'Not at all,' Thynne replies. 'I only carry out *your* toast. You gave the first executive officer, the King, and I gave the last executive officer. Jack Ketch.'

Laughter from some. Wintrige shrinks back into his booth and they don't try again.

He must have stopped working for the Customs Office for he never goes out. Sarah avoids him, wonders if he's listening for new treasons. Yet he writes nothing, talks to no one except waiters when he orders increasing numbers of dishes. All the scribbling he once did has ceased.

Sudden sunlight alerts her one morning. A clean underskirt unfolded from a drawer displays a slight black smear. Thumb-sized. She holds it to her nose, sniffs burnt tobacco.

He's been in her room! Searching for the incriminating letter of course. Has gone through all her belongings, which now she checks minutely, finding all carefully replaced: books, pamphlets exactly where she'd set them, her few clothes apparently undisturbed. Yet everything *fingered* by him.

She runs to his bedroom, wakes him from dingy sleep. Shouts at his head half buried beneath pillows.

'*Wake up*! You've been in my room, gone through my things!'

'What is this? I'm asleep, Sarah.'

'Then *wake*!' She would hit him but couldn't bear the touch. 'You've been in my room, gone through everything. Looking for that letter no doubt.'

'No worse than going through all *my* things in order to steal it! And *you're* in *my* room, now! But I told you, the letter was a decoy. I don't care about it. You're imagining it. You know I spend the days downstairs. When would I have done it?'

'You left a mark on my clothes.'

His hand shoots out from the bedding, grips her wrist.

'How do you know it was my mark and not some *close friend* of yours? Some *beau*. If your clothes are dirty it's because of your dirty life.' He pulls her hard towards him.

'Let go of me! Let go!'

'No! You've come to my bed. I'm your husband.' He grasps her shoulders, draws her down over his bulk, struggling to keep her there while she beats at his chest and face with her left fist, her right arm trapped between her body and his.

'Drab! Whore! I *will* have you!'

Protecting his eyes with one hand, he raises his knees behind her to lever her onto her back. She pitches her own weight against his, propelled by revulsion and an odd sense of surprise that she never resisted him before. In the struggle, her hand becomes free and though he has hold of the other, she clutches at the bolster behind him, heaves it over his face and presses. To blot out his features, those lips, eyes, is all she would achieve. She doesn't think to kill him and in any case she hasn't the strength.

Gasping, he breaks out, thrusts her onto the floor. She runs from the room, bruised, breathless.

Now, she locks her door each day, as well as bolting it at night. Tries not to think of him. He continues as before, half hidden downstairs, silent from breakfast till supper. If by accident they catch each other's eye, shafts of resentment make her look away. She recalls a phrase from the first days of their marriage: *forgiving nature*. That was it. He'd said she reminded him of his mother and grandmother who brought him up. Their colouring. Their forgiving nature. She'd wondered what he meant. Now she knows: they forgave him *whatever he did*.

As evenings end, small explosions of hatred arise from his corner in the coffee house. Eyebrows are raised at the sounds, noses tapped, winks and looks exchanged, for they've certainly noticed the scratches on his face. Then, when the house is empty and all have retired for the night, he begins

207

his verbal attacks outside her bedroom. Complains about their married state, her obligations. On and on. Accuses her of theft, adultery.

'By rights you should be hanged, Sarah. At least transported. You'd be glad of my existence after fourteen years planting potatoes with other felons in the Antipodes.'

She refuses to reply; sits stiffly upright on the other side of the door, willing him away.

Gradually he replaces wheedling with shouts. Some nights he bawls, hammers the door and threatens violence to it. She has another bolt fitted; knows constables won't intervene without the presence of blood. He curses her, condemns her. Even weeps, laughs and weeps. It's unlike anything from their previous life: she remembers his mesmeric murmuring before their marriage, how rarely he spoke after it. Perhaps he really *did* want to be an actor. Or were these genuine tears? Eventually she gets into bed the moment she reaches her room, curls down tightly under the blankets, struggles for sleep.

Waits, taut, for the performance to cease; waits for the night's quiet, where love, remorse and hope dwell beneath dreams.

*

All of a sudden he stops. Comes out of his booth, stations himself imposingly at a table near the fire. Drinks coffee as soon as it's brewed, demands the day's dishes as soon as they're cooked. Keeps the waiters running.

Cook touches Sarah's sleeve. 'Miss Battle, Mr Wintrige do eat a lot. More'n any other. Do I tell John to say to 'im *no*? Will I put smaller on his plate, mebbe?'

'We cannot ask a waiter to say no, Mrs Trunkett. And he'd soon see if he was getting less than the others. I can do nothing about it.'

'Says here,' James suddenly announces from his prominent place, clearing his throat noisily as if about to address the Commons, 'two new spacious squares are now forming on the Duke of Bedford's Bloomsbury estate, Russell Square and Tavistock Square.'

Men turn to stare. Apparently the man is transformed.

'And,' assuring himself of their attention, 'at the north end and adjoining the new road, a very handsome dressed nursery-ground and plantations are already enclosed and laid out.' Will he ride to hounds in his plantations, do you think? Ha hah!'

An exaggerated yawn. No other comment.

'Northwards of these it seems there's to be a road of one hundred and sixty feet wide in a direct line formed through the joint estates of the Duke and of Lord Southampton, from these buildings to the junction of the two London roads to Hampstead, saving the circuitous and unpleasant routes, either of Tottenham Court Road or Gray's Inn Lane.'

'We *know*, Wintrige. We know all about it. And we've seen it for ourselves! The whole area is a mess of works.'

'How can I know what you've seen for yourselves?' he counters. 'I don't possess special powers.'

Nudges from some. Wasn't he employed by the *government*? Special powers of a sort *there*. Or perhaps he wasn't. Nobody knows. The man's an oddity.

'If you hadn't hidden away all this time you might have heard us talk about it. Incessantly.'

'Come now.' The voice of Lyons who knows what it's like to be put down. 'Mr Wintrige has decided to join us. Let us welcome him.'

An embarrassed shifting in seats. A muddy quiet. Wintrige scoops up the last pastry crust, soft in gravy, gobbles, pushes away his empty plate.

'I'll read about the riot instead. You'd rather listen to news of *de*struction than *con*struction!' He laughs, his mirthless eyes sliding from one man to the next.

'You'll set Thynne and Bullock at each other like cocks, if you do.'

'Then we'll ask Cook to pluck 'em and roast 'em,' he retorts, looking for others to laugh with him. A snort, a snigger.

Someone has always read from the newspapers in Battle's. Not that people can't read for themselves as once was the case, but it's useful to be able to hear the latest story while warming one's hands round a dish of coffee. And now that there are evening papers and weeklies it's pleasant to listen to many different events and scandals. As long as the reader's voice is tolerable and he doesn't lard the article with too many tedious witticisms. James Wintrige tends towards monotony and his humour limps.

But he's seated early, grabs the first morning paper and reads from it while men begin to wonder what exactly they might fancy eating in a couple of hours.

'Here is the text of the Lord Mayor's handbill concerning the rioting,' he says loudly. 'Addressed to us all.'

'We'd better hear it then, Wintrige.'

'Whereas the peace of this city has been, within these few days, very much disturbed by *numerous* and *tumultuous assemblies of riotous and disorderly people*,' he says heavily, 'the magistrates, determined to preserve the King's peace, and the persons and property of their fellow citizens, by every means which the law has intrusted to their hands, particularly request the *peaceable* and *well-disposed inhabitants of this city*,' looking up with meaningful emphasis, 'upon the appearance of the military, to keep themselves away from the windows, *Mrs Wintrige*.' He stops, waits; they all watch as Sarah, poised in the middle of the room while he reads, rushes out in a fury.

'Away from the windows, as I said; to keep all the individuals of their families and servants within doors; and, where such opportunities can be taken, to remain in the back rooms of their houses. Well now, gentlemen, we welcome the presence of the military, do we not?' They assent to that. 'And Combe wants us to back away from the glass. You fellows at the window, move your stations! Make yourselves comfortable by the fire. Perhaps some of you will not return home awhile. I am fortunate in being able to remain here.'

'This is not *new*, Wintrige,' Thynne bursts out, jutting his spicular chin. What a terrible bore the man is! It was better when he lurked behind the curtain, speechless. 'We had it all much worse twenty years ago with that madman Lord George Gordon. Then they were rioting about papists not bread.'

'And we were all perfectly safe here,' says Bullock. 'The mob were too busy dosing themselves with gin at Langdale's to bother running down Change Alley.'

'And turning the distillery into a heap of ashes, don't forget.'

'That's when Miss Battle's mother was killed, wasn't it?' someone asks.

'For those who dare not leave,' Wintrige declares, 'Battle's will provide breakfast without charge.' They see him gleaming with magnanimity and roll their eyes.

Sarah stands in her father's old office, now hers, her knuckles pressed on the table, staring at the shuttered window.

Addressing her publicly is bad enough, let alone calling her Wintrige, the name she hates. In particular she abhors the tone in which he reads aloud, scathing, triumphant, the tone of the government organ, his favourite newspaper. The voice of the man who deceived her utterly, who fooled those he convincingly claimed to support.

In the darkened room fury distils into despite. But despising helps her understand what he did before, if not why he's like he is now.

He aped radicalism as spy's cover. His revolutionary murmurings to her maintained consistency but also served to get himself a wife who would support him, while he kept his spy's pay secret. Marrying the daughter of an anti-Jacobin, in other words, the enemy, improved his standing with the Corresponding Society who thought it an admirable disguise. And somehow he saw he would succeed with her, sensed her rebellion against Sam's crass views purely from observation. That was perceptive of him.

What he *hadn't* calculated was the power of the ideas he now openly pronounced treasonous; ideas spouted with supposed conviction and borrowed rhetoric when he was a spy which nevertheless took root like trees. He misunderstood her entirely. Credited her with nothing except apple cheeks and the forgiving nature he'd imposed upon her. Her generous supply of food and drink.

Of course she remembers the *sound* of the mob with horror, the roar of fire, the sight of capering figures on Newgate's roof. But her mother and Newton were killed by soldiers, not rioters. She treasures still her conversion in St George's Fields, bathed in the emotion of a crowd bent on reform and justice.

And since then she'd learned from Tom. Learned everything from Tom.

The rioters are right. She hardly needs refer to the pamphlets and books that stand upright on the chest in her room like a small altar. Wheat prices rise each year: everyone speaks of it. Farmers and meal men profit, bakers charge great sums for bread. Not everyone speaks of *that*, though the people think of it, dancing and singing when flour mills burn down.

She sees for herself. The handbill pasted in haste:

Those Cruall Villions the Millers Bakers etc Flower Sellers rases Flowe under a Comebination to what price they please on purpose to make an Artificall Famine in a Land of plenty.

Bony beggar women slumped against doorposts, their children too famished to play with stones in the gutter.

*

James puts on weight. It crosses her mind that he might be mocking her, for surely her pregnancy has begun to show. But it's not that. His cheeks fill out in rapid distortion, ever more frog-like, though his eyes sink into pouches. His long fingers fatten. The men become used to him. Their hostility reduces to banter, though his 'wit' generally fails to make them laugh.

He finds another way to amuse.

'Wintrige, have you eaten the steak yet? Mrs Trunkett has excelled herself today, I can vouch for it, man.'

'So far I've only drunk the turtle, Bosanquet. Not a trace of mutton in it. Unlike some. Oh glorious broth! I'll take your word about the steak. John!'

213

The waiter brings fried steak and a plate heaped with potatoes. A second bottle of claret. When he's finished he swears it's so good he'll take the whole lot again.

'Lest I forget the savour of it.'

'That's it, Wintrige! And you'll want more claret, surely. Dick, get the man another bottle. No, no, on *me*. The man needs fattening up. Look at him! Anyone'd think he'd been starving on the heath all his life.'

They watch, grinning, a little queasy, but soon competitive in their offers. It becomes a daily occurrence in the timetable of drinking, eating, sparring, business and bonhomie, to encourage him gradually to raise the record. Wintrige's capacity increases with his expanding gut, with his pleasure at the attention he gains.

'Now, Wintrige, my turn to read to *you*,' says Bosanquet, addressing them all. It says here that a young woman in North Curry, that's Somerset, has eaten, listen to this: *six pounds of pork* and vegetables and so forth. Doesn't specify how much vegetable. Then *seven* four-penny eastercakes, all eaten with great ease, it says and washed down with three four-penny glasses of brandy. What do you say to that?'

Wintrige's mouth is full. Lyons answers for him. 'Reckon he's easily surpassed the drinking and the meat. You should eat more cake, Wintrige.'

Sarah can no longer ignore what takes place. Sam would have welcomed it, of course, for the cost of James's consumption is paid for by those encouraging him and the number of men who stay longer to watch, buying more drink for themselves. As word gets round he'll become an attraction.

She accosts him one night as he lurches to bed.

'James, you must stop this excessive eating and drinking.'

'Why?' the word slurs.

'You'll eat me out of house and home.'

'Rubbish! You're rich as a duchess. Which means I'm rich as a duke. Rich as a duchess you are *and* as fair!' He lunges. Stumbles against a wall.

'For God's sake, James!'

'In whom you don't believe.'

'Do *you*?'

'Tom Cranch was an atheist.'

'Don't!' She covers her ears. 'Don't *ever* mention his name. You're not worth a single hair on his head. You will stop your guzzling, your drinking. Control yourself!'

'I shall take my pleasures as I can. Be glad I'm not *whoring*! Unlike *some,* snuggling and fumbling in other men's beds. *You* could hardly deny me visits to the *bagnio*. An adulterous wife who denies me! What else do I have but the delights of the palate?' He begins to sob.

'You are become a *spectacle*. They egg you on. Soon hoards will press to come and watch. The place will be overrun. You're no better than the Wonderful Pig Father wished he'd had in the place.'

'Let them come! They love me!'

She moves away to lock the coffee house door and he shambles after her, arms vaguely flailing.

'I'll stop. I swear. Come fuck me and I swear I'll stop.'

*

A man asks to see Sarah.

'William Pyke, apothecary. Friend of Tom Cranch.'

She takes him into the office, opens the shutters, shows him a seat but he will not take it.

215

'The package you sent us was passed on to me. The evidence against James Wintrige.'

'I'm glad it's in the right hands. I knew the messenger would find a way. What can you do, Mr Pyke?'

'It is too late to do much,' he says. 'You will know the Society has been dismembered, Mrs Wintrige.'

'Yes. Please don't use that name. Although there has been no divorce I don't regard myself as married to him.'

'I understand.' He is melancholy; long downward lines incise his face. 'If we had known earlier...'

'I found the letter just before I went away with Tom. We opened it on board ship, when of course we could do nothing. At first in Philadelphia we knew no one to whom we could entrust it. And when we did, nobody was returning to England. People only fled *from* England.

'Tom wanted to write to you but worried his letter of warning would be seen by the wrong people; besides, without the evidence it might itself have been thought false. The times were bad, the Society already in danger. We decided it was probably already too late. Was that not so?'

'Yes, indeed it was. And when I received your package here a while ago, we were all in hiding because of Hadfield. Did Tom speak of us, Miss Battle?'

'He did.'

'Of Hadfield? Harley? '

'Yes. And you, Mr Pyke.'

'Harley has fled. Hadfield is in prison following his attempt on the King. He fired at him in the royal box in Drury Lane.'

'I did hear of it.'

'They've put him in an asylum from which only death will rescue him.'

'Poor man.'

'This is a delicate question, Miss Battle. You need not answer it. Did you not ever suspect James Wintrige when you were first married to him?'

'No, Mr Pyke. No, I didn't. You will find that hard to believe, but I was young, stupid. Knew nothing. Knew not what a marriage was. He spoke so little and I believed whatever he said. No, I never suspected. For a while I thought *Tom* was the spy! Oh, if only I *had* suspected it.'

'It is better for you that you didn't, perhaps. It's a hard thing for a wife to tell on her husband.'

'But if I had, what would you have done then?'

'Alerted everyone in the Society. Expelled him from it. Nothing else. We could hardly have brought a government spy to justice.'

She sits.

'You must not blame yourself, Miss Battle. It is *we* who were at fault. We in the Society, the Society that was. We should have known, should have noticed. We were complacent, asleep! He seemed too foolish to be a spy.'

She shakes her head.

'He *played* at being a fool. With me he played the serious thinker. I think he wanted to be an actor, you know. He liked the theatre, certainly. And *still* he plays!'

'The letter you found showed Wintrige for what he was. For that we are most grateful. What we don't know is how much damage his spying did. No doubt he contributed to the destruction of the Corresponding Society. We'll never discover how many his reports consigned to prison.'

She covers her face with her hands.

'Miss Battle, please. It was not my purpose to upset you. Quite the opposite. I came to *thank* you for sending us the evidence. And also the few of us who remain ask to be allowed to provide any help you might need. You are to call on us, please.'

She looks up. 'Thank you. That is very kind.' Sees his glance shift inwards.

'But I have also come for myself. May I sit?'

'Of course.'

'I am near despair, Miss Battle. We have been crushed; there is no future. A few rash men and boys risk their lives in futile revolution. They will achieve nothing; will be caught and hanged.

'I miss Tom Cranch. We all do. His purpose never wavered. In his absence we have disintegrated too easily. He had enthusiasm, wit. Of course, he was an idealist, for which some criticised him, and he was impetuous, certainly, but he had courage. I doubt I have such strength, but it would help me to hear about it. To hear about him.'

Her mind floods with sadness. Can he know how much she longs to talk of her beloved Tom? Suspects he does.

She smiles at the forlorn apothecary. Tells him all about America.

3

Sarah's child is born in high summer when Change Alley is at its most fetid. She's attended by a man-midwife recommended by Pyke. He encourages her through a long labour with plentiful brandy and a novice's anxiety: it's only his second birth.

The baby is a girl whom she names Eve; who is fussed over by Mrs Trunkett, Dick, the waiters, the kitchen maids, so that now and then Sarah must send them away in order to gaze on the child herself. The child who is proof that she hasn't dreamed her brief life with Tom; that he was real, not a fantasy of perfection. Was he perfect? Of course not, though in that short time he seemed so, their unsanctified marriage blessed by love, by passion.

Pyke called Tom impetuous. Robert thought him an innocent, worse, culpable. True, he put himself in danger, and after he died she sometimes thought to blame him. That had not lasted. She loved him for the very idealism and energy that made it imperative he include the docks among all the work places in Philadelphia where he distributed his rousing pamphlets, so full of hope. The docks where yellow fever arrived on ships from the South.

How much more good might he have done? How much

more happiness would they have had? She despises her craven self-pity, at least will not expose the child to the sight of it. But misery in the heart of the night is an old way, well walked since childhood, not one she can banish.

In moments of quiet she contends with her oscillating feelings.

That Tom will never know his child is a great sorrow. That Eve will never know her father is another, but Sarah intends to tell his daughter everything about him until he almost lives again. Sometimes grief is countered by the child's resemblance to Tom, his colouring, bright eyes, seemingly easy contentment. Suckling the baby, she laughs with remembered pleasure, weeps at her loss.

Dick and Mrs Trunkett run Battle's quite well for the month's lying-in. They keep Wintrige away from her; she supposes he's sulking. She employs a nurse, a motherly woman obscurely related to the man-midwife, and in due time is back downstairs supervising the running of the coffee house. Eve lives in the nursery, constantly visited by her mother who is determined her own childhood will not be repeated. Her daughter will not be raised among idle men, careless and ridiculous in their pravity; she will not be ignored by her mother, her earliest playmate a puppy on the filthy floor. Sarah sings and plays with her baby, whose laughter is catching. Reads rhymes by Blake, that poet Tom knew:

Merry, merry sparrow!
Under leaves so green;
A happy blossom
Sees you, swift as arrow,
Seek your cradle narrow
Near my bosom.

Pretty, pretty robin!
Under leaves so green;
A happy blossom
Hears you sobbing, sobbing,
Pretty, pretty robin,
Near my bosom.

In a few years Sarah will find good education for her. Only through education can women become independent said Constantia in the *Massachusetts Magazine*. Only through education might they hope to do something more worthwhile than work in a coffee house. She thinks of the night she addressed the Democratic Republicans in the Indian Queen, blushes at the memory. How little she knew. Yet Tom had faith in her. The notes for the pamphlet they were to have written lie locked in a drawer.

It's as well the child is not a boy for she would have searched perpetually for Tom's replica. Her love for Eve, her joy holding the dark, sweet baby, echoes with lament.

All about, London seethes. Hunger, resentment, loathing. Charcoal crawls over pavements, handbills and chalk scrawls cover walls:

K— G— and the farmer are busy crambing the empty stomachs of the poor with Bayonets

Crowds collect, swarm, face the Yeomanry united, no longer split between Jacobins and Monarchists. Women organise great protests outside Coldbath Fields prison, their husbands locked in damp cells without heat or light, legs ulcerated by frost.

Wintrige catches her arm one night. He's been waiting for her in the shadows.

'It is time you saw sense,' he blurts.

He is fleshy and shambling, his legs uncoordinated through accumulation of weight. They have kept out of each other's way for weeks, but Sarah is aware of his behaviour, has had reports from Dick and Mrs Trunkett.

'Miss Battle, you be best buy 'im off,' Dick advises.

'What do you mean?'

'Tell 'im there's more food and better at Slaughter's and you do pay 'im to go there.'

'Dick, would that it were so easy! I'm *married* to him. There's nothing I can do.'

'Oh.' He wrings his arthritic hands.

In the dark corridor, Sarah tries to pull herself from Wintrige's grasp.

'It is time *you* saw sense, ' she cannot help retort. 'Let me be!' But his clutch is tight. 'I shall call out for help. They've not all gone yet.'

He lets go. 'Sit and talk with me, Sarah.'

'There is nothing to talk about. But I'll repeat my wish that you cease making a spectacle of yourself.'

'You *benefit* from it since they buy more coffee and liquor. And so I earn my keep. But why do I speak like this? It is all mine anyway!'

She is almost out of hearing when he calls after her. 'Your child! Your child should have a father. Come, Sarah. Let us live together and bring up the child. I shall be a good husband and father. I promise.'

'Your promise is worthless.'

He shouts at her: 'They think it's my child. If you want to be respected it *must* be mine.'

'They know perfectly well she's not yours. And they forgive me. You will have nothing to do with my child. Never ask me again.' She hurries to the nursery where she has a bed alongside Eve's cot. Locks herself in, takes the baby in her arms, wipes tears where they fall onto the tiny forehead and rocks them both to sleep.

She is woken briefly by studied moans from Wintrige's room, followed by snores.

*

Men pour in to watch Wintrige. Dick and the waiters abandon their earlier attempts to ignore him, since much of the food and drink he consumes is bought for him by others.

To the relief of many, Wintrige drops his newspaper readings. His role is that of clown, entertainer: to astonish, to hold the crowd. His timing is precise, they watch in suspense. Will he actually eat *all that*? Will he down yet another bottle of port without puking? He spins out consumption like a storyteller, expressing uncertainty, near disaster, satisfaction, obscene delectation, through the movement of his eyes and brows, through a range of subtle hums and sighs. Between dishes he crows, boasts.

'Oh what a tedious life I led in the customs house!' An imaginary actor's existence appears. 'Oh, what ennui in the theatre! What boredom compared to the anticipation of another of Mrs Trunkett's pies, her lardy paste and steaming kidneys! Who needs a woman when you can thrust your fingers into puddings and suck on jellies!'

A roar of delight from his audience.

'How the juices ooze! Lick, lick, lick!' He squeals with pleasure. 'And another bowl of Mrs Wintrige's punch, John!'

His limbs and digits thicken, his face and body swell, his clothes gape open. Each evening the effort begins to tell, he groans as he chews, soaks a towel with sweat that sheets his lurid red face.

Bets are laid, increasingly large sums won. Winners usually hand a proportion to Wintrige himself, placing it next to the by now senseless man slumped, snoring, among licked-out bowls and plates, drained bumpers.

When Sarah insists the twice-daily event take place out of the way, upstairs, she is politely, firmly denied. And then Wintrige breaks a record, eats a whole menagerie of meat and fish. Clown becomes hero. Unknown to her, bills are posted by cronies of Dick who, for all his affection for Sarah, has never lost his loyalty to her father.

Heroic Consumption!
Watch the great Eater and Drinker J. Wintrige
Beat all known Records!
Battle's Coffee House, Change Alley. Twice daily.

How Sam would have loved this show: its money-making monstrousness.

''E'll be laughin in 'is grave,' Dick says, to Mrs Trunkett's disgust, 'rubbin' 'is bones togever wiv glee.'

Nor are Mrs Trunkett and Sarah the only people to loathe the spectacle. Handbills are torn down or defaced:

Shall the Poor starve while the Spy stuffs himself?

His shameful secret, so carefully kept, is scrawled on walls. How do they know? But who cares now that he was once a spy? The Corresponding Society is defunct. The fist is closing on conspiracies.

Sarah is helpless. More and more she retreats to the nursery where, the sound muffled, she feeds Eve or plays with her. She is too distracted to read; instead she handles the books brought back with her from Philadelphia, lovingly opening them, holding the pages to her nose, scenting the lees of that life. How different it was! Each day, each night revealed its own new colour, its richness. Everything she did emerged from love, from confluence.

There was no falsity, no coercion, unlike in childhood when she had been compelled to take over her mother's role, her life dominated by Sam. Then Wintrige manoeuvred her into a marriage that failed to save her from her father and imposed its own bleak tyranny. Now, he's dropped the bleakness, seems, absurdly, to have linked arms with the ghost of her father and imposed a dictatorship of repulsive misrule.

Yet she had tried ways of escape before: the world of conspiratorial laughter in which she lived with Ben Newton; her deluded belief that she'd escape Battle's through Wintrige; flight with Tom as soon as he offered it. 'Come with me,' he'd said, embraced her and they'd gone.

But how can she extract herself from this present vileness? She can think of no way to do it. She longs for quiet, for love, for Tom. For Martha's companionship. Relives those joyful, short-lived days; murmurs the tenderness to her gurgling baby.

*

In retreat one day she stops before a picture. She's passed it often without noticing, for surely it's just a pretty country maid? The expression catches her. It's an engraving of a young woman, flowers in her hair and hands, singing perhaps, her face and dress slightly disordered. It *isn't* just a pretty country maid. A delicate desperation looks out of the frame.

She wonders about this young woman. Who has engraved it, who painted her in the first place? It's not a picture Sarah knew as a child. Her father must have bought it when she was in America, but from whom? She looks through the account books, finds purchases made soon after she'd left, from an engraver, J. Young, Little Russell Street:

2 Morocco-bound portfolios	*60 gns*
Engraving, coloured, framed	*8 gns*

Of course, the portfolios were those *Amorous Scenes* she failed to get Dick to burn. She supposes Sam bought the young woman with the flowers to appear respectable.

She writes a note to J. Young who replies that yes, indeed, he both engraved and painted the original of the *Ophelia* he sold to her father, Mr Samuel Battle, and that he has many more engravings in his series of Shakespeare's women if she'd care to visit Little Russell Street.

She's welcomed into the shop by the same young woman in the engraving. Without the flowers, pretty; not disordered, though not calm.

'Yes,' says Lucy Dale. 'I was the model for all Joseph's paintings of the women in Shakespeare's plays. Well, except for Emilia, of course, but that's a small part. I know the plays so well now, you can imagine! He read them with me or told me everything there is to know about them. The paintings were so popular he made engravings and I coloured them in for him. People are always asking for the engravings. Some even buy the whole series! The paintings are mostly all sold, I'm afraid. He has the sketches for them, though. Perhaps he could paint one or two again from those sketches, if you were interested.'

She pours out her words as though she's not spoken for days.

'I am interested,' Sarah says, drawn to the puzzle of the girl.

'Shall I fetch Joseph? He is at home today. He will tell you about the series and what he might be prepared to do. Whether he could reproduce any of the paintings. I wouldn't need to sit again because of the sketches. Besides, I cannot look at all the same. I am much older and I have a child now.'

'Oh, I can assure you you are quite recognisable. But please do fetch your husband.'

When, momentarily, Joseph and Lucy stand together, Sarah knows she's seen them before. But Lucy leaves the room and Joseph, in lively mood, soon dazzles Sarah with information about the subjects. Though she read slowly through *Macbeth* in the early days of her marriage to Wintrige and had learned more from Tom, she has never been to the theatre. Joseph suggests a price and she agrees to buy paintings of Cordelia and Desdemona, whose stories, as told by Joseph, move her much.

'I feel certain I've seen you before, Mr Young. You and Mrs Young.'

'It is not likely, Miss Battle. We rarely go anywhere together.'

Sarah is driven home in a hackney, pleasingly distracted from the horrible events in the coffee house. She suddenly remembers when she saw Mr and Mrs Young: on her return from Philadelphia, when she disembarked at Wapping. The girl with the bag frantically searching every passing face. The tall man, his fair hair tied back, remonstrating with her, pulling her away. Not consoling her.

4

On the anniversary of Tom's death Sarah remains downstairs supervising the waiters, interfering in the kitchen, even standing behind the bar for an hour or two taking orders. To lock herself all day in Eve's nursery, crouch on the floor and sob her sorrow into the floorboards would be inadmissible luxury.

However, later she allows herself to write to Martha.

Battle's Coffee House, Exchange Alley.
26th October 1800

My dear Martha,

I am sure your sister Mary will be happy to read this letter to you.

It is a year since my beloved Tom died. I remember the day so clearly, every moment of it. I shall never forget your kindness: I do not know how I would have lived afterwards without you, Martha.

I have a dear child, Eve, now more than three months old. I wish that you could see her.

Oh Martha, if only you lived here: how we could talk and laugh together! Would you and Willie come if I sent money for

228

your passage? Please think seriously about this; I'd do it so
gladly.

I hope that you and Willie are both in good health.
In fond remembrance and hope,
Your friend,
Sarah Cranch

She seals this letter and encloses in a cover addressed to R.
Wilson, Bookseller and Publisher, Zane Street, Philadelphia,
writing separately to Robert:

Dear Robert,

Before Tom died I promised him I'd do what rapid illness
prevented him from accomplishing. After his death I was too
upset to carry it out. Now, a year later, I ask you to consider
what he would have said to you had he lived.

Martha is your lover and the mother of your child. Treat her
as you should, not as a servant. Best of all, marry her once
you've divorced your wife under the Pennsylvania divorce law
of 1785.

In attempting to persuade you, Tom would have admitted
that he and I were not married, there being no divorce law
available to me in England and my having not yet become an
American citizen. You will know that nevertheless in truth,
indeed in God's eyes, we were man and wife. Certainly we
would have been legally married had we been able.

I trust that you are in good health and will give consideration
to this letter as you would have done to Tom's own words.

Sarah Battle (Cranch)

*

When the year ends customers demand a sight of Sarah's child to accompany their Christmas dishes.

'If we are to obey the King's proclamation and reduce our consumption of bread and abstain from pastry, let alone use economy when feeding our horses, how can we enjoy ourselves and celebrate the birth of Our Lord, Miss Battle?' Thynne asks, his smile a hair crack in a wine glass.

'We can drink! No proclamation against that,' says Bullock, stouter and breathless as he ages, 'and let us admire that babe of yours, Miss Battle, whom we trust will charm us as much as you do!' Thynne and Bullock agree: a wonder!

A semicircle the size of Wintrige's girth has been cut in a table so that he can sit closer to his plate. Sarah finds a time when Wintrige's head has dropped upon the ledge of his stomach in urgent sleep, whirls around the coffee house with Eve in her arms, fast enough to escape comments about resemblance to her mother Anne or even Sam. In her mind Eve can only resemble Tom or her own younger self. When a note arrives from Joseph Young, she is glad to hand Eve to the kindly, doting nurse and deal with his request.

He'd like to visit Battle's, he says, to see where the paintings might hang and how they should be framed. She is surprised by this attention to detail, suspects he hopes to persuade her to commission more. And why not? Much of what hangs on the walls should certainly be replaced. The large, embrowned mirror in which men once adjusted their wigs, but now, wigless, preen themselves with remarkable vanity; the notice of rules and orders governing conduct: fines for swearing and excessive arguing, never imposed within her memory; cheap prints of faded landscapes; framed cuts from Laroon's *Habits and Cryes of the City of London*, grime-grey.

Joseph arrives at a bad time. Someone has laid a bet of five hundred guineas against Wintrige eating the day's supply of turtle soup, a fowl smothered in oysters, an entire leg of mutton with caper sauce, boiled onion and mashed turnip, a salad, a huge bowl of syllabub, dessert of nuts and candied fruits and a three-pound cider cake, washed down with claret and two bottles of brandy. Wintrige has begun on the soup, each spoonful noted by a gleeful circle around his table.

'And what if I just fancied turtle soup *myself*, today? Did you think of that, Chaloner, when you laid down your money?' says a man in mock annoyance. 'Nothing left of it!'

Wintrige is tackling the leg.

'Oh! Oh! The fat! Let me die of it!' His frog chin is spotted with capers.

Do frogs have chins?

Joseph's attention is caught.

'You know I make satires, Miss Battle?'

'I saw some in your shop window, yes.'

'This scene is perfect. It would sell well and act as advertisement for your coffee house.'

'No! Please don't think of it, Mr Young. This spectacle is entirely against my wishes. I have tried to prevent it, but have failed. We have plenty of custom.'

They watch as Wintrige, his face purple, abandons his knife, takes the mutton in his hands.

'How this man holds his audience! Who is he, Miss Battle?'

'James Wintrige.'

'He'd have everyone watch each mouthful. Such determination! He seeks fame, adoration, would like nothing better than to appear in a print.'

Sarah is aware of an intelligence in Joseph Young in strength not unlike Tom's, though in nature different, arrogant and wayward. He lacks Tom's intense, mercurial energy; projects instead a tall man's easy confidence.

'I've observed so many in their cups or eating, smoking,' he continues. 'Enjoying themselves. I've drawn so many. This man is not like them. Something drives him on. What is his occupation?'

'This is his occupation.'

'But what used he to do?'

'He, he once worked in the Customs Office. Actually, he spied for the government.'

'Good lord! First he shuns attention, living in the shadows and now he seeks it!'

'We must decide on the best wall for your paintings, Mr Young,' she says, to turn the subject. Nor can she bear to confess who Wintrige really is. 'Perhaps, if people like them as much as I'm sure I shall, I might decide to buy others.'

'It's hard to think that those keen to watch a man stuff himself like this would care a jot for paintings of Shakespeare's women.'

*

Sandwiches are taken off the bill of fare at Battle's when the Brown Bread Act comes in, for who'd eat a sandwich made from coarse crumb in place of a pleasing wheaten loaf? The kitchen maids are put to more onion-slicing and fish-descaling.

After winning the five hundred guineas himself, Wintrige takes to his bed for three days, carried there by his supporters, since his legs, vast though they are, won't hold him. While Sarah is pleased he's out of sight, for the first time in her life she feels a strand of pity for him, though it's tangled with despising. She never loved him, had once admired him, or rather, had fallen under his strange frog-like spell, had quickly learned dislike, disgust. Watching him with Joseph Young, she sees the desperation she's chosen to ignore, the craving for applause.

But how can she be kind to him when she denied the dying Tom as he looked at her with such longing? When she couldn't, wouldn't smile at the man who'd smiled at her always. Tom, whom she loved with her soul. Loves with her soul. She'd put her pain before his need in a moment of selfishness. She will never forgive herself.

Battle's customers, those not siphoning financial information, making deals, reading as many newspapers as they can, are at a loss without the entertaining guzzler.

'Do we know exactly what ails him? Has he been bled?'

'Don't be a fool, Rothesay. Excess, the simple ailment, excess!'

'Can we be sure it isn't something worse? What if it's locked jaw? The poor fellow may never be able to eat again!'

Lyons pipes up. 'They cure locked jaw with electricity now.'

'This is another of your philosophic fantasies, Lyons.' Bullock pinches his lumpy nose, still trying to press it into a more seemly shape.

'By no means. I have it on good authority. A small receiver is filled with electrical fluid, discharged through the jaws of the affected person and the jaws fly open instantaneously.'

'And is the affected person capable of *closing* his jaws after that or is he forever agape?'

*

Joseph comes again to Battle's and then often. Sarah wonders if he is secretly making sketches of Wintrige and will produce a finished series despite what she said. However, he asks for her and she drinks coffee with him while he describes the painting he's working on for the newly bared walls of the coffee house, the dramatic moment he's trying to portray.

He's amazed to learn from someone that she's married to the monstrous Wintrige. Wonders how it can possibly have come about, surely not from choice, respects her too much to ask. Briefly he's sorry for her, soon prefers impressing her, finds her responsive to his knowledge, tries to overcome the shades of scepticism he detects. She particularly likes to talk about sketching and caricatures, seems to have known an artist once, who she thinks was very skilled. Says she'll show him some of his work one day.

Of course she believes he's married to Lucy, which for the moment he won't correct. Not only is it not true, but Lucy is not living in Little Russell Street.

He'd returned from Wood's to find her and the baby gone. There was a note:

I am going to William Digham.
It is better that we do not live together. Lucy

When he awoke thirty-six hours later, dry, hungry, grimy, he was relieved not to see her paleness, her expression of hurt and incomprehension. Her lingering love that so irritated him. Relieved not to hear the baby's bawling. What she wrote was true. He had need of her no longer.

Digham is endlessly kind to Lucy, relieving Joseph of the necessity to placate, to explain. He has no idea what the old man says about him, but although when he does go to Paternoster Row, she still sometimes looks in that worshipping way, she's more interested in news he might have about Matthew. Which he rarely has.

Two rooms at the back of Digham's on the second floor serve as bedroom and nursery for Lucy and the sadly named baby, Matthew. At first the old engraver refuses rent from her, but then agrees that she continue to limn his prints and that she sell them for him downstairs in the shop to pay for her keep. Moreover, she's graduated to topography, at last, colouring scenes of ruined abbeys, sublime Welsh mountains.

Digham is too generous to remind Joseph of his original warning against living with Lucy. Joseph has always valued the old man's opinion when it's one he wants to hear. But in any case, he has forgotten. His increasing success cheers him, feeds his confidence. Yet there's a dullness. It's like coming across a sheaf of drawings, brown and cockled by damp. There's nothing he can do about it. His relief at Lucy's move doesn't remove his acid sense of worthlessness. Wood's palls. Fanny fancies another man. Fanny Lobb. Fanny Loblolly. What did he expect?

For the moment it's Battle's that contents him. He's found a patron, a place to display his work and an intriguing woman, like neither Lucy nor Fan.

*

Summer, and the melancholy William Pyke pays Sarah one of his occasional calls. Apart from the recommended man-midwife, she has not accepted any more of his offers of help.

'Not now, Mr Pyke. But in a few years, when Eve is old enough to learn I shall ask you to help me find a school for her. Or, if none exists, for most girls' schools teach little more than French and dancing, then good scholars. I can teach her everything I know, but after that I would have her taught as men are. Tom would have wished it.'

'Ah yes. I shall be happy to help. Meanwhile, Mrs Cranch,' he smooths down his sparse white hair, 'I'll tell you about Thomas Spence, the bookseller, you know. I've been attending his trial. A man after Tom's own heart.'

'I've heard the name but know nothing of him.'

'He's being tried for seditious libel in his book, *Spence's Restorer of Society*. I tell you especially, because in it he recommends the abolition of all private land, an idea which I know was dear to Tom. A courageous man, who speaks well, is thought somewhat mad, but not so mad he can't be sent to Newgate, as no doubt Tom would have been had he remained in this country. Perhaps you should take consolation in that, my dear.'

'You are kind to think of me, Mr Pyke.'

'I also must warn you of the particular stir being caused by Mr Wintrige *outside* the coffee house. I fear you may be unaware of it. Look. You may not have seen this.' He shows her a defaced handbill that he has removed carefully from a wall.

Unbeaten!

The Hero shall win another Wager!

5 bottles of Port

5 dressed Capons

5 broiled Eels, buttered

2 Legs of Mutton

5 Plum Puddens

5 mincemeat Pies

1 Whole Cheshire Cheese

To be Consumed by Jas. Wintrige all at One Sitting!

Enquire at Battle's, Change Alley

It was defaced in two places:

Let poor Men eat Dust!

And in a different hand:

Kill and cook Wintrige!

'They have been posted liberally in streets all about here. And many have been written upon, understandably, by hungry men. But remember, summer is when crowds gather.'

Sarah is shocked by this danger. Furious with Dick whom she suspects as author of the handbill. She knows too well about mobs. And a few weeks ago, angry crowds entirely demolished the disused Queen of Bohemia, once a Corresponding Society tavern, on the rumour of a murder. Inside, surgeons using the abandoned building for anatomical study, escaped with their own lives, leaving behind cadavers and instruments of dissection. What better excuse for the hungry to attack Battle's than a man within, gorging himself on monstrous meals?

William Pyke offers to remonstrate with Wintrige but it is hopeless.

'His mind is fixed, there's no moving him,' he says. 'All you can do is stop the handbills, keep him out of view of the windows and hope he becomes too ill to continue. It seems hardly right for me, an apothecary, to speak so!'

A freak storm strikes the metropolis. Thunder, lightning, a hurricane; torrents of rain flood the streets. The Strand becomes a foul canal, coaches and shop-fronts splattered with mud and dung. In the court of common pleas, Westminster, rain smashes a skylight and pours down on the assembled wigs. Men rush into Battle's through sheets of water and stand about, steaming.

Sarah, made nervous by the threat of mob attack, is in the nursery with Eve. The child, almost a year old, hides her face in her mother's hair to shut out shocks of light, the crack and boom so close, like houses breaking up.

A kitchen maid knocks, puts her head round the door.

'Miss Battle, please to come downstairs. Dick do ask it.'

'No, Bessy. Eve needs me, as you can see. Whatever's the matter? Is the building flooded? Are people trying to break in? Surely they won't do it in this weather?'

'Nobody have broke in, Miss Battle.'

'Then please go away. I shall come down when the storm is over.'

Later, when Eve is soothed, Sarah leaves her child sleeping with a perfect quiet that makes her weep to see, descends to an unusual hush in the main room. The storm is over, the steaming men have left.

'Miss Battle,' says Dick, somehow older and more arthritic since she flew at him about the handbills. 'Mr Wintrige it is.' She looks over and sees he's not there. Retreated to bed again, she hopes.

'Mr Wintrige be in your office, Miss Battle. Please to come wiv me.'

In the office the shutters are drawn and Wintrige is lying on his back on her desk, papers and account books piled to one side.

'Is he dead, Dick?'

A surgeon she has met before speaks up. 'Your husband has had a fit, Mrs Wintrige.'

Dick clears his throat loudly and prods the surgeon, who begins again.

'Mr Wintrige has had a fit, *Miss Battle*.' He holds a candle over the great bulk, indicates the slight rise and fall of the chest. 'He still breathes. His heart beats, if slow and distant. He is not dead, but it is my belief he will not wake.'

In dim light, close to the man from whom she's kept away so long, Sarah sees the mass of broken veins hatched across his fleshy face, as though a cat has used it for a scratching post. Colossal legs have burst their stockings. She's shocked by yellowed skin.

Six men carry Wintrige to his room where he lies like a giant puffball turned to stone. Someone prevents Dick from pouring liquid down his throat. With regular bleeding Wintrige lingers on for fourteen days, until one morning Dick says: 'he 'ave slid away, Miss Battle.'

A post-mortem reveals no disease other than a wrecked liver. It is said that just before the fit he almost succeeded in drinking six quarts of punch. That he ate and drank to excess for months is taken into account. The man was no lunatic. Nor was it a case of cynorexy, pure greed, insatiable appetite like a dog. Wintrige had enough education to know the likely consequences of his excessive consumption. His actions were deliberate. According to the witness Lyons, he had recently said: 'If it were now to die, 'twere now to be most happy', after finishing Mrs Trunkett's pound cake with raisins and brandy. The verdict, *felo de se*, however, causes much dispute and discussion in Battle's. Dick, though not within Sarah's hearing, agrees with it and claims Wintrige ate and drank himself to death for the unrequited love of Miss Battle.

It is some time before the image of Wintrige's bloated, immobile body and distorted expression fade from Sarah's mind, some time before she can separate revulsion from relief.

5

Sarah's release from the burden of Wintrige has an effect that surprises her: she dreams of Newton. Her earliest days with him. It's as though Wintrige's death delivers her from sorrow and care and permits return to the simple love of her childhood.

She looks out the sketchbook she'd kept for him the day he was killed, turns page after page of caricatured oddities, features exaggerated into hilarity, actions tipped over into farce.

Here are figures slumping over their drinks, enfolded in newspapers, gripping each others' collars in furious dispute, farting complacently, grinning into the steam of their coffee. Dick balancing a pyramid of dishes. Sam gathering fury. Itchy wigs, bursting waistcoats, watery eyes, bulging calves stretched out for admiration.

She feels again Newton's closeness when she presses her head into his sleeve. Smells dusty thread. Hums his tunes.

And here, on the final pages of the sketchbook, are the rioters with their bludgeons, their sacks of cobblestones. The tiny image of herself behind a lamppost, observing. Then a drawing she'd quite forgotten: infantrymen kneeling to fire, pointing their rifles straight at the artist. How prescient! Did he think of that sketch as he took her mother's hand and ran with her across Poultry?

She sees how skilled he was. As a child his drawing seemed like magic; now she knows that it *was* a kind of magic, innate, unforced, a talent. Like Tom's ability to talk to anyone in the street, to expound and inspire.

Yet Newton had had little success. She somehow knew it, even as a girl, for he never bought new clothes, lived off free coffee. Sat in Battle's all day as though he had nowhere else to go. What would have happened to him had he not been killed? Would his luck have improved? She doesn't think so, doesn't think he would have succeeded like Joseph has.

She will show Joseph the sketches, for it's wonderful that she knows another artist. She may ask to see some of his own satires, which, from the few she's glimpsed, are more ferocious and grotesque than Newton's. She's adjusting to Joseph's arrogant manner, so different from Newton's, but he's an interesting man and she likes him.

*

Philadelphia, 17 February 1801

Dear Sarah Mrs Cranch,

Mary write my words. I so pleased when your letter come I cry for joy. I miss you in the house. You and Mr Cranch. I so happy about your baby. I wish I see her. Mr Wilson he not let me and Willie go to England. Willie grow tall and big. Blue eyes turning brown.

Maybe we come one day Sarah Mrs Cranch. Mary say pray God Almighty. I say it too. Mr Wilson say he glad Mr Jefferson president. That man he still visit Mr Wilson.

Your friend,
Martha

The very sound of Martha's voice comes back to Sarah when she reads the letter and imagines her dictating to her sister. Although she's hardly allowed herself to hope, the news of the continuing rule of Robert depresses her. Nor is there any reply from *him*. Martha's presence in Battle's would have lightened everything, helped maintain connection to her life with Tom. Martha could have told Eve about her father, and she herself would have escaped Robert's tyranny, even if she didn't see it that way. Sarah feels a great weariness, a sadness she finds hard to hide from her child.

A few months later the public mood lifts, with peace soon to be signed between England and France. Crowds take the horses from the carriage of Bonaparte's Aide-de-Camp and pull it through Bond Street and St James's Street to Downing Street, almost overturning it in their excitement. Squibs, rockets, bonfires illuminate the night, pistols are fired out of sight of the Watch, surging crowds demand Lights! Lights! in every window, smashing those houses still in darkness, pelting them with mud and brickbats.

Battle's resounds to toasts and cheering, twice as much punch is drunk, French wine is in high demand. Sarah, musing amidst the uproar, unable to rejoice, is astonished to hear that Joseph Young's wife would speak with her.

The girl stands in her office, a child sleeping against her shoulder. The candlelight is poor yet Sarah recognises the frantic look she noticed once before.

'Mrs Young! Sit here. Will your baby wake?'

'I hope not. Miss Battle, I can think of no one to turn to except you. I already ask so much from Mr Digham, you see. You and I know nothing about each other, but I think you are kind.'

'What is it, Mrs Young?'

242

'Please call me Lucy. Though I pass as Mrs Young, Joseph and I are not married. Nor do I live in Little Russell Street any more.'

'I see. Tell me what's troubling you, Lucy.'

'It's my brother. I have a brother, Matthew. He has been arrested. Once before he escaped arrest, but this time, this time they've definitely caught him. And now...' She bursts into tears and wakes the baby who also cries.

'Lucy, soothe your baby back to sleep, then we'll lie him on the sofa here and you can tell me about your brother.'

*

They see Joseph ever more rarely at Digham's place in Paternoster Row. In Little Russell Street Joseph employs a man to operate his press, a woman close at hand to limn his engravings. No one replaces Lucy in the shop, but since he gave up producing portfolios for hire some time ago and wastes little time on satires, there are fewer customers. The demand is for his 'serious' paintings and prints. What visitors he has come to commission, must discuss pose and price with the artist himself.

As Fanny's desire for him expires, his thirst for the noisome, for harsh, warm gutter life dwindles. When his mind darkens he doses himself into oblivion behind shutters and soon the squalor of his rooms resembles that of the old lodgings in Albion Place. No one sees this but himself; his public person impresses, frequently charms.

'Lucy's upstairs with little Matthew,' Digham says to him when he ducks into the old engraver's shop one morning. 'I'm always pleased to see you, my young friend.'

'How are you, William?'

Digham conceals surprise at a question not often asked. There's something else his ex-apprentice wants.

'As well as I can expect at my age. Anhelous at times when I'm up and down stairs. Thank the Lord I have Batley to turn the star-wheel. Oh, short of breath!'

'Are you kept awake at night?'

'Very little. You know my sad history: I'm glad of a child in the house. And a pretty woman. Both are flourishing. It is better for them here even in this dark old place than with you, Joseph. That was always a bad arrangement. And you, you are free of course.'

'Yes. I'm becoming known. Money flows, William. You will be pleased to hear I've given up Wood's.'

'At last! What does your Sal or Moll say to that?'

'She's gone for someone else. Besides she's become fat.'

Digham peers up at Joseph. He thinks he can guess.

'Lucy had a visitor,' he says. 'The proprietor of the coffee house, Battle's. You know her, I think. Mrs Battle, is it?'

'Sarah.'

'Ah yes. Sarah Battle. A good, kind woman. And a looker, I'd say.'

'You would?'

'She hasn't Lucy's beauty. She's not immaculate: her colouring's too high, her nose too long. There's something of the selenite about Lucy I think occasionally: her pale perfection. Though like the moon, she always revives, grows full again. Sarah Battle, on the contrary, is of this world. And intelligent. I took to her right away, especially when she wanted to see my work!'

'She's buying the series of Shakespeare women for her coffee house. I'm painting a whole new set.'

'Hoho, you'll have asked a good sum, no doubt! And it

shows she has taste. A widow, I believe. Somewhat older than you, is she?'

'Oh, perhaps. Not much.'

'If she were nearer my age I'd make her an offer. Every man needs his cynosure, his guiding star, even if she's earthly. Perhaps *especially* when she's earthly. Not that any woman would want an old mole of a man like me. Who's limning for you now, young man Young?'

*

It's only the remnants that are taken at the Seven Stars, Bethnal Green, a spot north-east of the city walls remote enough for escaping madmen, for resurrectionists digging up bodies in the churchyard. Nevertheless a foolish place to meet, the publican well known for his opinions. The main conspirators are already in prison after the raids on the Royal Oak and the Nag's Head a year ago and on Thomas Jones's house, which they ransacked for papers, taking away sacks of evidence as well as Lizzie and her child, Edward.

Contrary to Joseph's belief, Matthew never went to Hamburg, but lurked in safe houses and unsafe ruins of houses, risking his life from falling beams, collapsing half-burned floors. Moving on every few days, he saw himself as a rat. Hated but hating, cunning. Uncatchable. As the hue and cry faded he sometimes came across a fellow United Briton or two, trembling in a cupboard in a tumbled building. Gradually a few of them dared meet together to plan and dream.

The Runners break down the door of the tap-room, grab the men by their collars, discover a cutlass and two archaic pistols. As he emerges, handcuffed, under the stars and glaring moon Matthew sees light-horsemen surrounding the tavern, swords drawn.

In Bow Street Police Office they're searched. A list in secret code is found. In soap-boiler Clarke's pocket scrawls from the memorable meeting with 'Captain Evans' the year before:

Newgit cobathfilds   clarkevell prisns   berricks
towr   benk   stop myul cochis

Lucy wouldn't recognise Matthew if were she to see him now. He has a beard, long hair, his clothes are filthy. He is taken before the Privy Council, called together at a disagreeable hour.

The room is full yet silent. Fifteen Privy Councillors sit at a long green-covered table, hands clasped or fiddling with inkwells and pens, sifting papers, fingers tracing routes on maps, drumming impatiently. Messengers and other servants edge the room.

'You are brought here, Matthew Dale, on charges which may affect your life. You may refuse to answer, if the answer will criminate yourself.'

Briefly he is at a loss, intimidated into blankness. For a year he has barely said a word. More fox than rat, he's survived by speed of movement and decision. In safe houses he's been fed, given precious coins and sent on his way. Coins enough to pay a girl sixpence in a doorway and hasten off as she pulls down her skirts, or buy half a pint of shrimps, occasionally a pamphlet from a bookstall. His mind runs on iron lines, driven by hatred which surges now. He sees they are the same as the masters at the school, as his father. But he is no longer a boy, knows the exact worth of those before whom he stands.

'Pray, sir, what are those charges?'

246

'Here is the warrant. You are charged with the crime of high treason.'

'Sir, high treason is so general and indefinite a charge that I am unsure what you have in mind.'

'We cannot help that. Were you at the Seven Stars, Bethnal Green, on the night of February 18th?'

He doesn't answer.

'Mr Dale, you have not attended to the question asked of you.'

'Indeed I have, sir. I am considering whether to answer.'

'Well, Mr Dale?'

'I have decided to remain silent, sir.'

'Have you ever gone under the name of Mason?'

'Sir, I cannot answer any questions while I am still uninformed of the *exact* charge against me, "high treason" being so general and indefinite.'

'If you are innocent you have nothing to fear.'

'I'm not so sure of that, sir. As I'm ignorant what may be deemed high treason I don't know how far I may commit myself by an indiscreet answer.'

Sometimes he wants to laugh, sometimes to rush at them, jump on the table and strangle them with their silk cravats, his filthy fingers tightening the ends until their eyes pop out. But his hatred feeds an immaculate politeness. He knows he disconcerts them, his manner and education quite at odds with his present appearance and his no doubt reported activity.

At the end of the first day, it being around midnight, he has told them nothing; is taken by carriage to the Tower.

*

The governor of the Tower fails to smother his own discomfort. He's an anxious man in any case, chewing his finger ends at the presence of the deputy chaplain's son before him on the gravest of charges. With a military guard they march to the south-west tower. It's dark; other men are asleep.

Three floors up, they unlock a door and the governor addresses two warders: 'You are to remain in this room night and day. Hold no conversation with your prisoner, nor suffer him to go out of the length of your swords. You answer for his appearance at the peril of your lives.'

The warders are old, obedient but not unkind. Each one sleeps on a cot in a closet on either side of Matthew's bed. Matthew sleeps well, not having spent a night in a bed for some time. In the morning he finds the collar and cuffs of his coat, the padding of his neckerchief, the soles of his boots ripped open and sewn up again.

For a week he appears constantly before the Privy Council, maintaining pedantic politeness or silence. His days are patterned and although he is allowed neither books nor writing materials, he is not uncomfortable. He is given twenty-one shillings a week for subsistence, sends out for his meals. Each morning a woman lights a fire, boils a kettle, prepares breakfast, makes his bed, sweeps and cleans. There's more order to his life than he's had for years.

He feels keenly the irony of being back in the place from which he thought himself forever severed. He's not terrified, as many other prisoners must often be, rather is disgusted at his failure. No visits are allowed although the governor could hardly refuse a request from Matthew's parents. Partly he dreads, partly longs for the announcement of his father, to confront him, shame him. Is glad there's no weeping, snuffling mother.

Daily he stares out through each of his two windows at the river. Sees high tide, low mud, the great ships at anchor in the centre, wherries crossing, sails, oars, poles; gulls screaming unceasingly. Singles out particular boats and lightermen, wonders who is thieving, who planning to sail to America.

Imagines a boy and a stout, sweating, blackguardly lawyer. The hasty construction of a Tricolour with his earnest sister Lucy, about whom he rarely thinks. Did William Leopard ever get to America? Did he really hold radical views? His *Rights of Man* was greasy and bent: *someone* had read it. For certain the man was on the run: the signs he didn't know then, he knows now. The sour smell, stubble, eyes darting continuously round corners. And of course, he was after Matthew's money. His childhood is an embarrassing dream: he will forget it.

*

Sarah tries to help Lucy, though she cannot think what to do for Matthew. She shudders at the thought of Lucy's brother in the Tower, a traitor. There's no mention yet of a trial, no mention of the likely outcome of conviction. She remembers Pyke's words: 'a few rash men... futile revolution... will be caught and hanged.' If she can hardly bring herself to think of the word execution, what must take place in poor Lucy's mind?

There's no one with influence among Battle's customers, who, though they're mostly canny and make themselves money, have little power. She thinks it unlikely Matthew can even be visited, for the Tower is hardly Newgate, bad enough though that would be.

Listening to the tale of Lucy's life with Joseph, she feels pity and a certain fascination. It seems he was unkind, ruthless, yet also affectionate, declared he loved her, at first, anyway. Rushed to his mistress, returning to sleep off his debauchery and attack Lucy for complaining, sometimes for not complaining. The paintings and engravings of her that Sarah has now seen, show his admiration of Lucy's gentle beauty, yet he rarely calls on her, barely speaks to her. There's some small consolation to Lucy that Sarah, too, had a marriage that never was. Sarah says little about Tom, however: it can't help the girl fathom Joseph.

But at least there's William Digham, thinks Sarah. She observes the old man's calm and warmth, his patience, humour; the way, holding Lucy's child, he lets him tweak the spectacles off his nose again and again, pull the embroidered felt hat over his eyes. And Sarah's Eve is about the same age as Lucy's Matthew, so that by spring, 1802, no longer babies, they play together in the nursery at Battle's, pretend to read to each other from the tiny pretty books of *The Infant's Library*.

Joseph reveals no sign of his erratic behaviour to Sarah. He's egotistical, ebullient, but his conceitedness, arrogance, are eased by a youthful, fair-haired grace of bearing that pleases, and an attention to her she can't quite ignore. Knowledge of his cruelty to Lucy disturbs; she puts it aside. Then there's his great ability as artist and engraver. It wasn't difficult for her to agree to buy the whole series of Shakespeare paintings which he reconstructs from his sketches. They decide which walls are best for each canvas. With Wintrige gone, Battle's can finally become the superior coffee house Sarah always wanted it to be, where people can contemplate Shakespeare and the skill of Joseph Young.

His reputation is growing; he is even becoming grand. He paints portraits which he signs *Josephus Iuvenis pinxit* and, with the sitters' permission, rarely withheld, he engraves them too. The sitter displays the expensive portrait on his wall, while others enjoy the reflected glory of the engraved version on theirs.

It has been a long time since Sarah talked so much to an educated, intelligent man. Her longing for Tom plays its still-discernible ground beneath her thoughts, a passacaglia beating to her blood. At times Joseph displays a pomposity that she mocks. Yet she cannot help her bias: Joseph is an artist. She begins to feel an affection for him almost as if Newton has come again.

He orders brandy at Battle's one morning and, as he often does, asks for Sarah.

'I have met such an interesting man, Sarah. I must tell you about him. Jacques Garnerin. The Official Aëronaut of France.'

'Good Lord! Does he have wings?' A Newton comes to mind: what fun he'd have had with balloons! 'I suppose he wants you to paint his portrait and sell prints of it.'

'Much more exciting than that. He is planning an ascent in his balloon and I am to go with him and sketch. Think of it! London seen from the air in paintings and prints. Balloons are not new but sketches made from them are. Think of the fame!'

He bounces with enthusiasm.

'Now that we are at peace with the French, Sarah, assuming we trust Bonaparte, what a symbol it will be! A Frenchman and an Englishman flying over London together!'

'Cannot a woman go, too? I seem to remember the actress Mrs Sage went up in a balloon years ago. Neither the sky nor peace is the province of men alone, Joseph.' How absurdly prim she sounds!

'No, of course they're not. You needn't chide; do you think I am unreasonable?'

He doesn't expect an answer. Says: 'I'll suggest it to Jacques. And Sarah. You will be the perfect woman to accompany us. No! Do not protest! You have argued yourself into it.'

*

> Robert Wilson, Bookseller and Publisher
> Chestnut Street
> Philadelphia
> 4th March, 1802

Dear Miss Battle,

I received your letter somewhat more than a year ago and apologise for the length of time it has taken in which to reply, but you can imagine how shocked I was at the revelation it contained that you and Tom Cranch were not married. In addition, you will understand that I was hurt to have been deceived, even while I was doing my best to help you both when you first arrived and thereafter.

You will know I count myself a good Democratic Republican, though not a revolutionary. Some of the views you expressed yourself, while you lived here, were more than I could stomach, as you are well aware. I believe in God and in the divinity of Christ. I therefore cannot approve of your having lived with Tom Cranch as his wife, outside the laws of both God and man. Moreover, Tom's deception should have precluded his issuing 'advice' on my relationship with Martha. I bought Martha on my arrival in America in 1781. According to Pennsylvanian law, all who are slaves before 1780, as Martha was, remain slaves for life. Nevertheless I freed her, by manumission, and, having done so, I see no reason to elevate her further.

In view of the fact that you were not legally married to Tom Cranch, you will realise that I cannot return any of the money he put into my business, were you to think of asking for it. Of course I acknowledge that it was a most welcome investment at the time and one from which we all benefitted.

There is one piece of news about which I believe you will be interested to hear. The lawyer William Leopard was recently sentenced to a long term in Walnut Street Prison, having been involved in a street brawl in which a man was killed. Although there is insufficient evidence to prove that his was the fatal blow, there were many witnesses to his involvement in the affray. It is said that he was challenged by the dead man about blackmailing activities. I only tell you this because information has reached me that he was extracting money from you.

I am in good health, thank you, and trust that you are. Should you ever have a proposal for a book in my series of Pocket Guides, *it would certainly be given consideration by,*

Your erstwhile friend,

Robert Wilson

She almost laughs at this faultless hypocrisy. It's early summer, there's no fire in the grate. She burns the crushed paper among old ashes, watches its blurred disintegration.

*

Joseph brings two paintings and Sarah pays him. She is glad the improvement of Battle's has begun, though she wonders how long before smoke and steam dull the delicate colours' glow.

Today Joseph is peevish.

'It seems I am *not* the first artist to ascend in a balloon. Somebody came across a book and was pleased to tell me that it contains drawings from a balloon made seventeen years ago!'

'Are they drawings of London?'

'Ah. I think they flew from Chester.'

'Well, your fame will be none the less, then.'

She sees how very young he is, this tall, fair man, petulant like a child; how Lucy could never have influenced him. Yet his very childishness appeals to her. 'Joseph, I must talk to you. Come, let us sit over here.'

They move to a settle away from easy hearing, but Dick appears, arthritic fingers clutching at the waiter's cloth over his arm.

'A word wiv you, Miss Battle.'

'Is it important, Dick? Just now I'm busy. Please be brief.' She stands aside to talk.

'Them pictures you did want me to burn, Miss Battle,' he whispers hoarsely, 'them were drawed by...' Wild eye and brow movements indicate Joseph.

'Yes, Dick.'

A cunning look crosses his face. 'The men 'ere do know it's 'im.' He waves his arm to take in the whole coffee house.

'Mr Young has explained to me how artists turn their hands to all manner of work when they are young and poor. I'm sure the customers understand that. It was years ago, Dick. Mr Young is a respectable, well-known portrait painter now.'

Dick turns away, mutters about Sam Battle, balls in the sky, shakes his head like a palsy. Sarah is touched that he should wish to protect her reputation. But he was ever a supporter of Wintrige: though Wintrige is dead, Dick perceives Joseph as a usurper.

It's of no consequence. She sits down next to Joseph.

'I must talk to you about Lucy.'

'Oh, yes?' He is unconcerned.

'She is so terribly distressed about her brother Matthew.'

'Yes. I know that. A rash, desperate boy. What has she told you?'

'That he's imprisoned in the Tower for high treason, but she doesn't know what he's done. She's sure he's innocent. Is he?'

'How can I know? Probably not. Look, Sarah,' in lowered voice, 'I sympathise with many of their views. We need new ways.'

'I've seen real freedom in America.'

'You have?' He looks at her intently. Her usually animated face pauses, serious. They have never talked about such things.

'Where people speak their minds and publish without fear.'

He would draw her out of her thoughts, bring her back to himself. 'Once, I...'

'What will happen to him, Joseph? Is it as bad as someone once suggested? Can you tell me?'

'They are collecting evidence for the trial. He is like to be condemned to death.'

'Oh! Poor Lucy. Can *nothing* be done?'

'Nothing. There are those who petition, write letters, but it is hopeless. The government want to show they've rounded up all traitors, want to demonstrate success. They fear revolution, Sarah, so they will find a plot. Indeed I believe they already have. Then they will need names, a trial, punishment, bodies.'

'And what can be done for Lucy?'

'I don't know. Lucy has no trust in me: there is nothing *I* can do for her. Digham is kind.'

Sarah glimpses his ruthlessness. Remembers the moment when she'd wanted to reach out to the frantic girl on the quayside. Knows she must find some way to help her herself, for he is impervious: she has no notion how to move him.

'Don't think any more about it, Sarah. William will take care of Lucy. For years he was like a father to me; now he will do the same for her. You must concentrate on our flight. Oh, how I'm looking forward to it! It will be magnificent. You will be magnificent!' He looks at her with pleasure.

Her mood limps behind his.

'They say Monsieur Garnerin is very competent.'

'Of course he is! He has made several journeys and, I tell you, the man is fearless. What's more, Madame Garnerin, his wife, is herself a balloonist. For some reason she has not accompanied him this time, but he tells me a woman can be as intrepid as a man. There speaks a man of the Revolution, Sarah!'

'Good. Of course he's right. But I don't think *I'm* intrepid.'

'You need do nothing except stand in the basket and smile. And keep your balance. Surely you're not worried?'

'Sometimes I do worry, yes. Not for myself so much, but when I think of Eve.'

He would touch her face, but cannot.

'No need. All will be well. I feel absolutely certain all will be well.'

And it's true, he does. His mood is alight. Dullness, worthlessness have vanished in the presence of this woman, Sarah.

6

Wherever there's space bills announce:

The celebrated Aëronaut M André-Jacques Garnerin
will Ascend in his gas Balloon
at Ranelagh
on 28 June 1802 at 5 o'clock
during an elegant Afternoon Breakfast
given by the Directors of the Pic Nic Society.
M Garnerin will be accompanied by
the well-known Artist and Engraver Mr Joseph Young
and, to prove the Safety of such Travel to
Members of the Fair Sex,
the well-known Proprietress of Battle's Coffee House
Miss Sarah Battle

Sarah is nervous. The danger involved in the ascent is one thing, for, the news being out, people insist she hear of all the accidents that have taken place in the last twenty years. Yet, can it really be worse than crossing the Atlantic by ship? Endless weeks, threat of disease and wreck, perpetual sea roar, nothing but salt pork.

No, it's the prospect of appearing at Ranelagh before two thousand people that bothers her as much. What should she wear? She is warned how she will freeze as they ascend into the clouds, yet she'll not want to be wrapped in cloaks and muffs in June before a multitude of women in the latest fashions.

Monsieur Garnerin is too busy preparing the event to meet her, so Joseph, acting as go-between, discovers that when Jacques took up a woman, not his wife, with him four years before in Paris her charms were shown to good effect. Apparently Jacques is glad to hear that Sarah is handsome and says that she should wear whatever she likes. She swallows her annoyance at the thought of the conversation the two men have had about her, decides she'll pack a bag with two shawls and a cloak to put on once clear of the crowds, and turns her mind to the matter of what food and drink to supply for consuming in the upper air.

Sarah sees Joseph daily, for he stops work for the moment and constantly has some new detail about the flight to discuss with her. His presence is a diversion from the tedium of the coffee house, whose heavy, dark masculinity is already seeping into Eve's life, ready to choke her childhood. Eve will need to be rescued soon, though Sarah won't think of sending her away to school, to some doubtful establishment in Chelsea, for instance. If only there was an Academy like the one in Philadelphia, where they teach girls mathematics, geography, chemistry, natural philosophy. As yet she knows no solution. She tells herself that once the flight is over she'll talk to Mr Pyke and work out what to do.

Meanwhile, she comes to expect Joseph, knows exactly when he arrives from the cheers and heckles of the customers.

'The Conquering Hero!' they bawl with admiration and irony. Someone trumpets out the famous Handel tune.

'He's to fly off into the ether with our beautiful Sarah, you know,' they say to a newcomer.

'Good Lord! Why?'

'She says a woman can do it as well as a man.'

'Oh, one of those.'

'Not so. No bluestockings.' It's Thynne. 'She's always made up her own mind. Not like her mother, though now I think of it, making up *her* own mind got her killed.'

'Oh?'

'Mistakenly shot by militia in the Gordon Riots. But Sarah, now, she's a friend of this artist who's to sketch the city from the heavens. He's well known.'

'Can we spare her, I ask you?' says Challoner, one of those who still miss Wintrige.

'Just this once. They'll make a striking sight.'

Sarah's friendship with Joseph has become public, has become a pairing she never intended but is amused by, enjoys.

*

The day is hot and cloudy. Sarah and Joseph walk together through the crowd towards the enormous balloon, thirty feet in diameter, forty-five feet high, as big as a four-storey house, its alternate dark-green and yellow segments encased in a net, its oblong car draped in Tricolours and Union Jacks. On the ground around it is a cartwheel shape of barrels and pipes in which acid and iron filings have generated the hydrogen that fills the great globe.

Someone pulls at Joseph's sleeve and he turns impatiently.

'Young man Young,' says William Digham. 'I've come to wish you success.'

'William!' Joseph's grimace transforms. He wraps the old man in large arms.

'I've not seen you in a while, Joseph, but there's no need to suffocate me now that we finally meet!'

Joseph bows his head. He has neglected his beloved master shamefully.

'Off with you to your aërostatic globe. They're waiting. Do your best. I'm watching your fulgent star rise to its zenith.'

Jacques Garnerin waits for his companions in an elegant blue coat and French hat with the national cockade, chatting to bystanders and smiling, for all a showman at Bartholomew Fair, encouraging people into his booth. He is sinewy and slight, his noble nose and thin, sharp features wind-burned, his skin toughened like a sailor's. Behind Sarah is Eve with her nurse, and Lucy, wretched at the sight of so many Tricolours, holding little Matthew's hand. Sarah wears her best dress, its low neckline and short sleeves fashionable enough, and a large beribboned bonnet. She is red with heat and self-consciousness. It's not unlike the first day she stood at the bar in Battle's, when men scanned her perpetually till she felt skinned.

She turns to hug Eve and kiss the child who looks with bright eyes from her to the balloon and back, too young to understand, aware only of a vast murmuring, a heaving sea of smiles.

'I'll be back soon, my little one.' She steps up to the basket, wanting it all to be over.

Joseph bows to Lucy and of a sudden, perhaps to cancel that formality, ruffles his son's hair. Garnerin, the small, foreign entertainer, hands his two British aëronauts up steps into the car, springs into it like a boy. There's only just room, for in the centre is ballast, bags of sand marked in quantities from kilos down to grams, suspended by four cords from the hoop at the base of the balloon's netting. Attached to the car's ropes are a thermometer, impressive compass, telescope and a barometer for measuring altitude. Dick, limping on his arthritic hip, carries over baskets of provisions with the help of a waiter. There's applause. Battle's has provided the food and drink! All of which is stowed in lockers under the seat on which Joseph sits, cluttered about with pens, pencils, chalks, brushes, paint boxes, sketchbooks and blocks, perspective glasses and his own pocket telescope. Jacques calculates that large Joseph, his equipment, and baskets of food and drink will balance the weight on the opposite side of the car to Sarah and himself.

A band strikes up *God Save the King*. The Official Aëronaut of France, fidgeting throughout, stands to attention for the succeeding tune which no one recognises.

'But that is not the *Marseilleise*,' says Joseph, puzzled.

'It offend Napoleon. I told them they must play *Veillons au salut de l'Empire*. Soon he become Emperor.'

After four verses, during which it is the crowd's turn to fidget and chatter, Garnerin unhooks bag after bag of ballast, hands them over the side of the car until the captive balloon pulls at its tethers.

At last he signals, assistants untie the ropes, restrain the great ball by muscle power. The crowds hush.

. A sign, the ropes are loosed, a huge cheer breaks out, the ascent begins. Sarah feels the basket leave the ground, an upward pull through her body that makes her laugh out loud. Even as her child slips further from her, the little face blearing in her sight, her legs weaken with pleasure and she grips the car to steady herself. Jacques, so many successful flights in hand, moves about with panache, making the balloon rise slowly, letting it hang over the gardens for maximum effect. He holds a French flag himself, gives Sarah a Union Jack and with Joseph waving his sketchbook, they all three salute the crowds thronging the Gardens and all roads that lead to Ranelagh. The great vehicle moves massively, elegantly in a north-east direction, away from the packed banks of the river, from the waterworks, the creeks and sluice gates of Pimlico fenland. Still low enough for onlookers clustered in every window and house-top, perching in trees like cawing rooks.

Joseph, breathless with excitement, sketches rapidly as they sail over Green Park and St James's. Ducks peel from the lakes as the huge shadow passes. Westminster to the right, Charing Cross beneath.

'Look, Sarah. See the stocks?' he asks her.

'I hope there's no one in them.'

'It might cheer the poor prisoner to see us. At least it would distract the pelters. Here! Use my pocket telescope. I've not enough hands for it.' His steel spectacles have a second set of lenses, tinted, hinged up until needed, for all like mad eyebrows.

Everywhere upturned faces.

'Strand,' Jacques points out.

'The whores are lifting their eyes instead of their skirts,' Joseph says to him.

They move at speed between that road and the river. Or rather, road and river seem to move past below, for they feel no motion, borne at the wind's pace.

'Over there in the distance, are those St George's Fields?' Sarah asks Jacques whose thin brown finger traces a line on the map. She remembers the day, the shining day. Was it not June then, too?

'I think St George's Fields, yes. Now we release the bird.'

He opens a small wicker cage Sarah hadn't noticed and a pigeon with a tiny Union flag round one leg, a Tricolour round the other, flies out without hesitation.

Small boats jostle each other on the river. At this point there are no masted ships, held back by the multiple, stumpy legs of London Bridge. Anchored, the little vessels rock to the movement of their passengers who follow the balloon, cheer the pigeon's flight, soon lost.

Fleet Street, Ludgate Hill and the glory of a dome from whose pinnacle stone seems to cascade like water. They're so near they almost touch it.

'Who wouldn't give their eye teeth to touch St Paul's?' Joseph's pencil runs over page after page. 'If only we could stop!'

'No balloon have ever taken this route before,' says Jacques. 'Look at the people. They desert their houses like in an earthquake!' He reads the barometer. 'Three thousand feet. I keep it low for them.'

Cheapside. Sarah peers down. Somewhere near here is Winkworth Buildings, City Road, the place of her dismal marriage. Poultry, where her mother and Ben Newton were killed. Can she see Change Alley? Battle's in its dark corner? Her life passes beneath her.

The wind still carries them north-east. Such density of brick. Such insect-tunnel streets.

To their right, masts and sails appear beyond London Bridge.

'Look where they've pulled down the granaries in Tooley Street,' Joseph announces. Gulls screech. Foul grey smoke from a brick stack puffs up, floats away.

The Tower, flag flying. Matthew. Condemned. How will Lucy bear his death? And he, rash, rejected, loved, traitor, watcher of the wonderful flight like any other man, sees from one of his windows in the south-west tower the green and yellow balloon drift away from the city. Green and yellow: fine Irish colours, he thinks. Recently the United Irishmen have laid aside the national green and switched to yellow to protect themselves.

'I wish it would come over here,' he thinks. 'I'd climb in and sail the other way to Dublin.' His days are a monotonous nightmare of waiting.

Goodman's Fields, market gardens, pastures where cattle stand. The wind is blowing them due north.

'Now we ascend,' says Jacques, the city finally behind them, the fields and hamlets of the East End shrinking to dabs of colour.

'Madame Battle, you will feel the coldness *un petit peu*.' He unhooks sacks of ballast and throws them out.

They rise through cloud mass. Sarah shivers, reaches for her bag of winter clothes, two shawls, a cloak, gloves.

'Thermometer reads fifteen degrees,' says Joseph, ghostly in the mist, layer upon layer, three full shelves of cloud.

Then they are through: vast blue opens above and around. The quicksilver shoots up five degrees more than summer heat. Whiteness lies thick beneath them.

'Have we stopped moving?'

'*Non*, Madame Battle, we merely *seem* stationary.'

'We can see nothing against which to locate our movement,' Joseph remarks, his sketchbook temporarily abandoned, his tinted lenses lowered against the glare.

'Yes! You are right. And so we eat now. What have you brought for us, Madame Battle?'

They pull out the basket, balance plates on napkins on their laps, hold glasses cautiously, eat, drink, smile at each other.

Sarah is famished, having eaten nothing since early morning, and then, too nervous for more than tea. There's ham and cold fowl, Mrs Trunkett's best plum cake and three bottles of orgeat, wine and spirits too dangerous to take because of the air pressure. Balloons and champagne: those were the early days, before war with France.

Eat, drink and smile again. Monsieur Garnerin leaps up constantly to check ropes, instruments, his markings on the map. His mood is imperturbable, his movements disturbing.

'Jacques,' says Joseph, 'stop for a minute and tell us about your imprisonment in Buda castle.'

'No! It is without purpose. The past is finished, it is dead. I never think of it.'

'Oh, I can't agree with that,' Sarah says. 'You're quite wrong, Monsieur Garnerin.'

'The past, *c'est passé*! Today is important and tomorrow.' He checks the barometer.

Sarah catches Joseph's eye momentarily. Does he think that, too about the past, his own past, so conveniently abandoned? Yet she is glad he's there with her now, excitable though he is. Over months, they have become used to each other's ways, enjoy each other's presence, talk with pleasing familiarity.

He shows her his sketchbook.

'Oh, Joseph, these are wonderful! Look at St Paul's, the ships on the river. Even the people in the trees at Ranelagh. You seem to have drawn everything. Such skill.'

'You are not drawing me?' says Jacques, flicking through the pages.

'They'll make a most excellent book,' Sarah says, 'and increase your fame, too, Monsieur Garnerin.'

'Now that we are cut off from the earth by these clouds, Sarah,' Joseph says, 'are you afraid?'

'Madame Battle has no need to be afraid. I have much experience. I have ascended many times. You are safe, *Madame*.' Sinewy Jacques is practical, has never known doubt.

'I feel quite safe, Monsieur Garnerin, and not afraid at present, though a little apprehensive about the next stage, perhaps. It is a different world here. I begin to wonder if there ever was another.'

Jacques frowns, but Joseph says: 'Perhaps this *is* the only world and what we thought we knew before doesn't exist. I can see from your expression you don't agree, Jacques. You think this is nonsense. Sarah and I are Romantics. You, Jacques, are a man of science, a *philosophe*. You want to understand the workings of the world. You want to command it!'

'*Bien sûr*. Who does not?'

'It has never occurred to me to want that,' Joseph says.

'From up here I can understand what you mean, Monsieur Garnerin. From up here I could issue proclamations and orders! I feel like a queen.'

'Sarah, Jacques would command the *elements*, I think.'

'Whereas I see the world as one huge coffee house, you mean. Joseph, it was a joke. I imagined a cartoon of myself.'

'I'll draw it for you now. Look. *Queen Sarah Rules the World from her Aërostatic Globe*. I'll finish it later, and work the world into a giant coffee house. For of course, that is what it is!'

They pack away the meal, stow the baskets. Joseph has removed his greatcoat, both men take off their jackets.

Suddenly the clouds below disperse and the world appears. The whole country spreads magnificently beneath and beyond them. Sarah gasps and Joseph, elated, grasps her hand.

'We are in heaven, are we not? To look down like this is perfection. I never felt so happy!'

She takes her hand from his, gently, steadying herself on the basket.

'Madame Battle, you feel dizzy?'

'Certainly not, Monsieur Garnerin.'

'You feel well?'

'I feel exhilarated.'

They are fifteen thousand feet above a boundless land, which at first appears as swathes and blocks of greens and browns like a canvas in preparation. The balloon's shadow moves across it, the only cloud. Then they lean over the side and are amazed to see objects picked out in extraordinary clarity. Joseph insists Sarah use his snakeskin-covered pocket telescope, but even without magnification, they point out to each other ruts in roads, furrows in fields, thatch in hamlets, chimneys in towns. Their hearing, too, has sharpened strangely so that sounds reach them: the rattle of carriages, lowing of cattle, mewing of kites and buzzards, shouts of surprise and joy.

'This is remarkable,' Joseph says, 'quite remarkable.'

'When people ascend first time, sometimes they talk of God,' Jacques tells them.

'I can understand that,' says Sarah. 'The ordered beauty of the natural world.' That day at the Schuylkill River. 'But think of the thousands of lives below, the tragedies, pleasure, love, the sadness, and we can neither see nor hear any of them! Like the ship's captain who cares nothing for the mice on board!'

She thinks: 'My own life, too, is as nothing in the universe. Yet now for me each second is full, so full of everything that is happening, all that has happened.'

'Of course *you* don't believe in God, Jacques,' says Joseph. 'You are a man of the Revolution. For you, men are masters of the universe.'

'Not yet masters complete, Joseph. Not of the whole world. But *I* shall conquer the sky. Balloons first. And parachutes. I design a parachute. Madame Garnerin have jumped already.'

'How astonishing,' Sarah says. 'Was she not afraid?'

'She feel no fear.'

'Do you believe in a deity, Sarah?' Joseph asks, dipping his brush rapidly, sketching, scratching with his nail.

'A distant one. A first cause.'

'Well! I thought all deists were men!'

They ascend higher and a west wind drives them over a forest. Jacques is attending to the map.

'Here is the Epping forest.'

'The easiest thing to sketch so far, let me tell you. Look, it's like a great gooseberry bush.'

He daubs and streaks, trying out greens merging into blue, black shadows, a distant sift of cloud while yet the sun still burns.

They move rapidly, high, to the east.

In the huge blueness Sarah's senses are keenly alert. She feels her body glow with the sun's heat, her mind open so that past and future spread like a magnified map. She sees like a blade.

And knows what she must do. Suddenly. What she must do for Eve and for herself.

She must leave Battle's. Sell it. Its darkness and smells, closed, inward-looking, a standing pool, black, stagnant. She will take Eve away from its influence. Sail once more, for the last time, to Philadelphia. Live there, work there. Publish and sell books herself. Take up where Tom left off.

'I shall do what he did,' she thinks, 'what he would have done had he lived, what we would have done together. I learned something of the business there, enough to try. Sell cheap reprints, he said, so as to publish more pamphlets and unknown writers. I'll finish our pamphlet on women's education.

'I can do it with the money from selling Battle's; I don't need Robert Wilson. What was it Tom said about me? He thought I was wasted in the coffee house. *She will find a new way in this new world.* I shall!

'Lucy and little Matthew can come with us, live with Eve and me. And Martha will be there, dear Martha. She will help Lucy laugh. Yes. I shall do all this.

'Oh! It's like the moment when the clouds dissolved! I can see it all set out: Sarah Cranch & Daughter, Books and Printseller, Market Street, Philadelphia.'

Joseph notices the change in Sarah's face, her features seeming both to sharpen and to shine. An inner exultation. Sketches her as well as he can without her knowledge. No cartoon, he catches uplift, illumination.

The balloon moves with speed towards lines of light and dark.

He stands close to her. 'Sarah, look. We're approaching the sea, I'm sure of it. Before it's too late, before we descend, I must tell you something. I understand everything now.'

'How strange! I feel exactly the same!'

'You *do*? How wondrous! The light, the atmosphere, makes everything into a vision, doesn't it? You look so beautiful in this upper air. Like a goddess, serene and noble.'

She doesn't hear, exulting still. He hesitates, but only for a moment.

'Oh Sarah, I know now without doubt. I love you. You, Sarah.'

She stares, unseeing.

'This journey, sailing in the ether, has helped me understand. Lucy was just a model for my work. I had a mistress who satisfied me, but she was coarse. You are the woman I love. The only woman I *can* love. You are the woman I need. You are a widow, free to marry; Lucy and I never married so I am free, too. And I am rich now, Sarah. You need never work again. Let us marry. Will you? Say you will. Oh, say you will!'

She looks at him. This young man, strong in body, charged with feeling, charming, skilled, of whom she's grown fond in recent weeks. He, seeing only assent, clasps her to him and for a moment the embrace claims her: she has lived on memories for so long.

She pulls back.

'No! Good God, no, Joseph!'

Sees his shock. Regrets what she must do.

'You don't know me, Joseph. You know nothing about me, do you? Tom was my husband. Tom Cranch. Yes, he's dead but I shall be true to him always. For three years we lived as husband and wife though we couldn't be legally married. I am *his* widow, not Wintrige's. Wintrige was a spy and a liar. The marriage was a sham. I loved Tom from the moment we fled the country; no, much earlier, though I didn't realise it. I loved him then, I love him now and always shall.'

Oh, she is struck by sadness. To use his name to hurt! Fierce certainty subsumes it.

'I have decided to return to America. I shall sell Battle's and leave as soon as I can.'

Joseph, white, sways with the blow. Clutches the basket edge with both hands, for his vision has skewed, his mind is blind. He staggers. His bulk crumples, shrivels. His body is bones, his ecstasy a husk: he could be tossed out of the basket.

'I didn't know this. I didn't know. It's true I know nothing about you. I see you as I want to see you. A guiding star, a cynosure. Oh, what have I done? What have I done? You will hate me now. Oh Sarah, I'm sorry. How foolish, how crass! Will you ever forgive me? Please forgive me, Sarah! Sometimes my feelings overwhelm me; I cannot help myself. Then I regret it.' He groans heavily, covers his face with his hands, his head bowing down below his shoulders.

'*Joseph*!' Jacques shouts. 'For God's sake, we must descend. Look, *la mer, la mer*!' The wind has driven them eastwards, over the marshes of Essex, extremely close to the sea. At the same time a summer storm cloud wells up immediately beneath them, black, heavy with disturbance.

Although Jacques shows no sign of panic, indeed he never feels it, he is coolness personified, he must keep the worst from Madame Battle.

'*Il faut que nous passions a travers de ce drôle la*,' indicating the cloud. '*Accrochez vous ferme car nous allons nous casser le col*.'

'He says to hold on tight,' Joseph tells Sarah as Jacques pulls on a rope to open the valve at the top of the balloon. 'We shall have to pass through this storm.'

Gas spurts, they plunge down into the cloud and the squall's centre, beaten by wind and rain as they descend with sickening velocity. They grip the sides of the basket and Sarah cries out as a particular buffet hurls her onto the floor.

Both men help her up. '*Vite, vite*! We strike the ground in a moment,' Jacques yells above the wind. 'Hold the hoop, so. Lift the feet!'

The basket is held by a hoop attached to the net around the

271

balloon. Joseph lifts Sarah up, bids her hold onto the hoop for dear life, raise her legs, does the same himself. Jacques, monkey-like, jumps up, tucks his feet into the net, holds an arm out to Sarah and the three of them, new-fangled acrobats, swing from the massive gas-emitting globe as they hit the ground.

Sarah, her bonnet long gone, her dress soaked against her body, her muscles jarred, is too cold to cry. Survival is all. Gusting wind pulls the balloon across fields, the car dragging behind it at speed, banging over the ground, knocking against trees while they hang on to ropes with both hands, glad to be down, though jolted mercilessly. At last the grappling iron fastens its claw-hooks onto a tree stump.

'Madame Battle, you are well?'

'I am alive.'

'We could have done with your parachute, Jacques,' says Joseph, watching Sarah with fear.

'*Mais non*. Only madmen jump in this weather. *Regardez!*' People are running out of a nearby farmhouse and stand gawping and pointing. Not too close.

'Surely they will help, will take us in?' Sarah says.

Jacques and Joseph throw ropes towards them.

'Anchor us! Tie the ropes to your trees!' Joseph yells. The people stare. Some of the men confer with each other, gesture violently to the women who turn and run back to the house. A woman stumbles, shrieking.

'They think we are Napoleon's invasion! With our Tricolours,' says Sarah, for the Union Jacks blew off some time before. 'We are friends!' she shouts, 'please help us!' But her voice is lost in the wind's roar.

'They think we're devils dropped from the sky,' Joseph says grimly. 'I'll jump out and secure a rope, Jacques.'

'You cannot, alone, Joseph. You are not strong enough, even you. So much gas is still in the balloon. Many are needed to secure it. *Ils sont idiots, ces gens*!'

And then a sudden blast of wind grabs them like a hand, breaks the anchoring cable and with extraordinary speed shoots them hundreds of feet into the air. Tosses them back in the direction from which they came. The flight resumes just when they want it to end.

Jacques stretches for the gas-release valve rope, but it's out of his reach.

'It have slipped away,' he shouts. 'I cannot make us descend. We shall continue.'

Sarah pulls her cloak about her tightly to calm her shivering body.

'Madame Battle, have courage.'

'There is no braver woman, Jacques,' shouts Joseph, shaking with despair. 'But look, we all need courage now. We're being blown back to the coast.' He fastens the clasps of his sketchbook, wraps it in oilcloth, ties it firmly.

'At least what I have drawn may survive even if I drown,' he tells himself. 'Someone may find the sketch of her. It's the best thing I've ever done.'

'Put on the cork jackets. There will be ships, boats,' Jacques proclaims, confident.

Sarah longs for Eve, for Tom. Rejoices in her plan of hope and reuniting as the damaged balloon scuds rapidly towards a lucent sea.

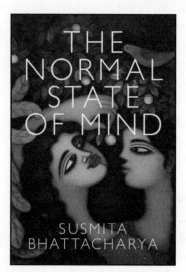
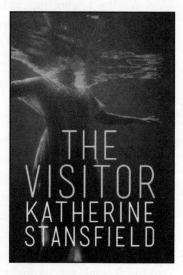

www.parthianbooks.com